Secrets of Twisted Souls

Alexandria Renée

ISBN 979-8-9931368-0-6 (paperback edition)

First Edition

Published by Sloane & Co. Publishing

Printed in the United States of America

This is a work of fiction. Names, characters, places, and incidents are
either the product of the author's imagination or used fictitiously. Any
resemblance to actual persons, living or dead, events, or locales is entirely
coincidental.

Dedication

Brendan and Brody,

No matter how far into the darkness you have to go to find your light, find it because you possess it, and when you do don't ever allow anyone to put that light out! No matter how high that mountain might seem you want to climb know, you can achieve anything your hearts desire, don't ever let anyone tell you otherwise. If you have a "gut feeling"—TRUST IT! Don't ever go against it, this is your truth. I wish I could have known this long ago, I have gone against it several times and every time I did, I regretted it.

Trust yourself! You hold the truth! Follow your dreams and live in your authenticity. Spread your love and compassion you both possess. Be kind, and sincere and don't let others take advantage of you or treat you badly. Show mercy and grace and stand in your truth. Ground and meditate often. Know your worth, because I know your worth and you both can achieve great things!

I have seen the trials and battles that you both have faced, please know your past doesn't define you. Stand strong and hold your head high, show the world who you are destined to be, not who others want you to be. See through the illusions and don't let anyone or anything hold you back! And don't hold yourself back!

Follow your dreams and love yourself along the way, and know I love you both more than you will ever know and I always will!

It's your story, don't let anyone else write it...

With all of my love,
Mom

Table of Contents

Chapter 1
The Forest's Embrace

Prophecy of the Sunblade

When iron falters & kingdoms fall,

A child of light shall heed the call.

With blade of dawn & soul aflame,

She binds the shattered crown to name.

D awn shattered the night with golden fire like a silent explosion, with sunlight erupting over the jagged ridgelines of the Dawnshire mountains. The citadel, carved into the highest peak like a sacred flame trapped in stone, caught the light first. Gold washed over its towers and spires that burned with brilliance, igniting stained-glass windows and holy terraces. For a fleeting breath, the palace shone like something divine—blessed by the Eternal Sun itself.

Alexandria paused at the treeline and looked back. From this distance, the citadel felt like another life—one burdened by duty, war, and expectations she had never asked for. Here, beneath the whispering canopy of the ancient forest, she could almost pretend the war didn't exist.

Her long dark hair flowed down her back like a silken waterfall, catching hints of copper where the sun kissed it. Her skin bore the soft glow of sun-bronzed warmth, a subtle contrast to the cold steel of her mesmerizing golden eyes—sharp, luminous, and unflinching. She wore finely crafted leather armor, tailored with elegance that whispered of royalty but bore the silence of the wild that was built to disappear amidst the leaves and shadow. In the palace she was a symbol. Here, she was a shadow moving between trees.

But her mind wasn't here yet—not fully. It remained tethered to the war.

The weight of it pressed heavily on her chest, tightening like iron bands with every step she took away from the citadel. The cries of the council still rang in her ears—arguments, reports, casualty numbers, and half-formed strategies. The map table had been stained with blood from a wounded courier just days ago, bringing word that the shadow-creatures had breached yet another border town.

How many more would fall before the Celestial Order could mount a proper defense?

How much longer before the golden fields of Dawnshire turned to ash?

Alexandria had seen the panic in the eyes of nobles who once laughed too loudly at royal feasts. She had seen mothers on their knees, praying under archways to gods that hadn't answered in centuries. The Eternal Sun still shone, but the light felt thinner, as if the gods were holding their breath, waiting to see who would fall first.

Whenever she closed her eyes, she would have many vivid visions. Not of glory, but of fire. Of shadows swallowing the towers of her home. Of screams. Where her dreams became her nightmares.

She exhaled slowly, deliberately.

Just a moment. She needed one moment without war clawing at her thoughts. That was why she came here.

Bellator padded up beside her. The great druidic hound's coat shimmered with mottled patterns of deep brown, midnight black, and snowy white, spots dotting her sides like a wild leopard. Her ears flicked forward. Her body buzzed with silent energy.

Alexandria touched the hound's side gently. "We'll be there soon, sweet girl. Then you can stretch out in the moss, and I can pretend, just for a moment, that we're not at war."

As they stepped beneath the ancient canopy, sunlight thinned to gold-dappled slivers. The forest accepted them with hushed reverence. The cool air clung to her skin, rich with the scent of moss, earth, and nightshade. Leaves whispered above, like the voices of ancestors lost in the wind. Here, the weight of her title loosened its grip. Here, she was just a woman with a dog and too many thoughts. Each stride into the woods dulled the sunlight around her, as if the trees themselves pulled her into another world—one untouched by war, untouched by expectation. Here, she was not a ruler's heir, not a symbol of hope to a desperate kingdom. Here, she was only a soul in search of stillness.

A low growl sounded beside her, familiar and soft. Bellator, her druidic hound—more sister than beast—walked at her side, her eyes sharp, ears flicking. She was always alert, always ready, even here.

"We're not far," Alexandria whispered, brushing her fingers against the druid's thick fur. "Just a little deeper. Then we can breathe."

The river's hum reached her first—a lullaby flowing over stones. But something felt wrong. No birdsong. No chattering squirrels. Just...quiet. Too quiet.

Bellator halted mid-step. A growl started in her throat, low and dangerous.

Alexandria went still.

Then came the sound—a sharp, ragged inhale. Not an animal. Human. Injured.

Bellator jumped in front of Alexandria to stop her from proceeding while she assessed the situation. As she moved toward the sound, a dark, evil presence lingered like a midnight fog. She alerted Alexandria to be careful as they did not know what was lurking around him. Alexandria had seen too much bloodshed in these past months, but this...this seemed different. He was alone. And alive. With caution, she moved toward him. Bellator growled low as Alexandria approached, her fur standing on end.

Moving silently through fern and root, she and Bellator crept toward the source. In the shade of an ancient willow, its trunk twisted like an old spine, lay a man. He was slumped against the roots, cloak torn, blood soaking the ground beneath him. A dark, charred-fletched arrow jutted from his ribs. But worse than the wound was the aura. Shadow spilled from him in curling strands, tendrils of corrupted magic that danced like smoke.

Bellator snarled and stepped forward, her body tensed, teeth bared. "Easy," Alexandria said under her breath, raising a hand. Her golden eyes locked on the man.

He stirred.

Then his eyes opened, brilliant green, fierce even through the pain. The whites of his eyes were too pale, his skin like porcelain dusted in frost. Silver hair, tangled and damp, framed a face that was both sharp and haunted. "Fantastic," he rasped, his voice hoarse but edged with sarcasm. "A sun-eyed princess and a leopard in disguise. Fate has a sick sense of humor."

Alexandria took a step closer, unimpressed. "You have ten seconds to explain why you're bleeding all over my trees before Bellator decides you're fertilizer."

He blinked slowly while smirking despite the blood on his lips, each breath labored. "Well, you don't look like a ranger. You look like regret."

"And you look like a curse that outstayed its welcome. What are you?"

He tried to push himself upright, groaning. "Wounded. Poisoned. Pissed off. That enough of a resume for you?"

Bellator snapped her teeth, stepping forward. "She moves fast," Alexandria warned. "You flinch the wrong way, she'll turn you into compost."

"Not the worst idea," he muttered, glaring at the ground. "At least I'd feed something decent."

"Charming," she deadpanned. "You always whimper this much when someone tries to save you, or is today special?"

"Save me? Is that what this is? You've got a hell of a bedside manner, sunshine."

"You're bleeding on sacred roots. I'm being patient. That's rare."

He groaned again, shifting slightly. "Didn't choose this grove, if that matters. Took an arrow trying to outrun something worse."

Alexandria crouched, careful not to touch the corrupted aura pulsing from his skin. "Blessed fletching," she murmured. "Whoever shot you wasn't just trying to stop you. They wanted you erased."

"Probably someone I insulted. I'm good at that."

"Clearly."

His piercing green eyes narrowed. "Call off your spotted demon before she rips out something I still need, or I'll gut her with my last breath."

Alexandria smirked. "Bellator, hold. He's got enough holes in him." The druid hound stayed tense, her eyes locked on him like a predator waiting for the excuse. "You don't belong here," she said. "This forest doesn't tolerate corruption."

"Neither do you, apparently. And yet...still talking to me. Curious."

"Cautious," she corrected. "Curiosity gets people cursed."

He coughed, blood flecking his lips. "Then stop flirting and finish me off."

"You think this is flirting? Gods help you."

He tried to laugh, then winced. "You've got a mouth on you, Princess."

"And you're bleeding out on my forest floor. I'd say I have the upper hand."

Bellator circled slowly, growling deep in her chest.

With a rasping laugh, short and bitter, he asked, "Then what? You want to play a hero? Heal the monster?"

Alex's eye twitched. "I want to know why something like you is crawling into my forest with an arrow in its side and no backup. Doesn't feel like a siege. Feels like desperation."

He met her gaze, wary but too weak to posture. "Don't help me." A flicker of something darker rolled beneath his skin. "It doesn't end well for you."

Bellator moved closer with a deep growl. He smirked, his eyes fixed on Bellator. "She hates me."

"Yeah. Good judge of character. You should be worried," Alexandria replied.

He chuckled, "If I was worried, you'd already be dead. And I'm not trying to die. Which is why I'm not letting you anywhere near my blood."

Alexandria rolled her eyes. "You think I want your nasty mortal insides? I'm trying to fix something before you become a walking infection."

"And yet here we are. You, broken and smug. Me, dying and pissed. Royal fairy tale." He cut his eyes up to her.

Alexandria smirked. "Oh, you're charming. Let me guess— emotionally unavailable and dying of pride?"

"I'm not a threat," he muttered. "At least not right now... It's getting worse. Whatever is attached to this arrow...whispers now."

She looked at Bellator then back at him. "Then shut up and let me help you before it starts speaking through you."

Reluctantly, he agreed. "Fine. But if that mutt so much as drools on me, I'm setting her on fire."

Bellator growled again.

Alexandria grinned darkly. "You'll be lucky if she doesn't eat your liver. Now, hold still, smartass. You're leaking darkness like a cracked vial of shadowbrew." She leaned closer, her eyes narrowing at the wound. The corruption pulsed, fighting the light. If she pulled the arrow out now, he'd bleed out. But leaving it...wasn't an option.

"We can't do this here. You'll die. I have a cabin nearby and supplies there. You'll survive—maybe."

His eyes flickered with something unreadable, but he remained tense. "I don't have time for this. I have somewhere I need to be."

"Not in your condition," she countered, glancing at the arrow. "You're losing too much blood. If it isn't treated, you'll be dead before sunrise."

He exhaled sharply, his frustration evident. "I can't afford to be delayed."

She met his gaze with a quiet intensity. "Then you're lucky I'm stubborn. Come with me, or I will drag you myself."

His brow twitched, a mix of irritation and reluctant amusement passing through his expression. "I doubt you could," he muttered, though the exhaustion in his voice betrayed him.

Alexandria crossed her arms. "Try me."

A muscle in his jaw tightened. He couldn't win this argument in his state. With a weary sigh, he relented. "Fine. But only until I can walk on my own."

She smiled—gentle, but triumphant. "Good. Now lean on me."

With effort, he allowed her to slip an arm under his, helping him to his feet. He gritted his teeth, and groaned as he leaned into her support. He was heavier than she expected, his frame strong despite his weakened state.

As they began their slow trek through the forest, he finally spoke again. "What's your name, Princess?"

"Alexandria."

A flicker of recognition passed over his face, but he quickly replied, "I'm Erythyn Darkbane."

She didn't question the hesitance in his voice, but she noticed it. Something about him felt...guarded. As if he held secrets woven deep into his being. "You said you had somewhere to be," she mused after a moment. "What is so important that you'd rather die on the forest floor than accept help?"

His grip tightened slightly on her shoulder. "Something bigger than myself," he murmured.

Alexandria glanced at him, curiosity sparking in her chest. "That sounds like a lonely burden to bear."

Erythyn exhaled, gaze fixed ahead. "It is."

Silence fell between them as the forest pulsed with life around them—crickets sang in the underbrush, the river whispered over smooth stones, and the trees swayed like silent sentinels in the night breeze. Yet, between them, unspoken tension simmered.

Alexandria tightened her grip on Erythyn's arm, feeling the strain in his body as they trudged forward, his weight pressing against her with every faltering step.

"You shouldn't be out here alone," Erythyn muttered, his voice low but edged with something unreadable.

Alexandria let out a soft huff. "Neither should you."

A ghost of a smirk tugged at the corner of his lips, but it faded just as quickly. He exhaled sharply through his nose. "I don't have a choice."

"Everyone has a choice," she countered, adjusting her grip as they maneuvered over a patch of gnarled roots. "Even in war, even in duty—

there's always a choice."

Erythyn winced as the arrow shifted, but he shook his head. "Not always."

The weight in his words stirred her curiosity. She glanced up at him, taking in the sharp lines of his face, the unkempt strands of silver hair sticking to his forehead. His features were hardened by something beyond mere pain—something deeper, more complex.

"What were you doing out here?" she asked after a pause.

His jaw tensed, his eyes flickering toward her before returning to the forest path ahead. "Hunting."

"For what? Trouble?"

A humorless chuckle escaped him. "It tends to find me regardless."

Alexandria sighed. "Yeah, I can understand that."

Erythyn's steps slowed slightly. "And you ask too many questions."

"If I hadn't, you'd still be bleeding out by that tree," she quipped, arching an eyebrow. "You're lucky I came when I did."

"Lucky," he murmured, almost to himself.

His gaze drifted downward, clouded with something Alexandria couldn't quite place. She studied him for a long moment. "Who are you really, Erythyn?"

For the briefest moment, his mask faltered. His lips parted slightly, as if he might answer, but then he shut his mouth and shook his head. "No one important."

Alexandria narrowed her eyes. "That's not true."

Erythyn clenched his jaw. "It is if I say it is."

She stopped walking, forcing him to halt as well. He let out a quiet grunt of protest, his breathing uneven, but she stood firm, her expression unwavering. "You're not 'no one.' No one fights through an injury like that for nothing. No one stares into the night like they're carrying the weight of the world on their shoulders unless it matters."

Erythyn's fingers twitched where they gripped his side, his posture rigid. "I can't tell you."

"Why not?"

"Because knowing me is dangerous," he muttered, his voice low and edged with exhaustion. "And you don't need another war to fight, Princess."

Alex's heart pounded at his words, but she didn't let them sway her. "Then it's too late for that," she said simply. "Because I already found you. And I don't abandon the wounded."

Erythyn searched her face, as if weighing her words, testing their truth. He must have found something in them because, after a long silence, he let out a slow, tired breath. "You're stubborn," he said finally.

"So I've been told," she replied with a small, knowing smile.

They continued their trek in silence for a while, as shadowy wisps drifted between the trees. Golden eyes gleamed from the shadows, belonging to creatures unseen, with fireflies dancing in hypnotic patterns, their iridescent wings leaving trails of sparkling dust in the thick air.

The wind carried faint whispers, not menacing but secretive, as if the forest itself held untold stories. Bellator, cutting her eyes up at Alex, made sure that she was not being foolish and using her discernment. Alexandria could feel Erythyn's body growing heavier against her, his energy waning. She wasn't sure if he would make it to the cabin before collapsing entirely. She tightened her grip on him, pulling him closer as they neared the cabin hidden among the trees. "Just a little farther," she murmured. "You'll be safe soon."

Erythyn exhaled, his voice barely above a whisper. "Safety is a luxury I haven't had in a long time."

Alexandria glanced up at him, her chest tightening at the raw honesty in his tone. "Then maybe it's time you found it again."

She noticed that Bellator ran off into the distance as she transitioned into one of her many forms. Suddenly, now embodied as an owl, Bellator landed on a towering tree as they approached the cobblestone cabin in the middle of the forest.

It had been built entirely from irregularly shaped cobblestone, each stone smoothed by time yet worn with cracks and moss-covered patches. The stones varied in shades of gray, brown, and green, tightly fitted together, though some had shifted slightly, giving the cabin a slightly uneven, rustic appearance.

The front door was an ancient slab of dark weathered oak, reinforced with rusted iron bands. A round, dusty window, fogged with age, rested near the top of the door, allowing a dim glow to filter inside. Around the cabin, the forest had begun to reclaim the land. Towering trees with thick, gnarled roots pressed close to the structure, their branches intertwining overhead to form a natural canopy. The forest floor was carpeted in layers of fallen leaves, soft moss, and scattered stones, some of which bore faint carvings from an ancient time.

Off in the distance from the cabin stood a towering stone wall that enclosed ancient ruins. The wall, weathered and cracked, was covered in creeping ivy and patches of moss. Its once-precise carvings were now softened by centuries of wind and rain. Some stones had crumbled, leaving jagged gaps where nature had begun to reclaim the structure. A massive stone archway, once grand and unyielding, now stood fractured, the edges softened by centuries of erosion. Vines and moss crept along their surfaces, weaving nature into the remnants of human craftsmanship.

Beyond, the wall held the ancient ruins that Alexandria did not allow anyone but Bellator near.

Without a whisper of wind, Bellator's hoot rose from the treetop like a call cast though the veil between worlds, a guardian's vow to hold the line while Alexandria stepped into the hush of the sacred cabin.

As Alexandria guided Erythyn up the steps and through the door of the cabin, he didn't pull away. When they stepped inside, the air was thick with the scent of aged wood, wild herbs, and a faint trace of something like magic woven into the very foundation. The large wall in front of them was made from ancient gnarled timber that seemed almost alive, the surface carved with shifting patterns of vines and glowing runes pulsing faintly in response to the movement.

The ceiling towered high, its beams intertwined with twisting roots and hanging lanterns filled with the soft enchanting glow from the fireflies that filled the room. A massive stone hearth dominated one side of the cabin. She held her right hand up in its direction and closed her eyes, muttering a silent call, and the fire ignited, burning with ever-changing hues—blue, green, and gold—casting dancing shadows across the room.

The furniture looked as if it grew straight from the earth itself. A sturdy wooden table, its surface polished smooth but still marked with the knots of grain of an ancient tree, was surrounded by mismatched chairs—some with curved legs that resembled roots, others adorned with carvings of mythical creatures. A thick fur-covered armchair sat beside the fire, its cushions plush and inviting as if it remembered every soul that had rested there.

Shelves carved directly into the walls held books bound in leather and strange, shifting materials, their titles written in languages long forgotten.

They made their way up the spiral staircase constructed of intertwined branches leading to a loft where a soft, moss-covered bed rested beneath the skylight. "You need to lay here. I will extract the arrow, and you will have a place to rest until you are healed," Alexandria said as Erythyn cut his eyes back to her, wanting to fight back though he didn't have the energy to as the wound had drained most of his strength.

He conceded and laid down on the bed. The glow of the moon and stars filtered through the skylight overhead as they cast silver beams that danced across the room, forming shapes that told forgotten stories. The cabin was silent, the wood creaking softly as the wind whispered through the trees.

Alexandria knelt beside the bed where Erythyn lay. His breathing was shallow, his face pale. The dark entity's curse had left him weakened, but she could still see the flicker of life in his chest. Though, she worried if he could make it through the night...

Chapter 2
The Cursed Arrow

The Song of the Moonlit Forest

In silver glade where wolves now tread,

The shadows dance where ancients bled.

Their voices hum through winding trees,

A lullaby to cease all pleas.

The arrow, lodged deep in his side, was the source of the darkness that lingered. She looked at the arrow, its shaft darkened by the cursed magic that had seeped into his veins. The metal glinted ominously in the low light, as if aware of its power over him. She took a deep breath, steadying her trembling hands.n

Erythyn groaned. "Ugh... The pain... It's unbearable!"

"I know this is hard, but I'm here to help you. Please, just hold still."

Erythyn wailed out in pain with a deep penetrating grunt. "Are you trying to kill me?"

"Really, you think I would bring you here if I wanted to kill you? You really are delusional!" She glared at him. "Hold on. This is going to hurt!"

The room felt colder as she gripped the arrow, her fingers brushing over the intricate carvings that swirled along its length. With a final glance at Erythyn, she started to pull the arrow free, the movement slow and deliberate. She gently lifted the arrow from his side, feeling a surge of energy coursing through her. Erythyn grunted once more, though a brief sigh of relief escaped him as his eyes rolled toward the back of his head, and he instantaneously passed out from the pain.

Alexandria looked at the arrow in her hand, crafted from the ancient wood of the sacred tree, glowing with a soft, ethereal light. The markings on the shaft seemed to pulse, resonating with the forest's magic. She carefully examined the arrow, noting the intricate engravings that told of its origin and purpose. The arrow was designed not only to pierce but to purify, to cleanse the darkness and restore light.

She recalled the stories passed down through generations, tales of how this arrow once banished darkness from the forest, infused with magical energy, holding the key to breaking a dark spell. With a deep breath, Alexandria gripped the arrow firmly. She stepped into the center of the room, the arrow glowing faintly in her hands. The shadows around her seemed to pulse, almost as if they were aware of her power.

She took a steady breath, feeling the ancient magic of the forest flow through her, connecting her to the land she was sworn to protect. With a deep focus, she raised the arrow high above her head. As she did, the air thickened with energy, the forest outside responding to her call. The ground trembled slightly, as if the earth itself was holding its breath. The light from the window grew brighter, surrounding the arrow with a warm, golden glow that intensified with each passing moment.

She spoke a single, ancient word under her breath, a word that had been lost to time but passed down through the royal bloodline. It was a word that called forth the purity of the forest, the untainted light that had been hidden away for so long. As the word left her lips, the arrow hummed with power, and a burst of radiant light erupted from it, filling the room and spilling into the forest beyond.

A soft crackling sound filled the air as the curse began to dissipate, its dark tendrils withdrawing from his body. For a moment, it felt as though the very room was stopped in time, waiting to see if the light would return to him. A faint glow began to emanate from Erythyn's chest, where the curse had once clung. Alexandria watched, her heart racing, as some of the darkness receded, replaced by the warm light of healing magic. The first signs of life returned to his face, a gentle color filling his cheeks as he began to stir.

Alexandria stood silently beside the bed where Erythyn lay motionless. His skin was almost translucent in the filtered morning light, stretched taut over high cheekbones and a strong jawline. His hair, pure white, fanned across the pillow like strands of winter silk. Beneath his closed lids, faint shadows darkened, and though he breathed, he did so shallowly—trapped in whatever battle still raged within.

She lingered there, her brows furrowed in thought. Her long dark hair, loosely braided over one shoulder, shimmered with the glow of the morning sun. Her golden eyes—piercing and ever observant—never left him.

"You look like death," she whispered. "But there's something still fighting in you. Something that won't give in." She took one last lingering look at him, his body still pale and cold. She knew he would need time to recover and that time was something she could not afford to waste. A soft creak echoed as the door swung open behind her. A breeze swept in, carrying the crisp scent of pine and frost. Alexandria turned away from the bed, exhaling quietly.

Bellator rushed down from the tree branch she was observing from, shifting back to her canine form. She stood waiting in the doorway, a druidic hound of imposing stature with a coat resembling the deep hues of the ancient forest, she was attuned to the unseen energies of the natural world and was alerted to a malevolent aura that clung to the stranger, stirring unease within her loyal heart. The hound's icy eyes were fixed on her mistress, full of concern.

Alexandria made her way downstairs and joined her, closing the cabin door gently behind her. Bellator whined softly and looked back toward the window, her ears laid slightly flat. "I know," Alexandria said, placing a hand on the hound's head. "I feel it too. There's something...wrong. It's not him exactly. But something surrounds him. A shadow that doesn't belong."

Bellator gave a low, affirming growl.

"I need you to stay with him," Alexandria added, crouching beside her loyal companion. "If anything changes—anything at all—you let me know. I don't trust whatever is clinging to him, but we can't let him face it alone."

Bellator leaned into her touch then licked her hand in quiet agreement. Her muscles tensed with unspoken worry, but she gave a final low bark of understanding.

Alexandria stood and looked eastward. A memory played in her mind of ancient tales told by the elders of the forest when she was just a young child—the ancient magical ice tree, deep within the ruins. Its waters, said to be imbued with the purest form of magic, could heal even the deepest of wounds, the most insidious of curses.

"I'll go to the Ancient Ice Tree. The healing waters may be the only thing that can help him now. The unnatural energy that surrounds him is something so dark and evil, this might be the only thing that can save him."

Without another word, she turned and slipped into the trees.

The forest beyond the cabin felt older than time. Sunlight filtered through the dense canopy in thin, golden shafts that illuminated dancing dust motes in the air. The deeper she walked, the more surreal the atmosphere became—colors seemed richer, sounds more distant. Her boots crunched over frost-kissed moss, each step accompanied by the distant call of unseen birds. Roots curled across the ground like petrified serpents, and above her, the trees groaned softly, as if murmuring in a language long forgotten. Ivy choked stone relics left behind by civilizations that no longer had names, and her fingers brushed one as she passed—a carved sun worn smooth by wind and rain.

As she moved, her thoughts returned to Erythyn. That pale face, those unnaturally piercing green eyes burning even in weakness. She couldn't shake the image. The darkness around him felt like a living thing —coiling, feeding. And yet, he hadn't lashed out. He hadn't begged. He hadn't asked for anything.

"Who are you really?" she murmured, stepping over a broken archway swallowed by brambles.

As she walked beyond the gate, she took in the beauty, the ruins stretching into the misty landscape. Towering pillars, broken and leaning, rose from the earth like skeletal remains. The ruins themselves rose like a forgotten kingdom. Crumbled archways cast long shadows over the stone pathways, now cracked and overtaken by wildflowers and creeping ivy. The air was thick with the scent of damp earth and aged stone, carrying the distant whisper of wind through the hollow corridors. A massive stone archway, once grand and unyielding, now stood fractured, the edges softened by centuries of erosion. Vines and moss crept along their surfaces, weaving nature into the remnants of human craftsmanship. The gate, once grand and imposing, was now rusted and half-buried beneath tangled vines. The carvings on its surface, eroded by time, hinted at an ancient civilization—faded symbols and worn inscriptions barely visible beneath the moss.

As Alexandria proceeded, the ground crunched beneath her feet. The eerie silence, occasionally broken by the call of a distant bird or the rustling of unseen creatures in the undergrowth, felt as though the ruins were watching, holding onto the echoes of the past, waiting for their story to be rediscovered.

In the heart of the ancient ruins, deep within the mystical forest, stood a breathtaking ancient magical ice tree, its branches shimmering with frost. Its bark was as white as snow, and its leaves shimmered like crystal. It pulsed with a quiet, eternal light, a living source of magic that seemed to hum in the stillness of the air.

She approached the tree with reverence, knowing that its magic was not easily tamed. She knelt before the tree, her heart pounding in her chest. She knew she was not just seeking water; she was seeking the very essence of the forest's power. She reached out, her fingers brushing against the ice-cold trunk, feeling the ancient magic stir beneath her touch. With a whispering incantation, she called upon the magic of the tree, her voice soft but sure, as if speaking to an old friend.

The ice tree responded, its branches swaying despite the stillness of the air. Slowly, a small pool of shimmering, ethereal water formed at its roots, glowing with an almost otherworldly light. She watched, entranced by its beauty, as the water sparkled, its surface undisturbed by the air around it, as though it existed in perfect harmony with the world.

Carefully, she lowered her flask into the pool, capturing the precious liquid. The moment the water touched the vessel, she could feel the magic surging through her fingertips, a warmth that contrasted with the frigid surroundings like the river beside it singing in a language only the oldest trees might understand. "Healing always comes at a price," she said under her breath, her eyes lifting toward the sparkling branches above. "I just hope he's worth it." She rose again, holding the vial close, the sunlight dancing within it.

The return back to the cabin seemed to take longer as Alexandria's thoughts consumed her. The conversation between her and Erythyn replayed over and over. The image of him collapsed near the river flashed in her mind like her spirit was trying to tell her something, though she wasn't quite sure what. Questions started to flood in. What was he doing in the forest to begin with? Where was he heading to? Who shot him with the arrow? Why did he seem so broken? Questions she didn't have answers to weighed on her like someone trapped inside with no escape. The forest was still and quiet, uncomfortably quiet with the heavy thickness of something ancient lingering in the distance. She couldn't shake it, though she proceeded anyway, pushing the thoughts out of her mind for now.

Her heart raced faster as she arrived. The room was dim and hushed, the only light spilling in from the cracked shutters casting long golden lines across the bed. The air was warm, tinged with the scent of herbs and sweat, and the faint crackle of a dying fire whispered in the corner. Alexandria stepped quietly inside. Her eyes immediately found Erythyn.

He lay sprawled across the bed, half-tangled in a linen sheet, his skin glistening with sweat. His chest rose and fell in slow, heavy breaths, each one laboring as if he'd been fighting battles even in his sleep. His hair clung damp to his brow, and his lips—soft, parted—seemed to murmur things only dreams could hear.

Alexandria froze at the foot of the bed, her gaze tracing the line of his jaw, the strong curve of his neck, the lean muscle along his shoulders. He had tossed aside his shirt at some point, leaving nothing to separate her from the broad plane of his chest, where droplets of sweat slid lazily down his ribs and stomach. The sight ignited something she hadn't expected—a deep, molten pull low in her belly. He was beautiful.

Infuriatingly beautiful.

She stepped closer, slowly and carefully so that she did not wake him. Her hand hovered briefly over his forehead then gently swept a strand of hair away. His skin was hot beneath her fingers. Feverish. But even in this vulnerable state, he carried a raw, simmering energy, like coals smoldering under the surface.

Why him? she wondered as her thumb brushed against his temple.

He was arrogant. Always had something clever to say, pushed her buttons just to see what would happen. And yet, she was intrigued by him and she was not sure why.

Maybe it was the way he looked at her like he could see through every wall she'd ever built.

She let her eyes travel over him again. The gentle rise of his abdomen. The way his hand curled instinctively near his chest, as if cradling a secret. The rhythm of his breath, so steady and alive.

Alexandria sat down at the edge of the bed, her heart pounding in her throat, watching the curve of his lips twitch faintly as he dreamt. She didn't dare touch him again. Not yet. Not when everything felt like it might burn down at the slightest spark. But the fire that burned inside her said she wanted to.

Not just his body—but the man beneath the bravado, the fire, the fierce, maddening soul of him.

And sitting there, with his head fevered, his breath whispering in the silence, and his skin bathed in sweat, Alexandria knew one truth with aching certainty:

She was in trouble...

She watched as his steady breathing reassured her that he was no longer in immediate danger from the injury, but she knew the curse still lingered in his body, hidden beneath the skin. Alexandria glanced down at Bellator, noting the tension in her posture. She whispered softly, ensuring Erythyn couldn't overhear, "I sense your unease, Bellator. Do you believe this darkness is inherent to him, or is it something external?"

Bellator emitted a low whine, her eyes reflecting concern. She nudged Alex's hand gently, guiding her attention to the faint, shadowy tendrils that seemed to wisp around Erythyn's form—visible only to those with heightened perception. Understanding her implication, Alexandria furrowed her brow. "An external force, then," she murmured. "Perhaps a curse or a malevolent entity seeking to exploit him."

Bellator huffed in agreement, her gaze never leaving Erythyn. Determined to uncover the truth, Alexandria resolved, "We must now perform a cleansing ritual. If there is a dark presence attached to him, we'll do everything in our power to dispel it."

Bellator's tail gave a slight wag, signaling her approval of the plan.

She walked to Erythyn's side, kneeling once more. She uncorked the flask and gently poured a few drops of the ancient magical water over his wound, watching as the liquid absorbed into his skin. The air thickened with the power of the water, and for a moment, she held her breath. As he lay there rugged, bare-chested, his flushed, almost glowing skin radiated heat. His chest was slightly damp with sweat. The moisture clung to his skin in a thin sheen as his body struggled to regulate the intense heat.

His muscles tensed, and his breathing was slightly labored. Suddenly, he reacted with an intense, instinctive response as his body jolted awake in a state of panic, his muscles tensing as if preparing for danger. His hand trembled as he reached out to grab her wrist, wailing in pain, yelling out to her, "What are you doing?" as she poured a second dose on the wound, pushing more forcibly against his ribs with her other hand.

He wailed out in agony. As the water seeped into the wound, his eyes started to roll to the back of his head as Alexandria tried to reassure him not to worry. "I am not your enemy. I can help you." His grip around her wrist loosened as he started to drift back into a state of unconsciousness.

Alexandria and Bellator then left to go down the stairs from the loft. She gave one last look over her shoulder to verify he was out. She was so intrigued by this man, though she didn't know why.

She proceeded down the stairs to make a soup as Erythyn had not eaten in days. Alexandria looked at Bellator. "You can go, girl. I'll be okay."

Bellator cut her eyes at Alexandria as if she was not quite sure she could handle him if he were to wake up.

"Really, I will be fine," Alexandria insisted.

Bellator hesitated but proceeded outside anyway. She then transformed again and quickly perched up in a tree so she could have a bird's eye view in case Alexandria needed her help. She let out a hoot so that Alexandria knew that her protector was watching.

Chapter 3
From Comfort to Chaos

Ode to the Druid's Guardian

Fierce of fang & steadfast might,

You stand between the dark & light.

Though flesh may fail & bone may break,

Your oath the world shall never shake.

*I*nside the cabin, bundles of dried herbs hung from the ceiling, suspended by twine that twisted and knotted itself as needed. Sage, rosemary, and lavender mingled with rarer enchanted plants, their scents filling the air with an intoxicating blend of spice and mystery. A large deep sink sat beneath a window framed by creeping ivy. The window offered a breathtaking view of the enchanted forest outside, where trees shifted ever so slightly as if breathing and fireflies danced in mesmerizing patterns.

On one side of the window, open shelves carved directly into the wooden walls held an eclectic collection of enchanted cookware. Copper pots gleamed with a soft inner light, delicate ceramic bowls and plates were etched with runes that subtly glowed, and glass jars were filled with preserved mystical berries. Alexandria walked over and grabbed a teapot to set on the fire. Its delicate golden sheen hummed softly, preparing the tea before a word was even spoken.

The kitchen radiated a sense of life, as if it responded once she entered it. Every object from cutting boards to ladles held a sense of magic, working together to create a space where cooking was more than a craft— it was an act of enchantment. With the tea kettle whistling, she reached to the shelf to grab a cup. As she poured her tea, she replayed the conversations she had with Erythyn over in her head.

"There has to be more to the story as to why he was in this forest to begin with, and I plan on getting to the bottom of it," she thought aloud.

As she glanced in the corner, a carved wooden pantry door, etched with ancient symbols, opened ever so gently on its own as if it had a mind of its own, knowing exactly what she needed. Some herbs, rare spices, and fresh vegetables from the garden levitated over to a large wooden bowl as she gathered and prepared to make supper. A wooden cutting board etched with ancient symbols floated overhead onto the counter in front of her.

She started chopping the vegetables and adding them to the pot, the warm, spiced scent of wild mushrooms and leftover liquid starlight water. She guided the wooden spoon slowly, practicing circles by her hands that knew the language of nourishment and magic, swirling the broth occasionally and tossing in a pinch of sparkling stardust. The potion-like stew shifted colors in response, turning to a luminous shade of golden hues.

As the stew thickened, the cabin was filled with a powerful aroma, and it hummed with a quiet living magic, as if the walls themselves were listening for the moment the meal was ready. She looked out the window to see Bellator, perched up on a branch, let out a hoot almost harmonizing with the bubbling pot. Alexandria continued to stir the pot as the stew thickened. The rich aroma of simmering stew—roasted roots, herbs, and something faintly sweet—was thick and comforting as it filled the room with the quiet ancient magic of the forest.

Suddenly, the peaceful atmosphere shattered in an instant. The rhythmic bubbling of the pot and soft crackle of the magical fire seemed distant, fading into a muffled hum. She heard movement coming from upstairs. Then a sudden collapse—a heavy thud, limbs hitting the worn wooden floor of the staircase leading to the loft. Erythyn tumbled down with a series of jarring thumps, each step catching an elbow, then a shoulder, then his head. A wooden chair toppled over in his wake, scraping harshly against the floor before slamming onto its side.

Alexandria froze for a brief moment and gripped the spoon tighter, her heartbeat loud and pulsing in her ears. The floating lanterns smeared into streaks of golden light as they began to sway at a rapid pace. Then the rush of movement—a sharp inhale, footsteps hurrying over toward her with hands reaching out. The peaceful hum of the cabin was broken now, replaced with hurried breaths, a whisper, and the flickering glow of firelight casting frantic shadows against the walls.

Erythyn pulled his arm back, throwing a dagger with brute force, aligning with Alex's head as she stood with her eyes closed, listening and feeling all the energy in the room. She heard the dagger cutting through the air and dwarfed her head to the left, causing it to fly by, piercing into the wooden wall in front of her. She quickly turned, throwing a green ball of energy out of her right hand, heading directly at him. He was thrown backward, crashing into a shelf, sending jars of glowing herbs and enchanted spices clattering down—glass shattering, powders puffing into the air like a ghostly mist.

It then turned into a frantic, chaotic chase as the scuffle escalated. "What are you doing?" Alexandria yelled out.

"What am I doing? What the hell did you put on me?"

"It's a healing medicine. You're crazy! *Stop!*"

"*No!* You put some sort of witchcraft on me, and now I am going to kill you!"

It had now become a scuffle between a force of good and evil inside the enchanted cabin. The battle wasn't just physical—it was a clash of ideals, their every move driven by opposing logic and beliefs. Alexandria fought with precision, seeking to defend rather than destroy. Her strikes were aimed at disarming and subduing rather than causing unnecessary harm, using the cabin itself—enchanted runes carved into the walls flaring to life, the floating lanterns darting and blinding and distracting, the very floor shifting beneath their feet to throw him off balance.

Her logic was built on protection, on preserving life, on preventing darkness from spreading. Erythyn, in contrast, fought with chaos and raw aggression, without regard for the damage he inflicted. He sought dominance, to overwhelm with brute force and dark trickery. He lashed out wildly, using his shadowy tendrils to knock over shelves, causing the room itself to become a battleground of flying debris and shattered glass. His logic was one of destruction—why waste time with restraint when fear and power could end a fight in an instant?

As they struggled, Alexandria tried to reason with him, her voice strained as she blocked a vicious strike. "You don't have to do this! This place is sacred. Don't let the darkness consume you!"

Erythyn scoffed, dodging and countering with a cruel grin. "Sacred? It's just another cage! Everything burns in the end. Why not speed it along?"

The battle raged—Alexandria fighting to protect, under the weight of their opposing forces, flickering between the warmth of her golden magic and the seething darkness of Erythyn's magic. Neither would give up easily, but in the end, only one ideology would shape the fate of the enchanted cabin.

As they wrestled for dominance, they both crashed through the cabin door, stumbling into the mystical forest beyond. Branches twisted overhead, their gnarled limbs creaking as if watching the fight unfold. Alexandria tried to gain distance, knowing the power the forest held could help her. But Erythyn was relentless, using the terrain to his advantage—shifting shadows, rolling in a thick fog, causing it to obscure the path.

Bellator flew quickly to a nearby branch, giving her an optimal bird's eye view in the event she needed to intervene, though Alexandria knew she must fight this battle on her own. They ended up on the edge of the river as it started to glow, its currents intensifying, the enchanted water pulsing with ancient magic.

Alex, breathing hard, steadied herself, knowing this might be her only chance.

Erythyn grinned as Alexandria hesitated, his voice dripping with confidence. "You're running out of places to hide."

Alexandria gripped her amulet with a spell forming on her lips. The forest started to interact with the fight itself—trees bending, the wind howling as if it was choosing sides. Glowing creatures darted through the air and were pulled into the chaos.

Alexandria was pushed to her limits as she called on a deeper, hidden magic of the forest—tree roots started curling up from barriers, vines coiling around Erythyn's legs to slow him down.

Erythyn, on the other hand, drew on darker powers, summoning an aura of shadow that warped the space around them. Time itself felt like it was bending, as if the very air was suffocating, making it harder to think or move.

The enchanted river acted as a source of Ashlynnwal, its waters shimmering with magical energy. As Alexandria tried to use it as a cleansing force, reaching into the river to draw out the magic to her advantage, the magic of the forest was wild—it didn't follow orders. It was a battle not just between two beings but between the very essence of light and dark, chaos, and order.

Erythyn's presence felt both ancient and powerful. His form shifted subtly in the flickering moonlight, a silhouette that was never quite solid, as if the shadows themselves were clinging to it. His eyes turned obsidian black, eerie bottomless voids that pierced through the darkness, reflecting light in unnatural ways. Long, gnarled horns twisted from his skull, curling like the roots of the ancient trees around them. Jagged, bone-like protrusions lined his spine, barely visible beneath the tattered remnants of what might have once been a cloak—or perhaps something more organic, a shifting, living shadow.

Clawed fingers flexed with an unnatural grace, each talon sharper than a dagger, dripping with a faint black mist that dissolved into the air before touching the ground. He rippled with strange energy. The trees closest to him were twisted, their bark now scorched with unnatural markings, as the forest creatures remained silent in his presence. As he moved, the forest itself seemed to recoil, leaves trembling, as the wind carried a sense of dread that lingered.

As Erythyn pulled back his right arm for another blow toward Alex, Bellator, the guardian of peace and balance, called out, "That is enough!" As her home and Alexandria were threatened, she became a wrath of the wilds with the veil between magic and nature thin. Bellator, perched upon an ancient bough of a towering oak, began to transform. She spread her wings wide, but instead of lifting into flight, her feathers started to shimmer, dissolving into streams of golden light.

The soft hoots gave way to an eerie, melodic hum, reverberating through the trees. The very air around Bellator bent and shifted as nature reshaped her form.

Chapter 4
The Gathering Storm

Fragment of the Shadowlord's Lament

I bore the crown & felt its weight,

Yet found within a hollow fate.

What victory when all is lost,

And souls lie frozen by the frost.

At the castle, The Prime Minister, His Excellency, Sir Valeric Astralhart—a noble and fearsome leader, bound by the duty to protect Alexandria and the realm from all threats, moral or arcane—sensed the battle as he rushed to a nearby towering window. Looking out toward the forest, his eyes were drawn to the sky, where he saw a dark force of energy turning ominous and stormy. Dark clouds rolled in, blocking out the light, with flashes of eerie lightning illuminating the shadows.

The air turned heavy and charged, filled with a sense of foreboding and power. An intense and brooding energy enveloped the sky, transforming it into a battlefield, with swirling storm clouds and bursts of lightning. The forces of good and evil created intense flashes, vibrant auroras, and thunderous sounds—an intense spectacle full of energy and power.

Prime Minister Astralhart rushed to the barracks to inform Sir Aldric Stormrend, General of the Supreme Elite Royal Guard, of what he saw. Within the stone walls of the barracks, the air was thick with the scent of oiled leather, burning incense, and the faint metallic tang of sharpened blades. He could see the Elite Royal Guards moving with disciplined urgency, their preparations a well-rehearsed symphony of steel and resolve.

Torchlight flickered against polished armor, casting long shadows across the vaulted ceilings as warriors fastened buckles, adjusted gauntlets, and strapped on their weapons. With great authority, Prime Minister Astralhart announced, "There is a battle in the skies over the forest!"

"Yes, sir, we are preparing now," General Stormrend responded.

Without hesitation, Prime Minister Astralhart replied, "Put the castle on lockdown immediately. Have the other guards prepare to disburse around the property and along the treeline. In case you need backup, they will be ready."

General Stormrend assertively responded, "Yes, sir."

No one else spoke until Brandell Blackthorn, Master of Weapons, broke the silence.

"Scouts reported it at dawn, a black cloud rolling in from the Enchanted Forest. They say it's alive."

Astralhart's jaw tightened. He turned to Sir Azareth Vossfyr, the Royal Guards Wizard, whose eyes already glowed with arcane awareness. "I felt it long before the scouts returned. Raw magic, twisted. It's corrupting the trees, leeching the light," Vossfyr stated.

A fresh rumble of unease filled the room. At the back, Elowen Duskbane, the Ranger from the wilds, stepped forward, his fingers brushing his bow. "Villagers fled the forest edge at first light. Whispers of people lost, screams cut short. And Princess Alexandria rode in there yesterday."

A collective breath filled the room. Finally, Drystan Nightbane, the seer, rose from his shadowed corner, his voice a hollow echo. "I...saw her spirit bound beneath that darkness. She calls for help, but I cannot reach her through a void."

Astralhart closed his eyes for a heartbeat. Then he opened them, steel in his gaze.

"So we know only this: a living shadow devours the forest, and our princess is trapped inside it. No more questions, only action," Astralhart demanded as he stepped forward, his hand sweeping across the rough-hewn map on the table. "Brandell, gather your swordsingers. Azareth, ready wards to shield our approach. Elowen, lead us to her path. Drystan, keep your sight on her soul. You ride at once."

Brandell's nod was crisp. Azareth's staff ignited in a flicker of blue flame. Elowen's boots scraped the stone as he shouldered his bow. Drystan lifted a pale hand, already whispering an invocation.

Astralhart turned back to the darkened window where the black cloud pressed like a living thing against the forest line. He muttered under his breath, "For Alexandria. No force on earth will keep me from her."

"Sir," Captain Stormrend replied. "Bellator is in the forest with Alexandria. My men are ready." As he scanned the room, he could hear the tightening of straps, ensuring every piece of armor sat perfectly in place. Some muttered battle hymns under their breath, a tradition meant to steel the soul before combat.

Others stood in quiet contemplation, their fingers tracing the symbols etched into their weapons, finding solace in the magic woven through them. Sir Astralhart moved among the soldiers, anointing their foreheads with sacred oil, murmuring blessings to guard them against whatever horrors lay ahead. The soft chime of ceremonial bells echoed through the chamber as he whispered final words of protection.

The captain strode through the ranks, barking final orders. "Check your weapons! Ensure your wards are intact! We do not enter the forest unprepared!" The warriors responded with sharp nods, their eyes burning with determination.

By the time the horn's call rang through the barracks, signaling their departure, the Royal Guards were no longer merely soldiers—they were the unbreakable shield of the kingdom, ready to step into the unknown depths of the enchanted forest and face whatever awaited them.

"My men are ready, sir. We will bring Princess Alexandria back," General Stormrend announced.

"God have mercy on you all!" Prime Minister Astralhart replied.

As the royal guardsmen dashed from the castle, their polished armor gleamed in the sun as they charged across the vast plains, the earth trembling beneath their feet. The scent of damp earth and wild magic filled the air as the forest loomed before them, its towering trees swaying unnaturally as if aware of the impending conflict. As they entered the magical forest, the atmosphere shifted; the dense canopy filtered the sunlight, casting morsels of light and shadow on the forest floor.

The guardsmen's footsteps became quieter as they moved deeper into the woods, surrounded by towering trees and the sounds of nature. Each step was filled with anticipation as they readied themselves for the looming battle.

Chapter 5
Awakening of the
Forest Guardian

The Lost Eulogy of the First Queen

She gave her all without regret,

Her name the Sun would not forget.

Through time may crumble stone & sand,

Her mercy rings through every land.

Deep in the heart of the forest, Bellator was perched silently in the limbs of an ancient ash tree as she had taken the guise of a spectral owl—her feathers swirling with the colors of dusk, her icy eyes piercing through the thickness of the forest. On the ground, Erythyn and Alexandria's clashing battle caused warping winds, forcing the leaves to shake from their homes like frightened birds.

In that moment, Bellator shifted.

Her feathers dissolved into green flame, and wings became arms wreathed in vines and thorns. Her form stretched, lengthened, until the owl was gone, and in its place stood a druidess, cloaked in bark-tone leathers that clothed her body each time she shifted into human form. She was sleeved in sacred tattoos that pulsed with the heartbeat of the forest. Her icy colored eyes shimmered with wild clarity. She dropped from the branch like a falling star, landing softly on the forest floor, blades of grass curled around her feet.

Bellator was now in the Forest True Form, a woman of power and undeniable grace.

She moved as wind through leaves—fluid, purposeful, and untouchable. Around her, butterflies of glowing amber followed, drawn to the magic that spilled from her like sunlight through the trees. Her presence smelt of earth after rain and wild blossoms tripped by moonlight.

In her hand formed a staff of twisted oak, topped with a living spring that loomed with every movement, a symbol of balance. As she walked, the ground responded: petals unfurled beneath her steps, and even the shadows leaned away in reverence.

Bellator was no mere illusion. She was the memory of the first grove, the guardian spirit of all things rooted, winged, and wild. Through her body, the forest spoke, fought, and defended.

Now, the awakened feminine form was nothing short of a divine manifestation—a living statue carved not of marble, but of earth, spirit, and ancient magic. Her figure was statuesque, both lithe and commanding, shaped by the wind's caress and the strength of ancient trees. She stood tall and proud, her limbs long and elegant, her muscles toned not through warfare but through the patient, enduring power of nature itself.

She wore armor of the forest—not forged, but grown. A bodice of woven bark shaped like overlapping leaves hugged her torso, flexible and unbreakable, clasped with knots of glowing amber. Draped over her shoulders was a long, asymmetrical cloak of moss and spider-silk threads, flowing and alive, catching light like dew on cobwebs at dawn.

Wherever she stepped, the forest responded, the earth rose slightly to cushion her, flowers opened, and even corrupted ground trembled before cleansing beneath her presence.

Bellator was not just beautiful. She was sacred, untamed, and primeval. She did not just represent the forest. She was the forest awakened, walking and ready to defend her realm with wrath wrapped in wild grace.

As Alexandria dropped to one knee beside the forest stream, her chest rising and falling with exhaustion, blood and sweat mingling at her brow, the battlefield still burned with the residue of dark magic. The trees groaned, their leaves curling in dread, and the stream itself recoiled from Erythyn's presence. The corrupted spirit towered nearby like a smoldering wound in the world.

Alexandria gripped the hilt of her sword, but her strength waned.

Then, they felt a tremor.

A pulse ran through the ground, not of destruction, but of awakening. The moss brightened. The shadows hesitated.

From the veil of hanging vines behind him stepped Bellator, in druidic form, now fully manifested. Her presence was a balm to the broken forest and a curse to Erythyn.

She didn't speak. She didn't need to.

The magic that flowed through her was both beautiful and terrifying, an echo of the forest's oldest memory and fiercest vengeance. As she walked, the air thickened with life. Roots wriggled up from the soil like fingers sensing prey. Flowers bloomed rapidly then snapped shut like jaws. The forest was no longer passive—it was hers.

With a flick of her staff. Bellator summoned a storm of roots and vines that erupted from the ground like serpents. These were not gentle tendrils. They whipped and coiled with sentient fury, cracking through rocks and stone. They ensnared Erythyn's limbs, anchoring him, strangling his shadows, pulling at the very darkness within him. Wherever the roots touched, his corruptive energy began to sizzle away, like acid on flesh.

Raising both arms to the heavens, Bellator called upon the light of the hidden moon. A beam of silver fire cascaded from the canopy, focused like a blade. It cut through Erythyn's illusion, piercing his wraithform and pinning him in place. The light was more than radiant. It was truth, and he could not hide his weakness beneath it.

The beam left glowing scars across his form, exposing the hollow echo of the soul he once had and lashing out with tendrils of corrupted shadow.

Erythyn, momentarily distracted by the sudden transformation, snarled, his shadowed form rearing back, smoke trailing like chains behind him. But Alex, ever in sync with Bellator, didn't waste the moment.

When Erythyn retaliated, lashing out with tendrils of corrupted shadow, Bellator danced through the battlefield with impossible grace. Each step sent leaves fluttering in her wake. She became partially translucent, like a spirit herself, her form fluttering in her wake.

Erythyn rose from the shadows, his voice a low rasp layered with a dozen echoes.

"So... The forest sends you, its favorite child. Do you think your vines and light can undo centuries of rot?"

Bellator stepped from the mist, glowing with forest wrath. "I am not sent. I am the forest. And you are a wound in its skin, Erythyn, one that will no longer fester."

Erythyn sneered, darkness twisting in his voice. "You speak of purity while hiding behind borrowed power. You were once a warrior. Now you play the druid's puppet."

She responded, her tone cold and steady. "I chose this path. Unlike you, I do not cling to pain and call it purpose. The forest offered rebirth —you chose corruption."

He circled her, conjuring shadows. "You don't understand what it is to fall. To lose everything and burn for it. I am not corrupted. I am free. No gods. No roots. No chains."

Bellator lifted her staff as the wind coiled around her. "Freedom without balance is chaos. And chaos without a soul is death. You came to unmake what breathes. I have come to reclaim it."

Erythyn roared his voice, shaking the trees. "Then come, forest witch! Let's see if bark and blossoms can bleed!" The forest trembled under the weight of their battle.

Moonlight pierced the thick canopy in broken shards, glinting off Bellator's steel as she ducked beneath a streak of searing crimson energy. Bark exploded from the trees in smoking splinters where Erythyn's magic struck. He moved like a wraith—swift, unpredictable—his cloak a dark blur between the trunks, his eyes burning with cold hatred.

Bellator breathed heavily, her sword clenched in both hands, her gauntlets scraped and blackened. She bled, but so did he. The scent of scorched earth thickened the air. All around them, the enchanted forest stood eerily still as if even its ancient spirits dared not intervene.

"You're running out of tricks," Erythyn hissed, stepping from the shadows, his staff glowing with a pulse like a heartbeat. "Yield, Bellator, or I will burn this forest to ash with you in it."

She didn't answer.

Instead, she planted her feet wide in the moss-laced soil. Her blade—a relic older than kingdoms—shimmered with latent energy. The runes along its length began to glow, one by one, like stars being born.

Erythyn faltered. "What are you?"

Chapter 6
When the Earth Swallows the Light

The Unseen Meridian

Beyond the line where day divides,

Here every truth in shadow hides.

The threshold hums with untold song,

Yet bids the brave to carry on.

rythyn's eyes widened, panic flaring too late. The ground beneath him fractured, roots unraveling like thread.

The ground trembled as Bellator drove her gleaming sword into the earth, her voice echoing with ancient words of power. The silver blade, etched with runes from the Old Tongue, pulsed with a radiant light that grew until the forest floor split open beneath her. A swirling portal yawned wide—an intended escape, a last resort. The air whirled and howled with arcane winds and the scent of scorched pine and iron as it drug the very magic from the air.

But from the shadowed trees behind her, Erythyn moved. His form, cloaked in shifting black, emerged like a phantom—his eyes burning with a furious hunger. As Princess Alexandria took one last glance at Bellator, her hand reaching out in trust, Erythyn's shadow-tentacles erupted from the gloom. They slithered through the air with terrifying speed and seized the princess in a suffocating grip.

"*No!*" Alexandria screamed, struggling violently. Her hair whipped around her face, her sapphire cloak flashing in the wind.

Bellator spun, lunging with an outstretched hand. "Erythyn! Let her go!" she bellowed, her eyes wild. Her fingers grazed Alexandria's as the dark tendrils dragged her back toward the portal.

A vicious snarl twisted Erythyn's face. "She is mine now."

With a last, desperate shriek, the portal engulfed them both, and then —it slammed shut. The earth sealed as if untouched, save for the scorched ring and lingering shimmer in the air.

Bellator fell to her knees, pounding the ground. "That portal wasn't meant for her..." Her voice cracked as she looked to the sky. "Goddess, no."

She stood slowly, bloody and weary, the forest around her whispering with the aftermath of chaos. Just then, the thunder of hooves and the sharp ring of armor filled the air. The royal guards had arrived. Cloaks fluttering, weapons drawn, they burst through the trees, surrounding her in protective formation.

"Commander Bellator!" shouted General Stormrend. "What the hell was that? We saw the light. Where is the princess?"

She stood frozen. "It happened so fast. Erythyn pulled her through the portal. He grabbed her at the last second."

"How could you let that happen?"

Bellator's jaw clenched. "Do you think I wanted this to happen? He struck with sorcery I've never seen before. The moment he whispered her name, the portal answered like the trees themselves bowed to him. I reached for her—I had her—"

Stormrend shoved Bellator back a step with wild eyes. "Apparently *not*! You're her protector! You swore your life for hers!"

Bellator grabbed Stormrend's arm as her voice dropped dangerously low. "And I will give it, if it gets her back. But right now, your rage helps no one."

Stormrend pulled his arm back. "Then where is she?"

Bellator replied, " I'm not sure! She was terrified, Stormrend. I saw it —just before she vanished. He's taken her somewhere that shouldn't exist. I told her we shouldn't help him. I felt it in the air—the old magic, sleeping just beneath the skin."

Stormrend turned toward the trees. "And now it's awake."

She stood shaking her head, "The portal was meant to send him to the far side of the forest, but when he pulled her in, it warped. I'm not sure it led where I intended. It was twisted by his magic."

Bellator's voice trembling with guilt. "The trees in this land, they remember. We must ride to the far side of the forest. It's the only lead we have."

Without hesitation, Stormrend turned. "You heard her! Ride hard! Find the princess!"

The guards spurred their mounts, a blur of metal and speed vanishing into the deep woods.

Bellator mounted Stormrend's horse and they departed, her silver cloak tattered, her armor dulled by the earlier battle. Her expression remained fixed, cold with focus, but beneath, it boiled in a storm of guilt and dread. She had failed to stop Erythyn. She failed to hold Alexandria's hand.

General Stormrend barked orders, sending search parties in radiating sweeps. Scouts moved swiftly through thickets, calling out the princess's name, their voices swallowed by the ever-thickening mist.

"Still no sign of them," one scout reported breathlessly. "No tracks, no scent, no trace of magic."

Bellator dismounted and dropped to one knee, pressing a gauntleted hand to the earth.

"Something's wrong," she murmured. "The trail ends here...and it's not just distance—it's time. The portal warped."

Hours had passed. The wind howled through the trees like voices crying out in sorrow. The forest offered no answer. And by the time the moon rose, it had turned blood-red, and they still had no further leads as to where the princess had gone.

Bellator started to panic. "Do you have any idea where the portal could have led with it being warped?"

He replied, "No. But I know who might. And I know that if we waste even a moment more arguing, she slips further out of reach. "

Bellator stood up with hope. "Who?"

With certainty he replied, "Astralhart! We must see him at once!"

By midnight, the exhausted company emerged from the treeline into the low fields outside Dawnshire Citadel. The towers loomed against the night sky, and banners hung limp in the still air. The city was quiet, unaware that the world had just shifted.

The gates opened without question, and the riders passed through, dust-caked and grim. Bellator didn't dismount until she was at the marble steps of the royal hall.

Travel-worn and grim, Bellator proceeded through the great halls with urgency. Her cloak still smelled of forest smoke. Guards and courtiers gave her space—they saw the fear in her eyes. She headed straight for the Prime Minister's chamber.

His guard tried to stop her. "He's in council—"

Brushing past him, she said, "Then I will interrupt it."

He tried to grab the door, but Bellator pushed through the doors to Prime Minister Astralhart's study.

The Prime Minister, an ageless man with silver hair braided in rings of gold thread, turned toward Bellator. His robes shimmered faintly with runes only visible when the light hit them just right. Astralhart turned around toward the doors. "Bellator, you return alone."

Bellator's voice trembled, barely held together by restraint. "She's gone. Taken by Erythyn, a dark entity. A portal—older than anything I've ever seen—swallowed them both. I... I couldn't stop it."

Astralhart stood silent, his expression unreadable as his eyes darkened with ancient understanding. "So it begins," he murmured.

Bellator, unaware Astralhart knew that name, stepped forward with fury flaring in her gaze. "You knew?"

Astralhart slowly raised a hand, palm outward. "Not this," he said softly. "Not like this. But I felt something...something that might awaken." He turned, his cloak brushing the stone floor as he began walking away. "Come. There's something I must show you."

They stood before the Prime Minister's hearth, a fire long gone cold. Astralhart extended a hand and whispered an incantation in a tongue older than the kingdom itself. The stone wall behind the hearth groaned softly, folding like mist, parting to reveal a hidden corridor. A cold draft spilled out—carrying the scent of damp earth, candle wax, and the weight of forgotten time.

Bellator followed him down a spiraling staircase carved directly into the bedrock. The torchlight cast moving shadows along the ancient stone, flickering against a circular chamber below. The room opened like the heart of a buried sanctum, its walls lined with tall shelves filled with sealed scrolls, weathered tomes, and strange artifacts encased in enchanted glass. The ceiling, a stained-crystal dome, portrayed the royal line as a celestial constellation—stars shaped into crowns, wings, and swords stretching across the heavens.

At the center, a raised dais glowed faintly, runes etched into the stone pulsing with dormant energy. Resting atop it, enclosed in a glass case, was a relic bathed in subtle moondust from Princess Alexandria's ancestors.

Bellator's voice came low, reverent. "What is this place?"

Astralhart's reply echoed softly. "A chamber known only to three monarchs and one Prime Minister in every age. Built by the first High Arcanist under oath and blood binding. Here, we keep what must be kept secret—even from the Royal Guard."

He approached the case and murmured three incantations. With each whisper, an arcane lock clicked open, releasing soft pulses of blue light. At last, the glass lid lifted on its own, revealing the items within.

Nestled in dark velvet was a key-shaped necklace, forged from moon-metal. The bow of the key formed a crescent moon, cradling a swirling opal that shimmered like a storm trapped in stone. The stem was etched with living runes, shifting when looked at, resisting comprehension. Its chain, delicate as spider-silk, gleamed like silver, yet felt impossibly warm to the touch.

Beside it lay a parchment map edged in silver thread, faintly glowing beneath Astralhart's fingers. It was tightly rolled in blue velvet and bound by a wax seal bearing the royal crest: a phoenix wrapped around an hourglass.

"When Alexandria was born," he said, "I made a promise to her mother that if the bloodline's curse ever awakened... We would be ready."

Bellator stared, breathless. "What is that?"

Astralhart lifted the necklace very delicately. "A Tracker's Sigil. But it's unlike any other. It does not trace the body—it traces the soul. The very presence of the wearer within the threads of the world." He laid the map upon a rune-carved table, smoothing it flat. At first, it appeared blank. Then he raised the necklace above it.

52

The opal began to glow—faintly at first, then brighter, pulsing like a heartbeat. A single glowing point flickered to life deep within the Enchanted Forest.

Bellator's eyes widened. "That's her heartbeat."

Astralhart nodded. "Yes. This tells us where she is—but more importantly, it tells us whether she's still bound to this world. As long as the light remains...she lives."

Bellator exhaled, relief flooding her chest, which was quickly replaced by resolve. "Then I'll take the map. And the key. I'll find her and bring her home."

He met her eyes grimly. "Bellator, you must know. I fear...she is no longer within our time. That portal bore the mark of the Time-Lost Realms—places stitched between past and present, made of memory and magic. Erythyn didn't just take her somewhere. He took her somewhen. He took her back."

Bellator's tone sharpened. "Then we go. Now. I'll take the elite guard and—"

Astralhart gently interrupted, placing the necklace fully in her grasp. "Take this. If you can find her, put it around her neck. It will sync her spirit back to this plane—and anchor her path for return... If she can return."

"I'll make sure of it," Bellator said fiercely, turning on her heel and racing up the staircase, the glowing sigil clutched tightly in her hand.

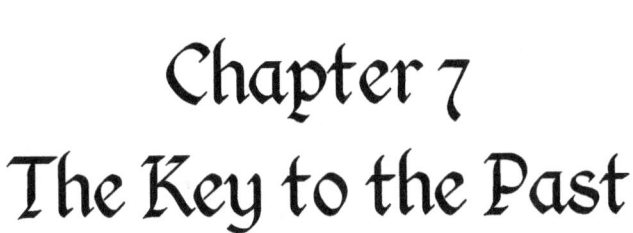

Chapter 7
The Key to the Past

The Promise of Dawn & Dusk

I bind my heart to both extremes,

To light that heals to shadow schemes,

In every clash of truth & lies

My solemn pledge shall never die.

Bellator and the Elite Royal Guard rode hard into the night. Guided by the glowing dot on the map, they returned to the clearing, the place where the portal had torn open. There, beneath the moonlight, the map pulsed brighter than ever. The tracker burned warm against Bellator's chest. The same spiral of scorched leaves remained on the forest floor, untouched by time or wind.

"She's here. The key says she's here," Bellator yelled to General Stormrend. "There's no one. No sound. No scent. Just...echo." As he glanced around, Bellator stepped into the heart of the spiral. She kneeled and placed a hand on the cold earth. The key around her neck thrummed louder.

General Stormrend walked closer. "We're standing exactly where it says she is. But there's nothing here. No magic. No trace. Just...ashes."

Bellator gazed into the distance. "Because she's not in this moment. She's somewhere behind the veil... Before the present ever happened."

General Stormrend quickly responded "Time magic? That's forbidden. Lost. The High Arcanist burned those tomes three generations ago."

Bellator turned her head towards him slowly and softly. "Not all of them."

As the morning sun rose, Bellator returned to the castle, wasting no time. She made her way to a part of the castle few dared enter—the High Library, a soaring chamber beneath the east wing, filled with scrolls bound in dragonhide and tomes written in languages long dead. She found Astralhart already there along with the Royal Elite Guards and the highest ranked spiritual leaders in the Celestial Order. Astralhart stood at a sealed alcove with no visible door, just a sigil of intertwined stars burned into the stone.

"You knew about The Time Lost Realms. About the way back."

Prime Minister Astralhart was still calm, but his eyes were weary. "I hoped we'd never need it."

Bellator leaned over. "We do now!"

He slowly nodded, placing a hand to the sigil and whispering, "Then may the old gods have mercy, as they have written the book foreknowing this time would come."

They stepped into the Timelocked Vault where forbidden knowledge was entombed and untouched by time. Runes crawled over the walls like vines. A single crystal pedestal sat at the center with a book, chained shut by a lock made of woven light.

Bellator didn't hesitate. She drew a dagger and sliced her palm, pressing into the book. The chains unwound, vanishing into smoke. The book fell open to a marked page titled, "Threads of the Vanished Hour."

She read, "To step through time is not to walk forward...but to unravel. One must echo the frequency of a soul already displaced—"

Astralhart interpreted for her. "The key isn't just a beacon—it's a tuning fork. If Alexandria is the melody, the key will let us sync in time with her."

Bellator stood at the center, now converted into a ritual circle, flanked by circle-weaving mages and astral navigators—the kingdom's last surviving temporal adepts. The Elite Guard stood by in silence, their weapons sheathed, their eyes hard with anticipation.

Astralhart placed the key around her neck. "You will not walk through a door, Bellator. You will become a thread, a strand flung backward through the weave of time. If your anchor fails or if you lose her signal—you may never return."

She pressed the ancient map against her chest and proclaimed, "I will not fail. I will not leave her stranded in the currents of time."

He met her steady gaze. "One more warning: when you find her, do not let the past ensnare you. It will seduce you with things that cannot be undone. Your only purpose is to bring her home."

A hush fell as the ritual began, soft voices weaving into a rising chorus. Runes at their feet flared to life, veins of light tracing the stones. The key over Bellator's heart blazed like a captive sun. The very air turned molten-bright, reality quivering on the brink of rupture. A silver rift tore open before her, revealing a forest unmarked by centuries, young trunks swaying in shadowed emerald.

"Hold fast, Princess," Bellator whispered, resolve steeled in her voice. She stepped into the light and then she was gone.

Chapter 8
Swallowed in Time

The Covenant Unbroken

No mortal hand can break the chain,

Nor tyranny its hold maintain.

For every dawn that wicked tries,

A vow returns to claim the skies.

*T*he soft whisper of wind in the trees stirred the younger forest like a lullaby sung to the ancient roots. Sunlight streamed through the dense canopy, dappled patterns dancing on the mossy ground, and a faint scent of blooming flora drifted on the breeze. Small creatures—rabbits with silken ears, fox kits with eyes like amber—gathered curiously around two unmoving figures. Birds perched on low limbs, tilting their heads, as if waiting.

Alexandria and Erythyn lay sprawled amidst the wild underbrush, both unconscious, their bodies slack with exhaustion. Here, in this untouched pocket of time, the forest had not yet suffered the scorch of war. Trees stood taller, proud and unscarred. Vines curled lazily around the unmarred stone of ancient ruins—monuments of a civilization long gone in their time, but here, alive and pulsing with mystic energy. Ornate towers climbed into the sky like fingers of carved marble. Crystal glyphs shimmered faintly across their surfaces. The air hummed faintly, like magic whispering just below the veil of reality.

Alexandria stirred first.

She groaned, propping herself up on her elbows with visible effort, her face tight with frustration and confusion. Her dark hair was tangled with leaves and twigs, her eyes disoriented as they darted around the unfamiliar landscape.

"What...the hell?" she muttered, voice hoarse. "Erythyn, wake up."

The man beside her blinked into consciousness, groaning as he rolled onto his back. His silver hair fell across his face, and his eyes, rimmed in weariness, met hers. "I'm awake. I think..." he rasped. "Where are we?"

She jerked upright, her fists clenching the earth beneath her as if she could drag him back through the portal by sheer force. Dirt and leaves tumbled from her dark hair, and her eyes blazed, wild with accusation.

"What the hell, Erythyn!" she snarled, her voice cracking with fury. "Do you have any idea how reckless that was? Pulling me through that damn portal!"

He stirred beside her, his silver hair falling across his brow as he pushed himself onto his back. His tired eyes met hers. "I'm awake. I think...Where are we?"

She shoved a handful of twigs aside, standing up on shaking legs. "That's what I'd like to know," Alexandria snapped, standing shakily. "This isn't the same forest. It's... It's too alive. Too clean. We're stranded in who knows where because you decided to kidnap me through space and time. Care to explain?"

Every muscle trembled with outrage. Dirt and leaves cascaded from her dark hair as she glared down at him. "Do you have any idea what you've done?" she hissed, her voice low and dangerous. The unfamiliar trees around them stretched up like accusing witnesses. "You tore me out of my world without so much as a warning. One second I'm breathing air I know, and the next, I'm suffocating under your damn magic!"

Erythyn rubbed the back of his neck, sitting up more fully. His silver hair fell in disarray, and for a moment his gaze faltered under the weight of her fury. "I... I didn't..."

She stomped forward, the ground trembling beneath her boots. "You didn't what? Didn't think? Didn't care? Because last I checked, I'm the one who's stuck here, thanks to your impulsive stunt!" She pressed a shaking finger against his chest. "My life is on the line, Erythyn. You owe me an explanation right now."

He swallowed hard, his shoulders slumping under her glare. "The portal was unstable," he began, his voice rough. "If I hadn't pulled you through..."

She cut him off with a bitter laugh, her eyes flashing. "If you hadn't pulled me through, I'd still be safe. But here I am, stranded in whatever hell you dragged me into."

He sat up slowly, scanning their surroundings. "I feel like I've been drained. Like my magic's been bled dry."

"Well, congratulations. I feel the same," she said bitterly, brushing dirt from her tunic.

They were still bickering quietly when the soft crunch of approaching footsteps stilled their voices. From behind a curtain of ivy emerged a figure—young, elegant, and robed in flowing fabrics that shimmered like woven starlight. She had hair the color of sunlit wheat and eyes that carried the glint of wisdom far beyond her years. Beside her walked a gentle doe and two fauns, their soft hooves clicking against the stone path.

The young woman halted a few paces away, her hands open in peace. "Are you injured?" she asked gently, "Lost? Where are you from?"

Alexandria and Erythyn exchanged a glance, both tense, wary. "You could say we're...a long way from home," Erythyn said carefully.

The stranger studied them for a moment, concern softening her features. "I am Ashlynn. What are your names?"

The name echoed in Alexandria's memory, brushing something buried deep inside. She said nothing, but a chill ran down her spine. Her face was puzzling. Like she couldn't quite understand where she heard that name before.

Erythyn responded. "This is Alexandria, and I am Erythyn."

"You look worn. Come. I can heal you, and we'll get some food into you. There's no danger here."

Still cautious, but with little choice, they followed her through the lush, blooming wood and into the heart of the civilization. Towering spires and graceful archways surrounded them, each structure pulsating faintly with magical energy. Crystalline walkways sparkled under their feet. Sky-bridges stretched from one marble building to another. This was the past, Alexandria realized in a slow dawning—this was the kingdom before its fall.

They were led to a chamber of light and crystal where the Ashlynn worked deft healing magic. Her hands glowed as they passed over their wounds and bruises, drawing out pain with a warmth that was both soothing and unfamiliar. To Erythyn's visible displeasure, a small ornate collar was fastened around his neck—light as air, but thrumming with

63

suppression magic.

"Precaution," she said softly. "There have been...troubles with dark magic recently."

Soon, they were seated around a low table laden with food—plump fruits, golden bread, and clear water that shimmered with a faint magical hue. As they ate, Ashlynn answered their cautious questions with kindness and clarity.

"This is Aelora," she explained, "our sanctuary in the heart of the forest. We've existed here for centuries in harmony with the land and its magic. But that harmony is fraying. Lately...something is stirring."

Erythyn leaned forward, her eyes narrowing. "What kind of something?"

Her expression darkened slightly. "We've been tracking a rogue wizard. A powerful one. He's been using black magic to tamper with animals—twisting them, enlarging them, filling them with shadow. His experiments are getting bolder. The creatures we find are no longer natural. We fear he's trying to craft the perfect entity. One that can absorb human desire—greed, rage, sorrow—and reflect it back, twisted and magnified."

"A weapon," Alexandria said flatly.

"A vessel," she corrected. "One that could be used to manipulate the masses, push them into despair. And in their weakness, he would rise. We fear he's preparing to use this magic on a human next. If he succeeds..."

She didn't finish the sentence. She didn't need to.

Alexandria's chest felt tight. "This wizard. Does he have a name?"

A beat of silence passed.

"They call him the Shadowlord."

The name echoed like a distant thunderclap. Erythyn's expression went unreadable, and Alexandria's gaze flicked to the far windows where the sunlight spilled in golden beams across the polished stone. Somewhere in this paradise, darkness had already begun to grow.

Neither of them noticed the way their host's features mirrored

Alexandria's—her eyes, her cheekbones, the regal set of her jaw. She was a bloodline unrecognized, a living thread to a forgotten legacy. The past was not done with them yet.

The sun climbed higher in the sky, casting its golden warmth across the tranquil valley where Aelora's civilization flourished. Unlike the fractured remnants Alexandria and Erythyn had known in their own time, this place pulsed with unspoiled magic—every vine, every carved stone alive with power and memory. The soft hum of enchantments wove through the air, a melody barely audible but deeply felt, like the heartbeat of the land itself.

Inside the chamber of healing, they rested on soft cushions near an open terrace that overlooked the crystalline city. Columns of glowing stone spiraled skyward, their surfaces etched with runes that shimmered like liquid stars. Walkways arched between buildings like strands of silver thread. The sky, impossibly blue, stretched above them—no trace of the ash or shadows that haunted their memories.

Erythyn sat with his back against a cool marble wall, his arms crossed, his eyes distant. The faint silver collar around his neck glowed subtly, dulling the edge of his power. He didn't like it. He hadn't said much since it was placed, though Alexandria could feel his frustration simmering beneath the surface.

She, too, felt unsettled. Not just by their mysterious arrival in this time, but by the presence of the woman who had helped them. There was something strangely familiar about her—her voice, her poise. Alexandria couldn't place it, but every time the girl smiled or tilted her head, a strange pang stirred in her chest. A feeling like déjà vu dipped in longing.

They sat together in a quiet corner, finally alone. The meal had eased the sharp edge of their hunger, and their wounds no longer ached. But their minds—still full of questions, still burdened with uncertainty—remained restless.

"So," Alexandria said finally, breaking the silence between them, "any brilliant ideas on how to stop a time-warping shadow warlord and get back to our own future?"

Erythyn raised an eyebrow. "I thought you always had a plan."

She gave him a sideways glance. "I usually do. But this...this is something else entirely."

He leaned forward, his arms on his knees. "We need to assume we were sent here for a reason. The forest didn't just spit us into the past for fun. There's something here we're meant to learn—or do."

Alexandria nodded slowly, chewing on her lower lip. "You're right. Whatever this Shadowlord is trying to create, it started here. In this time. If we stop it before it begins..."

"...then maybe we change everything," he finished, his voice low.

They looked at one another for a moment—two people bound by fate, distrustful of each other but more alone without the other. There was tension in the space between them but also a growing thread of understanding. They were both powerful. Both flawed. And, at least for now, they needed each other.

"We can't afford to fight anymore," Alexandria said more softly. "Not with each other. If we're going to stop him—and get home—we have to work together."

Erythyn's mouth quirked into something almost like a smile. "Truce?"

"For now."

They sealed it with a nod, not a handshake—neither trusted the other quite that much—but it was something. A beginning.

Moments later, Ashlynn returned with more herbs and a bowl of cool water. She knelt beside them, dabbing at the fading bruises on Alexandria's arm.

"You're both strong," she said. "The forest must have guided you here for a reason. It doesn't make mistakes."

Alexandria studied her as she worked. "This wizard you spoke of...

The Shadowlord. You said he's trying to create something. A perfect entity?"

Ashlynn nodded, her brow furrowing. "A being that could feed off human emotion, amplify despair, turn it into chaos. But the signs are clear: he's preparing to try the spell on a person next."

Erythyn's jaw tightened. "And once he does, there won't be any stopping it."

Ashlynn hesitated, then reached into a pouch at her side and withdrew a small glass orb. Inside it swirled with dark smoke, pulsing faintly. "This was recovered from one of the corrupted beasts. Traces of his magic. It's old, vile...But brilliantly crafted. He's not just any rogue sorcerer. He's a master of forbidden arts."

Alexandria took the orb carefully, her fingers tingling. The smoke coiled against the glass like it recognized her touch. A whisper crawled along the edge of her hearing—soft, indistinct, but malevolent.

"Has he been seen?" she asked, handing the orb over to her and forcing herself to pull her hand back.

"Not directly," the girl replied. "But he leaves signs. Ruined groves. Creatures turned into abominations. We believe he's hiding somewhere deep in the Nightroot Vale, where the veil between realms is thinnest."

Alexandria glanced at Erythyn. "That's near where we came through."

He nodded grimly. "Then we're closer than we thought."

"You want to go after him, don't you?" the girl asked.

"We have to," Alexandria said. "If we don't, we won't have a future to go back to."

The girl studied them, then gave a slow nod. "Then let me help you. I know this land. I know our magic. You'll need a guide if you're going to survive the Nightroot."

As night fell over the perfect city, Alexandria and Erythyn stood on a balcony overlooking the glowing skyline. The stars here were brighter, clearer. The air tasted of promise and danger.

"We do this together," Alexandria said, her voice firm.

"Together," Erythyn agreed, his eyes gleaming in the moonlight.

And far away, deep within the twisted heart of the forest, something ancient stirred—watching. Waiting. The Shadowlord's design was unfolding, and time itself had begun to bend around the approaching storm.

Chapter 9
Guardians of the
Vanished Hour

The Shards of Promise

From fractured oaths & broken pacts,

Through hands of those whose hearts steadfast.

The Sunblade's light shall be restored,

Its gilded truth shall cut discord.

The hours that followed passed in a strange quiet, filled only with the soft murmur of Aelora's ancient city at dusk. Lanterns flickered to life along spiraling bridges of crystal and silver, glowing with a light that wasn't fire but magic—warm and golden, like the breath of stars. Delicate windchimes made of enchanted glass sang in the breeze, casting a soothing lullaby over the rooftops. Citizens, dressed in flowing garments spun from silver-threaded fabric, moved gracefully through the city. Children chased light sprites that danced through the air. It was a world so peaceful, so breathtaking, that it almost seemed like a dream.

But beneath that surface, tension bloomed.

Alexandria stood with her arms folded across her chest as she watched the lights below. The city reminded her of stories her grandmother used to tell her when she was little—of a lost kingdom in the forest where everything shimmered with power and beauty. She had always assumed they were just bedtime tales.

Now, she wasn't so sure.

Something gnawed at her: This place, these people...seem all too familiar. Her soul couldn't shake it. The trees even whispered to her in ways they never had before. The magic in the air recognized her.

Behind her, Erythyn leaned against the stone archway, his arms crossed, silent but present. His mind wasn't on the city—it was on the collar around his neck. Occasionally, he'd reach up and touch it, as though trying to decipher its workings through sheer will.

"I can almost hear it," he muttered. "The way it blocks the shadows. Like standing in a room and hearing someone whisper your name from just outside the door."

Alexandria turned. "Stop fidgeting with it. You are not going to be able to get it off. It is there for a reason. "

"If I did, what would you do?" he asked, a wry smile tugging at his lips. "Blast me? Drag me back to Ashlynn?"

"Try me."

He chuckled softly and looked away. "You really don't trust me, do you?"

"No," she said flatly. "But I'm starting to understand you."

He gazed at her in the stillness.

Together, they stood for a moment, letting the silence stretch, their thoughts heavy. Both had seen too much darkness, too much loss. But here, in this slice of the past untouched by war, something had shifted.

"We have to stop him before he succeeds," Alexandria said at last. "If he finishes that ritual... If he creates something that can feed on desire and despair—he won't need armies. He'll just wait. Let people destroy themselves."

Erythyn nodded slowly. "That's the genius of it. He doesn't conquer. He corrupts. One whisper at a time."

"Then we don't have time to waste."

They turned as Ashlynn approached, wrapped in a flowing cloak of soft forest green. Her expression was calm, but there was a gravity to her gaze.

"I've been given leave to take you beyond the border," she said. "To Nightroot Vale. We'll need to move carefully. That place is alive, and it remembers everything."

Alexandria furrowed her brow. "Why would your people let us go? Why risk it?"

Ashlynn hesitated, then gave a faint smile. "Because I believe you're here for a reason. And because... I feel like I've known you both before. In another life, maybe. Or a dream."

The three of them prepared in quiet purpose. Ashlynn brought them supplies—food in enchanted satchels that would stay fresh for weeks, small charms to repel corrupted beasts, a map inked in starlight. She guided them to the edge of the city, where the polished paths gave way to wild earth and the music of the forest grew deeper, older.

As they stood at the threshold of the woods, Alexandria turned for one last look at the city behind her. Its towers gleamed under moonlight like a promise made in silver. She burned the image into her memory, knowing it would not survive the centuries ahead. This was what they would fight for. Not just the future—but the brilliance of a past worth saving.

The forest beyond the border was darker. The trees grew closer together, their roots tangled like secrets beneath the earth. Every sound felt amplified—the snap of twigs, the rustle of leaves, the low growl of something watching from the underbrush.

Erythyn walked beside her, quieter now. He had dropped the sarcasm, the smirks. His magic—normally a dark ripple at the edge of his presence —was dulled by the collar, but Alexandria could still sense the weight of him. He was like a caged storm walking beside her.

"You've changed," she said suddenly.

He glanced at her. "So have you."

They didn't need to say more. The silence between them no longer bristled with hostility—but with understanding. They were survivors, both of them. Warriors with cracked armor. And they had something in common now: they refused to let the Shadowlord win.

That night, they made camp beneath the boughs of a great weeping tree. Ashlynn drew a protective circle around them in silver dust, her voice humming ancient syllables as she layered enchantments over their sleeping place.

As Alexandria settled near the fire, she looked up at the stars— strangely bright here, unmarred by time, smog, or sorrow. And in the quiet, she whispered to herself, "We're going to stop him."

Erythyn, half-asleep beside her, replied without opening his eyes. "We'd better."

Far to the east, past the sleeping groves and winding rivers, something stirred.

A monstrous creature, twisted and stitched from broken animals and black spells, shambled through the shadows of Nightroot Vale. Its eyes glowed red. It sniffed the air. And behind it, in a cavern of obsidian and bone, a figure watched the stars through a crack in the stone ceiling.

The Shadowlord was waiting. His work nearly complete.

And Alexandria and Erythyn were no longer just visitors in the past.

They were its last chance.

The fire crackled low, casting flickering light against the gnarled bark of the weeping tree. Its drooping limbs rustled like soft sighs in the night breeze. Though enchanted wards shimmered faintly in the underbrush—Ashlynn's magic holding them like a quiet sanctuary—Alexandria found little rest.

Sleep teased the edges of her mind but never fully claimed her. Every time she closed her eyes, she saw flashes: creatures with too many eyes, roots pulsing like veins, cities burning under a sky stained violet with shadow. She sat up slowly, her arms wrapped around her knees, and stared out past the barrier into the darkness beyond. Something out there felt aware.

"You sense it too, don't you?" Ashlynn's voice was soft, from just behind her.

Alexandria didn't turn. "Something's watching. Waiting."

Ashlynn sat beside her, cross-legged. Her golden hair shimmered with faint starlight. "The Shadowlord's reach is long. Even if he isn't physically near, his presence lingers like smoke after fire."

There was a pause before Alexandria asked, "How did your people come to know of him? He wasn't born in this time, was he?"

"No. But the magic he wields... It's ancient. Forbidden. We believe he uncovered something buried beneath the earth—a relic or scripture left from a darker age. Whatever it was, it gave him enough power to rival entire warbands of spellcasters. And twisted enough to defile nature itself." Ashlynn's eyes hardened. "He works in silence. His army is not of men, but of beasts—enslaved and reshaped. He plays with hunger, emotion, and pain until his creatures are bound to him like limbs of his own flesh."

Alexandria looked over at her, her expression unreadable. "You speak like someone who's seen it firsthand."

Ashlynn nodded slowly. "I have. My brother fell to one of his creations—something that once was a stag. Its antlers had become thorns. Its breath was venom. He died saving others. That's why I'm here. Why I volunteered to guide you."

The quiet between them deepened. A bond forged not from shared history, but shared loss.

"I'm sorry," Alexandria murmured.

Ashlynn smiled faintly. "So am I. But grief, if left unchecked, becomes a weapon in his hands. That's why he must be stopped."

A few paces away, Erythyn stirred and sat up, rubbing his eyes. "You two planning strategy or swapping ghost stories?"

"Both," Alexandria replied dryly.

He joined them, his gaze sweeping the perimeter of their camp. "I had a dream," he muttered. "I saw a place made of bone and stone, with a sky like bleeding ash. And I was...there. Standing next to him."

"Ashlynn said his magic plays on desire," Alexandria said carefully. "What did he offer you?"

Erythyn didn't answer immediately. When he did, his voice was low. "Control. Not power—control. Of everything. Of what I am."

Alexandria watched him, really watched him. The anger she usually met him with was tempered now by something else—understanding, maybe even empathy. She realized then that Erythyn wasn't tempted by destruction. He was tempted by restraint. Because deep down, he feared his own strength.

"We'll make sure he doesn't get inside your head again," she said.

His dark eyes met hers. "If he does, you stop me. No matter what."

"I will."

The forest shifted around them, the silence pressing heavier now. Ashlynn stood, brushing dirt from her robes. "We should move. Dawn is still hours away, but the path ahead twists in ways not bound by time. Better to travel while the veil is thin."

They packed in silence, each of them carrying more than gear—regret, fear, resolve. The deeper they ventured into Nightroot Vale, the more the forest lost its color. Trees bled into one another in an almost painterly blur of shadow. The moon above grew hazy, as if viewed through thick, fogged glass. And beneath their feet, the ground grew spongy, riddled with roots that pulsed faintly like veins.

Eventually, the canopy parted, revealing a clearing unlike anything they'd seen.

At its center stood an enormous tree—twisted, skeletal, blackened like it had been struck by a thousand bolts of lightning and still refused to fall. From its gnarled limbs hung strips of cloth, bones, and glimmering runes that danced in slow circles, suspended in the air. The air itself hummed with chaotic magic.

"This is one of his sites," Ashlynn whispered. "A place where he transforms."

Alexandria moved closer, her boots crunching across old leaves and ash. The energy here was wrong—like it fed on hope and spat out emptiness. She bent down and touched the soil.

It was warm.

"He was here not long ago," she murmured. "He's close."

Erythyn stood very still. "Too close."

Suddenly, from the edge of the clearing, a howl broke the silence. The sound shook the trees, mournful and full of rage. Something charged from the shadows—something once a wolf, now bearing armor fused into its body, its mouth split far too wide, its eyes glowing red.

Alexandria summoned her magic, but it flickered in her hands—unstable, like the atmosphere resisted her. Erythyn stepped forward, a snarl on his lips, but his collar dimmed the dark sparks that danced on his fingertips.

"Ashlynn!" Alexandria shouted.

Ashlynn stepped into the center of the clearing and lifted both hands, her voice rising in an ancient chant. Light erupted from the ground beneath the beast, ensnaring it in tendrils of golden energy. It writhed, snapping its monstrous jaws, but the magic held.

"Go!" Ashlynn shouted. "There's a cave beneath the tree! That's where he's hiding his gate!"

They didn't hesitate. Alexandria and Erythyn dashed forward, finding a crumbling staircase descending beneath the cursed tree. The darkness swallowed them quickly, but they didn't stop.

They were no longer merely travelers out of time.

They were warriors on borrowed hours.

And ahead, in the silence beneath the earth, the Shadowlord was waiting—with a gate, a spell, and a monster born not of shadow... But of them.

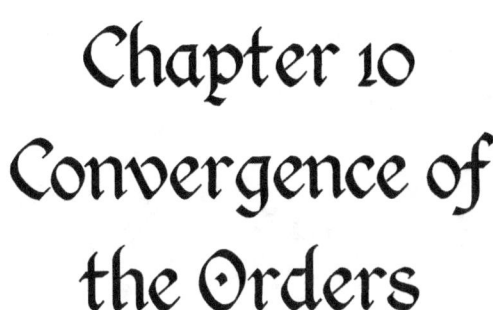

Chapter 10
Convergence of
the Orders

Alexandria's Vow

Forged in fire made of steel,

To the darkness I will not kneel.

Your shadows cross my given light,

I promise you I WILL win the fight.

P rime Minister Astralhart, his indigo robes streaked with gold thread and stardust, turned sharply on his heel, the sigils embroidered on his cloak catching the ambient starlight of the grand hall. The Celestial Chamber echoed with the heavy tap of his boots against the opalescent marble floor. He made his way to the pedestal beside the throne—a floating disc of silver-veined crystal, suspended in the air by ancient gravity-defying runes. As he ascended the steps, a low hum stirred in the chamber. The air thickened with ethereal energy.

Astralhart's gloved hand reached out and hovered over the pedestal, its surface swirling with constellations that moved like living maps. He closed his eyes for the briefest moment, channeling the deep magics of command, and then his voice rang out—deep, resounding, and absolute. "By the will of the Concordant Realms and the Authority vested in me, I summon the Celestial Order. Let the Council assemble. The Balance is broken. War has come."

The pedestal responded with a burst of radiant light, cascading outward in circular waves. Glyphs ignited in the air like stars being born —symbols of each Order: the Ryvarion, the Celestara, the Utheron, and more. Each began to pulse, signaling the call had been sent. Behind him, the great portal shimmered violently, unstable. Through it, the final images of Alexandria and Bellator faded: Alexandria, her spellfire halo still flaring with resistance; Bellator, sword in hand, her silhouette a fortress of unshaken loyalty. They were now inside the Rift, their fates tethered to the unraveling threads of the Realms. And that portal, once a sacred passage between dimensions, now wept sparks and smoke.

Astralhart turned his gaze upward. Above the throne, the Astral Dome peeled open, revealing the night sky not as it appeared to mortals, but as it truly was—alive, shifting, streaked with celestial omens. A comet screamed across the firmament, blood-red and too low. A bad sign.

The doors of the chamber creaked as the first of the Celestial Order began to arrive—manifesting through beams of light and folds in space.

Hooded figures, armored sentinels, wraithlike scholars of the Arcane Accord, and one, draped in feathers and shadow, descended in silence.

Astralhart did not flinch. His voice was a blade now. "Alexandria and Bellator are within the Rift. The Balance has not merely tipped—it has shattered. The echoes of the Void are rising. We will not falter. We must act."

A hush fell over the chambers. For the first time in a millennium, the Celestial Order would not debate.

They would prepare for war.

The Rift was not a place so much as a wound carved between realms where existence frayed at the edges. Once a controlled crossing point for only the highest sanctified mages and dimensional navigators, it now pulsed with instability. A jagged tear in the Weave of Reality, it flickered like a mirage between stars, whispering in forgotten tongues. Inside, time looped in spirals, space bent in half-remembered geometry, and light did not behave. Madness grew like moss. But within that madness lay power —raw, primal, and dangerous. It was here that Alexandria and Bellator were forced to enter, chasing a threat that defied all natural law. The breach of the Rift signaled something much darker than imbalance: the return of the Shadowlord, entities that once sought to devour the Realms by unmaking the laws of existence itself.

As the chamber filled with divine presences and eldritch energies, the members of the Celestial Order took their places in a wide spiral around the throne and pedestal. Each one brought a distinct presence—and a distinct reaction.

Clad in radiant gold, wings folded like blades of sunlight, the Celestara Guard were the militant protectors of cosmic law. Their commander, High Warden Serael, spoke first, her voice a clarion call. "We must seal the Rift. Our vanguard will hold the threshold with celestial fire. Alexandria and Bellator are not to be abandoned—they will have a path home—or vengeance." Her gauntleted fist rested on the hilt of a blade said to burn through lies themselves.

Robed in layers of hourglass-threaded silk, the Oathbinders did not speak immediately. Their Spokesage, Halcion, appeared flickering in and out of the present moment. Time danced around him. "The weave has bent...and frayed," he said. "If the Shadowlord returns, the future collapses inward. War is not the first act—it is the consequence. But so be it. We shall fortify the timeline's spine and hold the echoes at bay."

They began scribing sigils into the air—each one a vow against erasure.

Mysterious and masked, the Utheron were masters of illusion and shadowplay. They existed between layers of perception. Their leader, Mistress Shyra of the Obscured Path, floated barely above the ground, wrapped in cloth that moved like living fog. "War is loud. But shadows strike first. Let us root out the corruption that summoned the Rift from within. If the Hollow Sovereigns have allies...We will unmask them." Her voice carried secrets like poison—beautiful but deadly.

The Ryvarion's arrival was heralded by a rush of ocean wind and the scent of salt. These druids and tidecallers were bound to celestial currents and planetary oceans. Archdruid Callon, his waterlogged robes trailing sea foam, lifted his coral staff. "Even the tides recoil from this madness. The waters speak of drowning stars. But we will not kneel to chaos. We rise, like the flood." They would summon the seas to war if they must.

Astralhart watched them all, his eyes burning with fire. "The order must remember the Sunblade, the legendary weapon forged in the heart of the sun itself, our only true hope to defeat the Shadowlord. Only to be wielded by the chosen Champion of the Dawn, the one that is both of the kingdom and of pure heart."

The chamber trembled with silent consensus. The convergence was happening. For the first time in ages, all Orders were aligned. And yet, he knew this was only the beginning. The Shadowlord was stirring in the dark. And Alexandria and Bellator may have already been too far gone.

And so, the Celestial Order—once guardians of peace—stood at the threshold of war. No more deliberation. Action was ordained.

High above the convergence chamber, the Sigil of the Eternal Sun flared to life—a great symbol wrought of light and celestial fire, seen in the sky across every kingdom allied to the Order. It was the ancient sign of unity and war-readiness. The time for isolation was over. Every kingdom of the light now had a role to play.

The warhorns of Dawnshire rang like thunder from the heavens. As the military heart of the Sun Kingdoms, Dawnshire's Sky Bastions—great floating citadels—began to mobilize. Wings of sunsteel-clad paladins mounted solar drakes, forming the First Radiant Host, a force trained not just for battle, but for incursions into unstable realms like the Rift.

General Stormrend, commander of Dawnshire's vanguard, stood before his gathered legion with his blade to the sky. "We do not retreat. We strike with light. The darkness will remember who we are."

Their first mission: penetrate the Rift's outer border, stabilize a corridor, and retrieve Alexandria and Bellator—if they still lived.

Known for its golden fields and harmony with nature, Ryvarion moved not with steel but with seed and spirit. Their first act was to secure Logistical Sanctuaries across the kingdoms—massive living sanctums where the wounded could recover and the displaced could find refuge.

From the high mountain sanctuaries of Celestara, prayers were not whispered—they were woven. Their spiritual leaders began The Ninefold Chant, a sacred invocation of divine clarity meant to sever the corruption infiltrating minds and hearts across the Order. The Oracle of Celestara, veiled and radiant, opened the sacred Mirrors of Ascension—tools that reflected not the face, but the soul's state. Across the lands, priests and sages began testing all who served, rooting out the taint of shadow through divine vision and soul-trials. "Corruption does not announce itself—it lurks. And we shall find it before it festers." In secret, they also began scribing soul-binding oaths for the Order's highest commanders— to ensure they could not be turned.

Utheron, a kingdom of brilliant towers and alchemical skyforges, surged to life with blue and gold flame. Their scholars raced to stabilize arcane wards that could seal rifts, bind shadow-entities, and track the Hollow Sovereigns' manifestations. The Grand Arcanist Caelthor led the first team into the Hall of Convergences where alchemy, spellcraft, and divine theory were unified.

A council of sorcerers began building the Solarium Engine—a war-forged relic powered by distilled sunlight and cosmic ley energy, capable of burning away even shadow-touched anomalies. "We will not merely react. We will outthink the dark."

Meanwhile, a secret initiative began: researching what little is known about the Shadowlord...and the terrifying possibility that they cannot be slain, only contained. The Eternal Sun's light glowed brighter across the heavens. Temples rang bells of unity. Blacksmiths forged blades etched with radiant glyphs. Seers and children alike began dreaming of stars falling like tears—a warning, or perhaps a promise—and deep within the Rift, Alexandria stirred. Bellator's voice called out from somewhere far, far away. They were alive...but not alone.

The Celestial Order was making their first move. But the Shadowlord had already made his.

Chapter 11
A Truce in Time

The Sunblade

As darkness falls across the land,

My sword I wield in my hand.

For evil comes with all its might,

The Sunblade returns to finish the fight!

*T*he air changed the moment Bellator stepped through the portal. It wasn't just the light, though, that too had shifted—from golden dawn to a murky, uncertain twilight—but the feeling of the world around her. The portal behind her hissed shut with a sound like a dying flame, and silence rushed in to take its place, a silence that felt too still, too complete, as if the forest itself were holding its breath.

Bellator paused at the edge of a crumbling stone platform half-eaten by ivy, her boot heels sinking slightly into damp moss. She looked around, drawing her fur-lined cloak tighter. The trees here were tall, ancient things, their gnarled branches twisted like reaching arms. Fog laced the ground in thin, trailing sheets, coiling around her feet like curious spirits. She unrolled the map—glowing faintly with directional magic—and held it to the wind. It pulsed once with heat in her palm and pointed north, toward the heart of the forest where Alexandria had last been traced.

"Hold on," she muttered, slipping it back into her satchel. "I'm coming." Her voice was low, steady. But her eyes scanned the forest with a soldier's caution.

Bellator was exhausted. She had tracked for days before finding the gateway through the Weeping Stones, where the veil between times grew thin. She had fought through enchanted beasts, climbed shattered peaks, and bartered with stubborn forest spirits who refused to speak in anything but riddles. Her armor bore new scratches, her shield was cracked at one edge, and her sword had dulled from too many hasty, brutal skirmishes. But she pressed forward, every breath fueled by sheer will.

Alexandria was somewhere in this forest, and Bellator would find her —or she would never leave. She moved through the underbrush, her eyes sharp and ears alert for any unnatural sound. The birds here did not sing. The trees, though alive, whispered things she couldn't understand. There was a wrongness beneath the beauty—like perfume masking the rot.

Then she heard it. A low, heavy rustling. She dropped to a crouch behind a moss-covered stump, her hand on her sword hilt. The fog shifted ahead—rising, breaking—revealing something shambling between the trees. Her breath caught. It had once been a boar, she thought. Large, tusked, powerful. But this creature... It had grown impossibly large, its back bristling with bony spines. Its tusks were no longer ivory but blackened iron, veined with glowing crimson. Its eyes were glassy, swirling with darkness that pulsed like a second heartbeat. And something unnatural writhed beneath its skin—lumps shifting, bulging, as if more creatures were trying to claw their way out from within.

It snorted once, sending a wave of rot-scented air through the glade, and stomped forward, its hooves cracking old bones beneath the leaves. Bellator didn't breathe. Her fingers remained poised on her sword, but she didn't draw. Not yet. The map had warned her about the creatures changed by the Shadowlord—marked with red runes and driven mad by twisted enchantments. This beast bore one of those runes scorched into its side, pulsing with foul light.

As the creature lumbered past, Bellator slipped away—careful, deliberate—until she was a safe distance beyond its scent and sight. Her heart thundered in her ears, but her face remained still. Focused.

He's warping the animals now... Drawing from their instincts, weaponizing them.

She thought of Alexandria and the strange magic that linked her to this forest.

He'll be drawn to her like a moth to fire. I have to find her before he does, if he hasn't already.

By nightfall, the forest grew denser. The trees leaned closer, the roots gnarled like grasping hands. She passed a ring of stones that glowed faintly under moonlight—watching stones, used in old times to protect forest paths. But now, their glow was dim and tired, like the land had grown weary of its own defense.

Bellator's legs burned with fatigue. Her muscles ached. Her rations were gone. Every step felt heavier than the last, but she refused to stop. She passed the remnants of a skirmish—scorch marks on bark, blood dried black in the dirt, a shattered charm bracelet lying beside a charred log. She knelt and picked it up, rubbing her thumb over the broken wood beads.

Alexandria had been here.

The map pulsed again. Closer now. The thread between them was tightening. Bellator pushed forward through a tangled grove, using her sword to clear a path. The fog thickened again, and with it came whispers. Not from anything she could see—but from the trees themselves. Foreign, ancient words spoken too close to the ear. She didn't listen.

She walked through the whispers. Through the ache. Through fear. And then—just beyond a crumbling arch overtaken by ivy—she saw it. Torchlight. Faint, flickering. A camp. And silhouettes moving. Bellator dropped to one knee in the brush, pulling her hood up. Her breath caught in her throat.

Alexandria sat by a fire, her silver-blonde hair catching the light, her face grim with thought. Erythyn sat beside her, the glint of the collar visible. And there was a third figure—a young woman with regal poise and the unmistakable air of the Enchanted Forest bloodline. Bellator exhaled slowly. Relief and dread warred inside her. She had found them. But if she had found them—then others could too. The Shadowlord's reach was long, and time was running out.

The firelight danced across Alexandria's face, casting golden flickers through the soft locks of her hair. Her expression was distant, troubled— as her eyes were locked on the flames, her thoughts clearly elsewhere. Erythyn sat beside her, silent, his back against a tree, his expression unreadable in the shifting glow. The young woman, ever graceful, moved quietly along the camp's edge, tending to protective wards and checking her map etched with constellations from a time long past.

From the shadows beyond the firelight, Bellator watched. Her breath caught in her throat as she observed the trio, relief sent crashing into her chest like a wave. Alexandria looked well. Whole. Still herself. But she was sitting so close to him. Bellator's jaw clenched. Without announcing herself, she stepped forward into the clearing.

Alexandria's head snapped up. "Bellator?"

Erythyn was on his feet in an instant, his hands reflexively twitching as if reaching for power that no longer flowed freely. The faint shimmer of his collar caught the firelight.

"Alexandria, step away from him," Bellator said, her voice low but sharp, one hand resting on the hilt of her sword. "Now."

"Wait—Bellator—" Alexandria rushed to her feet, blocking her path.

"You've got three seconds to explain," Bellator growled, her eyes never leaving Erythyn. "Because last I saw, he dragged you through a collapsing portal without warning."

Erythyn scoffed and stepped back, his arms raised in mock surrender. "And you're welcome, by the way."

"Don't push me," Bellator snapped, taking another step forward.

Alexandria held up both hands. "Stop. Please. Just listen."

Bellator paused—barely—but she didn't lower her guard.

"He's not the enemy," Alexandria continued. "Not right now. That collar—" She pointed to the faintly glowing band around Erythyn's throat. "—is enchanted. It suppresses his dark magic. He can't use it."

"And I'm supposed to believe that?" Bellator's tone cut like a blade. "That he just volunteered to be muzzled like a rabid beast?"

"I chose it," Erythyn said flatly, "to prove I was serious."

Bellator's stare hardened. "Prove it to who? Because it sure as hell wasn't me."

Alexandria stepped between them, frustration and fatigue thick in her voice. "He's helping me, Bellator. And I need your help too, but not like this. Not with swords drawn."

Bellator's glare lingered on Erythyn a beat longer, but she finally stepped back, her hand loosening on the hilt. "Talk. Quickly."

Taking a deep breath, Alexandria gestured to the fire. They all sat again, though the tension was still coiled tightly in the air.

"We're in the past," Alexandria began. "Before the war. Before the Enchanted Forest was shattered. This is what it used to be." She glanced at the sky above—still soft with starlight, unmarred by the smoke and sorrow she knew from her own time. "We're standing in the ruins—but they're still whole. Still alive."

Bellator's brows drew together. "So you were thrown back in time!"

"Not thrown. Pulled," Erythyn muttered.

"Don't make me regret letting you sit near the fire," she shot back.

Alexandria interjected before either could rise further. "The Shadowlord is already at work here. He's using animals—corrupting them with dark spells, reshaping them into things that shouldn't exist. He's trying to perfect the process. To create something worse."

Bellator's expression darkened. "I saw them. On the way here. One was a boar—half-iron, crawling with shadow. I barely made it around without a fight. And another... It screamed like it was still part-human."

"They're getting closer," Alexandria said quietly. "More twisted. More unstable. But he's not done. This is still practice for him."

"He's trying to build an entity," Erythyn added. "One that feeds off despair, desire, greed—something that could infiltrate society by manipulating people's weaknesses."

"To conquer not through war," Alexandria continued, "but through decay. Corruption. And once he finds a human subject strong enough to survive the ritual... It's over."

Bellator leaned forward, her eyes burning with purpose. "Then we kill him now. While he's vulnerable. End it before it starts."

"We're trying," Alexandria said. "But there's more. We have someone with us. Someone who knows this world. Who's helping us."

She turned to where Ashlynn stood, quietly observing. "Bellator, this is Ashlynn. She's...she's an ancestor. Of mine."

Ashlynn offered a respectful nod. "I've pledged to help them. I know the forests, and I know the Shadowlord's patterns."

Bellator frowned, taking Ashlynn in carefully. The resemblance to Alexandria was uncanny—especially in the eyes. She offered a curt nod in return but didn't smile. "So what's the plan?" Bellator asked.

"We track him," Alexandria said. "There's a ritual site beneath the old tree in Nightroot Vale. He's still working from the shadows, still hiding. But if we can catch him before he completes the binding—we might be able to destroy the source of his power before it anchors to this realm."

Bellator was quiet for a long moment. She stared into the fire, her jaw tight, her hands curled around her knees. "And after?" she asked. "How do we get back?"

"We don't know yet," Erythyn admitted. "But if we stay too long, the portal back could collapse. The magic's not stable. This...this is all borrowed time."

Alexandria nodded. "We may only have days."

Bellator exhaled through her nose heavily, processing everything they were telling her.

"I don't have a choice." Alexandria stated with certainty.

Bellator looked at her again, the firelight catching in her eyes. "You're the only reason I'm staying."

"I know," Alexandria said. "But I'm glad you're here."

After another long pause, Bellator stood. "All right. I'm in. But I don't like him."

"Noted," Erythyn muttered.

"I don't trust him."

"Also noted."

"And if he steps out of line—"

"I get it, Bellator," Alexandria interrupted, her voice tired but amused. "He knows. We all know."

Bellator sighed, long and low. "Then let's get this done. Before we're trapped here forever."

Ashlynn turned toward the forest, her eyes distant. "Then we move at dawn. The Shadowlord grows bolder with each moonrise."

So, the four of them sat beneath ancient stars, the fire between them warming more than just the cold night air. They were a mismatched alliance of past and future, light and shadow, soldier and sorcerer. But for now, they were all that stood between the world and the storm to come.

The others had long since settled into a quiet, uneasy rest. Erythyn leaned against a tree, his arms folded, his eyes closed but not sleeping— ever the predator waiting for a threat. Bellator sat with her sword across her lap, her body still tense even in repose, her head bowed as if in prayer or restraint. Ashlynn had gone farther into the woods, meditating beneath the stars, her hands pressed into the soil like she was listening to the earth's oldest language.

Alexandria sat for a while, watching the fire crackle and spit embers into the night sky, until the silence began to press on her ribs like invisible hands. She rose quietly, careful not to wake the others, and stepped beyond the ring of trees that circled their small encampment. The forest, even at night, was alive with presence—though no animals moved, no wind stirred. It was not emptiness she felt, but something waiting.

She walked aimlessly at first, guided by instinct more than direction, until she found herself standing on a rise overlooking a glade bathed in pale moonlight. The trees here stood like silent sentinels, their silvered bark glowing faintly. A stream murmured somewhere beyond the rocks. Fireflies drifted in loose spirals above the grass, each pulse of light like a forgotten memory flickering back to life.

Alexandria knelt in the grass, her hands brushing the earth, and felt it —that pull. That strange, aching sense of recognition she couldn't quite name. It wasn't the place itself. It was something deeper. Something buried in her blood.

This is your home, the wind seemed to whisper. Not the ruins. Not the aftermath. But this.

She looked down at her hands, dirt under her fingernails, tiny cuts from brambles and battle across her knuckles. She wasn't a stranger here. Not really. The land knew her. The magic hummed when she passed. Even the trees leaned in a little, as if drawn to her.

I don't belong here, she told herself silently. Not in this time. Not in this peace.

But her heart disagreed.

Meeting Ashlynn had stirred something in her. It wasn't just the resemblance, though that alone had shaken her. It was the way Ashlynn spoke to the trees. The way her magic flowed not from force but from harmony. Alexandria had spent so much of her life trying to control her power, shape it, discipline it like a soldier. But here—in this time—magic didn't need to be caged. It was everywhere. In the air. In the stones. In her bones.

She thought of her people. Of the ruins they now lived among. Of the stories whispered in candlelight—legends of an age long gone, of towering spires and living rivers, of ancestors who walked in tune with the stars. Those stories had always felt like myths. Now she was living them. And it made her wonder—was she meant to witness this? Or was she meant to restore it? The idea terrified her.

She stood slowly, brushing off her knees, and looked up through the trees. The moon stared back, full and patient. Time here was soft, fluid. She could feel it pressing gently against her, not like a tide trying to pull her back—but like a hand on her shoulder. Steadying. Guiding.

What if the Shadowlord didn't just want to ruin the future? What if his goal was to corrupt the past, to rewrite it before it ever had the chance to bloom?

She pressed her hand to her chest. The answer wasn't just in defeating him—it was in preserving what was good and untouched. In protecting this golden seed of history before it could ever be destroyed.

A voice stirred gently behind her. "You feel it too, don't you?"

Ashlynn's voice was soft, threaded with the night breeze.

Alexandria turned. "Yes. I don't understand it, but... It's like this place is part of me. Like I've already been here."

Ashlynn stepped beside her, her eyes on the horizon. "Because you have. Maybe not in body. But in spirit. You are woven from the threads of this time. You carry its echoes in your blood."

"I'm afraid of what that means," Alexandria whispered.

"Don't be. The future isn't fixed, Alexandria. It's shaped by choice—and by those brave enough to change it."

They stood together in silence, two women born of different eras, yet bound by the same thread of legacy and defiance.

Alexandria didn't know what the coming days would bring. The Shadowlord's reach was growing. Time was thinning. The portal home would not wait forever. But for the first time in a long while, she felt something stronger than fear. She felt purpose.

Chapter 12
Shadows of the Heart

The Silent Concord

Speak not in words of black or white,

In whispered truce twixt dark & light.

For true discourse transcended such claim,

The soul's own voice will stake its claim.

Alexandria finally returned to camp as the moon reached its peak. The others were still asleep—Bellator lying near the fire, her hand loosely on her blade, and Erythyn leaning against the tree with his eyes shut, his breathing deep and even. Ashlynn had resumed her meditative position by the roots, her presence silent but alert.

Exhaustion pulled at Alexandria's limbs like lead weights. She laid down near the fading embers, tucking her cloak tightly around herself, and allowed sleep to take her in slow, heavy waves. At first, there was only darkness. Then, the forest came.

But it was not the one she had walked through. It was twisted. Dead. The trees were blackened husks, their branches clawing at the blood-colored sky. Rivers ran thick with something darker than water. In the distance, ruined spires crumbled as though mourning their own forgotten greatness. Alexandria stood in the heart of it—alone. She turned, trying to find the others, but there were no sounds. No animals. No wind. Just silence, deep and total, pressing against her like an ocean of shadow.

And then she heard it. A voice, low and echoing, neither male nor female, rising like smoke from the roots beneath her feet.

"You are not too late... But you are not early enough."

The ground trembled. Ahead, the ruins of Aelora—once proud and gleaming—rose from the dead earth. But they were hollow now, crumbling towers veined with corruption, glyphs cracked and weeping black light. In the center stood a tree—the tree. The Great Ice Tree from Dawnshire. But now it was fully consumed.

Its bark oozed shadow. Its limbs reached across the sky like broken fingers. Hanging from them were people—or what was left of them, their faces frozen in anguish, their eyes glowing faintly as if still alive. One of them looked like Erythyn. Another—she couldn't breathe—another looked like Bellator.

She stumbled back, her heart hammering. A voice deeper than the earth rose from the tree, its tone like stone grinding on stone.

"He is almost ready."

From beneath the roots, the ground cracked and split. A hand rose—pale, monstrous, but unmistakably human in shape. And from the shadows, a figure began to emerge. Cloaked in a mass of writhing tendrils, its face hidden behind a mask of bone. No eyes. No mouth. Just the void. But she knew who it was. The Shadowlord.

He didn't walk—he glided across the deadened ground toward her. Each step he took left behind twisted growths—flowers that bloomed and bled in the same breath. She tried to move. To run. To summon magic. Nothing came. He raised a hand, long and skeletal, and pointed toward her heart. Suddenly, she was bound—thorns wrapping her arms, her legs, her throat. She couldn't speak. Couldn't scream.

"Do you know what I need to perfect my creation?" the voice whispered —not from his mouth, but inside her head. *"Desire. Regret. Legacy. I feed on what you bury."*

He stepped closer. And now she could see it—underneath the mask, his face shifting. One moment it was her father. Then her mother. Then her own.

"You carry the blood of the forest," he hissed. *"What better seed to grow the end?"*

He raised a hand. Darkness coiled in his palm—glowing with the same runes as the animals. The same cursed light. Then—a scream cut through the air. One that wasn't hers. A voice she knew.

"Alexandria!"

It was Ashlynn's. Everything exploded into light. The nightmare shattered.

She woke with a gasp, jerking upright, sweat slick on her skin and her chest heaving.

Bellator stirred immediately. "What is it? What happened?"

Erythyn opened one eye, his expression suddenly alert.

Alexandria swallowed hard, wiping the cold from her brow. Her voice was raw. "A vision. A warning. From him." She looked to Ashlynn, who was already moving toward her.

"The Shadowlord?" Ashlynn asked quietly.

Alexandria nodded. "He's almost ready. He spoke to me. He showed me what he's creating. He's not just twisting beasts anymore. He wants something more." Her gaze swept across her companions, her voice low and full of urgency. "He wants a person. Someone to carry the magic. To become his final vessel."

Bellator's eyes narrowed. "Who?"

A beat of silence. Then Alexandria whispered, "I think... He wants it to be me."

No one spoke. The wind stirred the trees above them. The forest held its breath again. And time, ever fleeting, continued to unravel.

Several hours had passed. The camp had gone quiet again.

Bellator, worn from days of relentless travel and sharpened tension, had finally succumbed to exhaustion. She slept deeply, her body curled near the fire, her sword laid carefully beside her like a loyal animal. Ashlynn remained on the outskirts, beyond the warding circle, speaking softly to the trees—drawing on their magic, perhaps listening for their secrets.

The fire crackled low in the center, casting a soft glow on Alexandria's face as she sat near it, her knees drawn to her chest, her thoughts a maelstrom. She hadn't slept since the vision. Couldn't. Every time she closed her eyes, she heard his voice again—

"You carry the blood of the forest. What better seed to grow to end?"

It wasn't just fear that stirred in her now. It was doubt. The idea that maybe he was right. That maybe she was the perfect vessel for the end of everything. A soft movement to her left caught her attention.

Erythyn. Sitting down beside her, his arms resting loosely on his knees, his eyes darker than the night. "Couldn't sleep?" he asked, his voice quiet but not teasing for once.

Alexandria shook her head. "Didn't want to."

He studied her for a moment, then looked toward the fire. "The vision. You saw him."

She nodded.

"What did he say?"

Her fingers tightened around her knees. "He wants to make something more powerful than what he's made with the animals. Something that can feed on people. On what they want. What they fear. And he...he said I'd be the perfect vessel. Because of what's in me. My connection to the forest. My blood." She turned to him, her voice raw. "What if he's right, Erythyn? What if he's been watching me this whole time? Waiting?"

Erythyn was quiet for a long beat, then leaned forward, resting his elbows on his knees. "He's not right," he said softly. "He's clever. He twists truths until they break. That's what dark magic does—it finds a weakness and whispers to it until it thinks it's strong."

She looked at him, the firelight casting shadows on his face. "And what about you? Don't you hear him too?"

"All the time," he admitted. "But I don't listen anymore. I spent years being told I was nothing more than my power. That I was a weapon waiting to go off. The truth is... I was tempted. Not by destruction, but by the idea that someone wanted me to be more. Even if it meant becoming something terrible."

Their eyes met—hers shining with quiet pain, his with something more complicated. Shame, perhaps. Or understanding. "I never wanted to be saved," he continued. "But now... I think I want to be chosen. Not by fate, not by some darkness, but by someone who sees more than the worst in me." His voice trailed off, and the quiet that followed was thick with things unsaid.

Alexandria turned away for a moment, trying to gather her thoughts —but something pulled her back. A fragile tether between them, growing tighter. Her voice was barely above a whisper. "I used to think you were dangerous," she said.

"I am," he replied, just as quietly.

"But not in the way I thought." She hesitated, then reached out—not touching, just close enough that their hands nearly brushed. "You've changed, Erythyn."

He smiled faintly. "So have you."

As Alexandria sat close to the flames, the edges of her cloak drawn around her like a shield, her mind was a storm of thoughts—memories of battle, visions of a broken future, and above it all...him. Erythyn. The dark force she should have feared, the one who had once brought chaos, and now...confusion. Safety. Heat.

She didn't know when it started, this pull toward him. It was subtle at first, like gravity shifting beneath her feet. But tonight, it felt unbearable.

Her heart thudded in her chest, each beat louder than the wind weaving through the treetops. He looked at her, mesmerized by her golden eyes as they caught his—startled, uncertain, but unmoving.

Without a word, she moved closer beside him. Closer than she'd ever dared. Her eyes searched his. "I know there's still light in you," she said, her voice barely above a whisper. "Even if you don't believe it."

Erythyn exhaled slowly, like something inside him had cracked open. "You don't know what I've done," he said, his voice low, gravelly. "What I've become."

"I don't care," she said, her hand brushing against his. "Right now, in this moment, I see you."

Their fingers touched—tentative, electric. A breath caught in his throat. He looked at her mouth, then back into her eyes. And then, something snapped. He moved—sudden, magnetic—and his lips found hers.

The kiss started like a sigh—soft, aching, restrained. A meeting of mouths that trembled with unspoken words and forbidden desires. His lips were warm, firmer than she expected, yet careful, like he was afraid he might break her. Her hands slid up, her fingers tangling in the collar of his cloak, pulling him closer.

Erythyn let out a quiet, shaky breath against her lips before deepening the kiss. It became hungrier. Desperate.

Years of guilt. Months of tension. Days of almost touching. All of it unraveled between their mouths. His hand slid up her back, his fingers pressing into her through the fabric of her cloak, drawing her into him as if the space between them was agony. Her other hand rose to cup his cheek—his stubble rough beneath her fingertips—and she felt him shiver at the touch.

When they finally pulled apart, it was slow—unwilling. A breath between them, lips still brushing, foreheads pressed together. Both of them stunned by the gravity of it.

Erythyn's voice was hoarse. "You shouldn't... You shouldn't want this. I've done so many things, Alexandria. Things I can't undo."

She touched his cheek, forcing him to meet her gaze. Her thumb traced just under his eye. "I'm not asking you to undo anything," she said. "I'm asking you to fight for what's still left."

He stared at her, his eyes burning with a mix of sorrow and something dangerously close to hope.

The fire popped beside them, sending a cascade of glowing embers into the air like shooting stars, but neither of them moved. The world could burn around them, and it still wouldn't have pulled them apart.

Not tonight.

Chapter 13
When Wolves Clash

Dirge of the Shadowguard

Once they stood with hearts ablaze,

Now they march in ashen haze.

Bound to serve his silent will,

They guard the dark that kills them still.

Morning crept slowly over the edge of the horizon, the sky painted in streaks of silver and pale lavender. Birds remained silent. The wind was still. The forest, normally awake with its own ancient breath, seemed to pause—as if it too sensed what was approaching.

Bellator stirred first. The scent of cold ash from the dying fire tickled her nose as she blinked awake, her senses immediately sharp despite her fatigue. Years of battle, of relentless vigilance, had trained her to rise quickly, quietly, and without the grogginess of a true sleep. She reached for her sword instinctively then paused. Something was off. Her eyes scanned the camp—and locked on the pair still asleep near the fire.

Alexandria was curled slightly inward, her dark hair falling across her face, her head resting gently on Erythyn's shoulder. He had slid lower in the night, his posture relaxed for once, one arm loosely across his lap—but their closeness was unmistakable. Comfortable. Intimate.

Bellator rose silently and walked over, her boots crunching lightly on the dry pine needles. She nudged Alexandria with the back of her gauntleted hand—not rough, but pointed.

Alexandria stirred. "Mmm...?"

"Up," Bellator said. "Now."

She sat up slowly, blinking the sleep away, then caught sight of Bellator's expression and stiffened.

"I—it wasn't what it—"

"We need to talk."

Alexandria followed her a few paces away from camp, brushing stray twigs from her cloak, her cheeks still pink from sleep—or something else.

Bellator folded her arms, her tone flat but edged. "So...when exactly were you planning to tell me you were getting closer to him?"

Alexandria exhaled sharply. "It's not like that. Not exactly."

"Oh? Because from where I stood, it looked pretty exact."

"I didn't mean for it to happen, Bellator. I didn't even realize it was happening. It's just... We talked. And for once, he wasn't hiding behind that arrogance. He was real."

Bellator stared at her. "He's dangerous."

"I know," Alexandria said. "But he's also different now. He's trying. I've seen him at his worst, and even then, he held back. He didn't have to. But he did."

Bellator's jaw tensed. "And what happens when that collar fails? Or worse, when he convinces you to take it off?"

"I'm not stupid."

"No, but you're tired. And you're carrying more weight than anyone should. That makes you vulnerable. I've seen it before. He'll use it."

Alexandria didn't answer. The truth was more complicated than either of them wanted to admit. And just as the conversation threatened to fracture further—

—a low growl rippled through the trees.

Both women froze.

From the shadows beyond the camp, a massive shape emerged, the underbrush rustling violently beneath its weight. The wolf stepped into the clearing, silent but for the grinding of bone plates fused into its flanks. Its fur was matted with tar-like darkness, and its eyes—once blue, amber, or natural—now gleamed a sickening red, glowing faintly with corrupted runes that pulsed like blood magic.

Its snarl exposed jagged teeth, too long for a natural wolf. Spines protruded from its back, and its paws left scorched tracks on the earth as it padded closer to the sleeping camp.

"Alexandria," Bellator hissed. "Wake them. Now."

Alexandria spun, sprinting back to the fire. "Erythyn! Ashlynn—wake up!"

Erythyn jolted upright at the urgency in her voice, instinctively reaching for power—but the collar reminded him quickly of its presence, humming against his skin. "What is it?"

Before anyone could answer, the wolf leapt. Bellator was already moving.

In a blink, she surged forward, her body glowing with soft green light as she shed her humanoid form. Bones shifted, armor fell away, and fur sprouted across her limbs. A massive wolf—sleek and powerful with silver-streaked fur and eyes like blue fire—landed squarely in the corrupted creature's path, snarling.

The two wolves collided in a tangle of fur, fang, and fury. Bellator drove the beast back with raw strength, her jaws sinking into its shoulder as they rolled across the clearing.

Erythyn leapt to his feet and threw his hand forward, conjuring a barrier of shimmering light—not dark magic, but raw kinetic force, repurposed through the collar's filter. It surged up just in time to catch a blast of corrupted fire that the beast expelled from its gullet, shielding Alexandria and Ashlynn.

Ashlynn raised her arms, her voice weaving a spell like song. Vines erupted from the ground, lashing out and wrapping around the beast's hind legs, trying to pin it down.

Bellator, still in her druid form, used the moment of stillness to strike again, her fangs going for its throat.

But the creature shrieked—not in pain, but in anger—and burst free, throwing Bellator back against a tree with a heavy thud.

Alexandria ran forward, her hand glowing with her magic—pure and radiant—before she thrust it into the ground. The light spread outward in a wide arc beneath the wolf, burning the corrupted markings along its legs. It howled, twisted in midair, and began to retreat into the trees.

"Don't let it escape!" Ashlynn shouted.

But it was fast—wounded but not dead. In seconds, it vanished into the fog.

The silence afterward was thick and ragged. Bellator shifted back into her human form, crouched and panting, blood trickling from her brow.

"Everyone okay?" Alexandria called, rushing over.

"Still breathing," Erythyn muttered, dusting off his cloak.

Ashlynn nodded. "It wasn't fully transformed. A scout, maybe."

Bellator rose shakily, wiping the blood from her cheek. "He knows we're close."

Alexandria looked toward the forest where the creature had fled. The burned patches of earth still smoldered with foul energy. "He's watching us," she said. "We need to move. Today."

Bellator caught her eye, and the tension of their earlier conversation still lingered. But for now, it was buried beneath something more urgent. The hunt had begun. And the Shadowlord was done waiting.

The clearing still smelled of scorched moss and burned corruption. Smoke coiled low over the earth, mingling with morning mist. Erythyn crouched near the edge of the trees, inspecting a patch of dark residue left behind by the retreating wolf, his fingers ghosting above the burn marks. Ashlynn moved silently around the perimeter, whispering soft spells to mend the broken wards, her face pinched in quiet concern.

Bellator sat on a flat stone, wiping dried blood from her brow. Her wolf-form had taken most of the blow, but shifting back always left her bones aching, her body hollowed. Alexandria knelt beside her, silently dabbing a salve across a bruised shoulder.

For a while, neither spoke.

Then Bellator sighed—long, slow—and gave her a glance that was more tired than sharp. "You've gotten stronger." Alexandria looked at her, surprised. "You fought like someone who knows what she's protecting," Bellator added. "Not someone just reacting. You made decisions. Smart ones."

"I didn't think. I just...moved."

"That's what instinct is," Bellator said. "And leadership. You used your power to protect—not just to fight." She paused. "I saw that in you when you were young. Just didn't know if you'd survive long enough for it to take root."

Alexandria gave a small smile. "Was that a compliment?"

"Don't get used to it," Bellator muttered—but there was a flicker of warmth in her voice. The silence stretched again, but it wasn't uncomfortable. Just heavy with meaning.

"I'm sorry," Alexandria said softly, dipping her gaze. "For not telling you about Erythyn. I should have."

Bellator stared at the treeline for a long moment, then nodded. "Maybe. But...you were right."

That pulled Alexandria's gaze back. Bellator went on, her voice rough with reluctant honesty. "There's something different in him. Something controlled. He still makes my instincts bristle, but...he didn't hesitate back there. He shielded you first. No delay. No calculation."

Alexandria's chest tightened. "I don't know where it's going... whatever this is between us. But it's not about power. Or manipulation. I see him, Bellator. And he sees me."

Bellator gave her a long look. "Then if he breaks that trust—he answers to me."

A grin tugged at Alexandria's mouth. "Wouldn't have it any other way."

Bellator stood, wincing slightly, and stretched her shoulder. "Rest's over. That wolf's trail won't stay warm for long."

Alexandria rose with her, a new light in her eyes. Determined. Grounded.

They walked back toward the others, where Erythyn and Ashlynn were waiting. The group had formed an unspoken circle, something in the air now tighter—bonded. Forged by fire.

Ashlynn met them with a grim expression. "That creature... It wasn't just altered. It was marked. A servant, not a scout. It was watching us. Listening."

"Then the Shadowlord knows where we are," Alexandria said. "And what we're planning."

Erythyn added. "He's baiting us. Trying to pull us in unready."

"Then we don't give him time to prepare," Bellator replied. "We move. We follow the trail. We finish this."

Alexandria nodded, her fingers tightening around the hilt of her blade. "The corrupted path leads north. Toward the Vale. That's where he's anchoring the spell."

Erythyn stood and adjusted the collar around his neck. "Let's make sure it's his tomb."

The group gathered their gear. The air had shifted now—no longer still. Their footing was steady. Their hearts aligned. Ahead, the corrupted forest stretched like a living labyrinth, the last pieces of the Shadowlord's dark plan unfolding just out of sight. But they were ready.

This time, they would bring the storm.

Chapter 14
The Poisoned River

The Sunblade's Awakening

When shadows tremble at fledging dawn,

The sword of suns shall be reborn.

Its gold-kissed edge & tempered fire,

Shall pierce the veil & lift the pyre.

Months had passed, and Alexandria and Erythyn had grown closer, much closer, their connection undeniable. They confided in each other unspoken things they had never shared with anyone else. They were falling in love, a connection each of them had a hard time accepting but yet embracing at the same time. Each of them had such a sad, dark past, neither one of them able to fully trust anyone and always on guard. Until now when they were slowly starting to break free from the past that had a hold on them.

Many long, relentless, and cruel months had passed since Alexandria, Bellator, Erythyn, and Ashlynn set out on their quest to find and stop the Shadowlord. The four had seen the seasons change as they hunted him across forests, ravines, and cursed ruins. They had fought creatures twisted beyond recognition—beasts whose minds had been corrupted, whose eyes no longer reflected life but only the dark will of the one who had enslaved them.

But the most dangerous change had come not from beyond the kingdom's borders—but from within its very soul.

The protective barriers once spun by ancient magic had begun to falter, their once-impenetrable strength now riddled with unseen cracks. Through these invisible tears, malevolent spirits crept like smoke into the hearts of the towns, unseen but deeply felt. They slithered into homes beneath the veil of twilight, their presence marked only by flickering candlelight, unexplained chills, and the gnawing feeling that something— something cruel and watching—lurked just beyond the threshold.

In the villages and cities alike, fear took root.

Mothers clutched their children tightly, refusing to let them stray too far from the hearth. Marketplaces once filled with laughter now stood tense and quiet, bartering whispered over shoulders, every face pale with suspicion. Friends became strangers, their eyes narrowed with doubt. Had they been touched by the spirits? Were they one of them now?

Doors were sealed long before dusk. Lanterns were lit not to chase away the night, but to stave off the whispers—those ghostly murmurs that seemed to come from nowhere and everywhere at once. Prayers echoed softly behind shuttered windows, desperate chants to gods long silent. Livestock turned up mutilated, wells ran dry or tasted of ash, and shadows moved where they should not. The townspeople no longer trusted the peace of morning. For even daylight held a lingering unease. And still...the Shadowlord remained out of reach—elusive, untouchable, like a specter laughing behind the veil of despair he'd cast upon the land.

Each time the group drew close, it seemed something would pull them away—a distraction, a false lead, or an ill-timed misstep. They couldn't see it, not yet. That the missteps weren't always accidents. That someone among them—Erythyn, quiet and watchful—was keeping secrets. He didn't understand it himself, not fully. Only when Alexandria got too close to finding the Shadowlord, something inside him pulled back. A voice, a flicker of dread. He loved her. God, how he loved her. But something was wrong, and he couldn't stop it.

Then one dusky afternoon, the veil lifted—if only slightly.

Bellator had taken to the wilds alone, her senses sharper in her wolf form. The wind was still. Too still. No birds. No insects. Not even the rustle of leaves. That silence was unnatural.

She crept through the underbrush, her paws silent against damp earth, and paused behind a thick pine. Her icy eyes narrowed.

There he was. The Shadowlord stood at the edge of the river, his hood low, his face a smudge of shadow and light. In his gloved hand, he held a dark vial that glowed with an eerie, greenish light. With slow, precise movements, he uncorked it and poured it into the flowing water.

Bellator's breath caught in her throat. The river—their river. The one that flowed through every village, that fed every well, every field. The poison slithered like oil across the surface, shimmering unnaturally. She turned and ran. Faster than she'd ever run before. She transformed back to her human form as she returned. "Alexandria!" her voice trembled. "He's poisoning the river."

Alexandria froze. "Where?" she asked.

"Come, I will show you. This might be our chance!" Bellator replied with urgency.

"But we need to wait for Erythyn and Ashlynn to return. It is just the two of us." she responded.

"Alexandria! We don't have time to wait. We need to see where he goes. This could be our only chance. He is poisoning everyone, and they don't even realize it yet," Bellator replied, concerned and determined.

Alexandria responded, "All right, but we must stay hidden. We cannot let him see us, or it's going to be bad. We have no backup."

Bellator could see Alexandria's hesitation. "I understand, but I'm asking for you to trust me. He can lead us back to where he has been hiding. We will stay hidden."

Bellator's words hung in the air, and Alexandria sighed softly. There was no denying the truth in them: they couldn't remain idle when a chance to help existed, even if it meant risking everything for humanity.

They decided it was now or never and headed off. The forest groaned around them. Bellator sprinted ahead, her breath ragged, her muscles coiled like a predator's, every step pounding the forest floor in a thunderous rhythm. Behind her, Princess Alexandria's cloak snapped in the wind, her braid whipping across her shoulder as she ran, every heartbeat thudding like a war drum in her chest. The air itself felt taut—charged—laced with something darker than fear.

Birds erupted from the canopy in frantic bursts, black silhouettes against a rapidly dimming sky. A cacophony of wings and shrieks cut through the trees as if the forest itself cried out in warning. Twigs snapped. Leaves rustled in an uneasy rhythm. Somewhere far off, something howled—low and unnatural, neither beast nor man.

Alexandria's boots slid across moss-slick roots, but she didn't slow. Her eyes flicked to Bellator's broad figure ahead—her guardian, her anchor—guiding them deeper into the emerald gloom with terrifying speed. The trees thickened, their twisted limbs clawing at cloaks and hair, whispering with the wind in strange, ancient tongues.

"We're close," Bellator hissed, her voice breathless but focused.

A heavy fog was rising now, not from the ground but above the river. The closer they drew, the colder the air became. The warmth of spring had vanished—swallowed by a creeping chill that clung to their skin and sank into their bones. Then they broke through the treeline—and there it was. The river. Once pure, once sacred. Now—a corrupted vein through the heart of the kingdom. The water no longer shimmered with the clarity of moonlight. Instead, it rolled thick and slow, coated in a dark sheen that caught the last light of dusk like slick, poisoned oil. It slithered atop the surface—rippling unnaturally, like something alive. The scent of rot and iron choked the air. Insects buzzed and dropped from the sky mid-flight, twitching on rocks. Frogs lay belly-up along the shore.

Alexandria staggered to a halt beside Bellator, one hand braced on her chest as her breath caught. "This isn't just poisoning," she whispered, her voice shaking. "It's desecration."

Bellator's eyes narrowed, scanning the opposite bank. "He was here," she murmured. "Just moments ago. I felt him." She stepped forward, vigilant. "I saw the shadow. Hooded. Cloaked. But..."

She trailed off.

The bank was empty. The reeds still swayed from a presence that had vanished like smoke in the wind. No tracks. No sound. Only the stench of corruption remained. "Gone," Bellator breathed. "He was right here."

A raven croaked overhead, circling once—twice—before vanishing behind the treetops. Alexandria drew her blade. Not because it would help but because she needed to feel something solid—something she could trust in the face of so much dark silence. A branch cracked behind them. They spun—but saw nothing. Only the forest. Only the river. Only the knowledge that they were not alone. And that the Shadowlord was always one step ahead.

Back at the camp, the forest hummed with tension. Dusk was falling fast, the sky brushed with molten gold and bruised purple, casting long, watchful shadows between the trees. A hush had fallen over the camp, unnaturally quiet—too quiet.

Erythyn stepped into the clearing first, his cloak damp with dew and travel dust clinging to his boots. Ashlynn followed, her golden braid loose from the wind, her hands stained faintly with herbs and soot from the apothecary in town. He stopped dead in his tracks. "They're not here," he muttered.

Ashlynn scanned the empty space where the fire should've been stoked, where Alexandria's traveling pack should've rested against the moss-covered stone. "Where are they?" she asked, her voice tight.

"Alexandria said they'd wait for us." Erythyn turned in a slow circle, his jaw tight and nostrils flared. "She wouldn't just leave without a word —unless something forced her to."

Ashlynn crouched low, running her fingers through the flattened leaves and faint indentations in the earth. "Two sets of tracks. They left in a hurry."

Erythyn's gaze darkened as he clenched his fists. "Damn it. Bellator must've sensed something." He turned away, pacing toward the edge of the trees. "We were gone too long."

"They looked worried before we left," Ashlynn said, straightening. "Even back in town, people were whispering—'The river's changing.' 'The birds are migrating early.' 'Something's wrong with the soil.' The townsfolk are frightened. The world is shifting."

He nodded grimly. "I felt it. Like a pulse beneath the surface. Something is stirring."

Ashlynn narrowed her eyes toward the darkening forest. "You think the Shadowlord is moving again?"

"I don't think," Erythyn said, eyes glinting in the dimming light. "I know."

A look of concern came over Ashlynn's face. "Then we can't stay here."

Erythyn turned toward her, his voice sharp with resolve. "No. We go after them. Now. I don't know how long they've been gone, or where they were heading—but I'm not leaving them alone out there."

He knelt, his fingers brushing the prints left behind. "Bellator took point. She was running. Fast. Something scared her."

Ashlynn pulled her cloak tighter around her shoulders. "Then we follow. We catch their trail and don't stop."

He stood, unsheathing the long, curved blade at his hip. "If he is near them, I'll rip him apart."

Ashlynn touched his shoulder. "We'll find them, Erythyn. Just...don't let the rage take over again."

He paused for a beat, then nodded. "Let's move."

They plunged into the forest, the canopy above swallowing the last remnants of day. The path was uneven, slick with moss and covered with thorns, but they moved with quiet purpose. Ashlynn murmured small spells under her breath, runes flickering along her palms to light their way without fire.

Around them, the woods whispered—branches creaking with unseen weight, leaves rustling though there was no wind. Far off, an owl screeched. Then silence again. Too much silence.

"I hate this stillness," Ashlynn muttered. "It feels...watched."

Erythyn slowed then touched the bark of a twisted elm. "I know this trail. The river's close. Bellator used to patrol it when we first arrived."

Ashlynn frowned. "Why would she take Alexandria there?"

"She wouldn't unless there was no other choice."

They moved faster, urgency mounting with every step.

"Alexandria is so damn stubborn," Erythyn muttered, half to himself. "She thinks she can fight him without me."

Ashlynn gave him a sidelong glance. "You think that's why she left?"

He said nothing for a moment then finally admitted, "No. She left to protect something. Someone. Maybe me."

Ashlynn's steps slowed just slightly. "And who protects her?"

That question hung in the air like a noose.

The forest around them thickened, and the sound of water began to whisper ahead. Erythyn's stride grew longer. "We're close."

"Then we'd better hurry," Ashlynn said, her voice tightening. "Because whatever led them into this—wasn't done with them yet."

Chapter 15
Wounds of the Forest

Prophecy of the Darkened Crown

He who wears the dark-edged crown,

Shall see the seas & stars fall down.

Yet in a heart untouched by fear,

The Lightblade's gleam may yet appear.

eeper into the forest, the Shadowlord was gone. Only the dark gleam of tainted water remained. "He can't be far," Alexandria said, her voice hard with resolve. They continued onward to find him. They trekked through the forest along the river. Until they stumbled across something unexpected. A narrow, nearly invisible path wound toward the foot of the mountains. A thick wall of brush stood between them and what looked like solid rock—it was at that moment a wolf, black as midnight, emerged. Bellator froze. Alexandria's hand went to the hilt of her blade. But the beast didn't attack. It slunk away, revealing what was hidden: a cave entrance, sunken into the stone.

Alexandria glanced at Bellator. "We wait." They knelt in the thickening of the trees as the night was fastly approaching. The trees whispered above them. Insects sang, and the wind smelled of river rot. Then, he emerged. The Shadowlord stepped from the mouth of the cave, with a vial in his hand.

Alexandria's pulse quickened. She turned to Bellator. "He's going to poison the river again."

Bellator's eyes flicked toward her, calm and razor-sharp. "It's just us. We need to be careful. Quiet."

They moved closer—low, silent, like shadows in the brush. Then a voice cut through the air. "Alexandria!"

Erythyn.

Too loud. Too sudden.

The Shadowlord's head snapped toward the trees. His eyes locked onto Alexandria—and time itself seemed to falter. Bellator leapt, shifting mid-air into her wolf form, her teeth bared. Ashlynn shouted a spell, casting light through the darkness. Chaos erupted as the Shadowlord summoned his own creatures—wolves, slick with shadow and seething rage. And still he stared at Alexandria. His hand rose. A crackle of dark magic bloomed between his palms, growing brighter, denser, until he hurled it across the clearing.

"*NO!*"

Erythyn threw himself forward with his arms outstretched. The blast hit. The world shattered.

Alexandria was thrown like a doll, her body limp as it slammed against a tree trunk. Her head struck with a sickening crack as she crumpled to the ground, blood running from her brow.

"Alexandria!" Bellator's scream ripped through the forest as she shifted back quickly and ran to her side. Her body was limp as she gathered her in trembling arms. Ashlynn was down too, dazed but breathing. Cuts lined her arms, but she stirred.

Erythyn...changed. Something inside him snapped. The collar around his neck, the one he never spoke of, sparked and smoked. With a roar of pure fury, he ripped it off and flung it into the dirt. His eyes—wild, glowing, something ancient and broken—fixed on the Shadowlord. He charged. But it was too late. The Shadowlord had vanished.

But Bellator didn't wait to see the outcome. Alexandria's breath was shallow. Blood pooled beneath her. She fumbled for the key around Alexandria's neck then unrolled the ancient map they'd carried for months. Her fingers smeared blood across the ink, but the spell still ignited.

The air rippled as a portal tore open beside them. "I've got you," Bellator whispered, tears spilling down her face as she pulled Alexandria into the light. And in a flash, they were gone. Back to their time. But not to safety. Because no spell could undo the damage done. And Bellator didn't know if her dearest friend would live to see the dawn.

Smoke still lingered in the air, curling in the aftermath of the blast. Unable to capture the Shadowlord. Erythyn stood amid broken trees and blood-soaked earth, his chest heaving. His knuckles were scraped raw, his sword arm limp at his side. The collar—his collar—lay in the dirt, sparking, lifeless. Torn off in a fit of rage, it no longer hummed against his skin. No longer whispered to him in soft, manipulative tones.

But even without it, the darkness had not left him. It had simply taken root. His eyes scanned the clearing. No sign of Alexandria. No trace of the portal Bellator had opened. Only the memory—seared into his mind—of her broken body in Bellator's arms. Blood trickled down her forehead. Her eyes closed. He didn't know if she'd still been breathing. And Bellator had left him. Just like that. She'd made the decision, and in one breathless moment, Alexandria had vanished from his world.

Gone.

She was the only person who made him feel like he was more than his past. More than the thing chained to a collar and whispered to by shadows. She had looked at him like he was still human. Still worthy. And now she might be dead.

A raw, animalistic sound tore from his throat. He staggered forward and drove his fist into the nearest tree. Bark cracked. Blood smeared. Again. Again. Until his hand throbbed, and the tree leaned away from him like it feared what he was becoming. The wolves were gone and so was the Shadowlord. The night was eerily still. Even Ashlynn, who had regained consciousness and limped away to find help, had left him alone. Alone in his fury. Alone in his grief. The dark part of him stirred. The part that the collar had muted but never silenced. It rose now, hungry and seething, feeding off the rage and heartbreak pulsing through him like wildfire. He didn't fight it. He let it come.

Erythyn fell to his knees, his teeth gritted, his hands trembling with power that was no longer restrained. Darkness bled from his skin in thin wisps, curling around him like smoke. The ground beneath him darkened. The air thickened. His mind spiraled. And somewhere deep in the woods, something...felt it.

Days had passed and the forest had grown colder. Not in temperature, but in silence. The kind of silence that lives in the bones and whispers that something is dying. The trees held no birdsong. The rivers murmured low and sickly.

And Erythyn was losing himself.

He hadn't seen Bellator or Ashlynn since that night. Since the explosion. Since Alexandria had been torn from him, bleeding and unconscious, cradled in Bellator's arms as the portal swallowed them whole. Since he'd been left behind—alone, broken, burning. He didn't even know if Alexandria was still alive.

Every night, he replayed it. The way her body had flown like a leaf in a storm. The way her head had cracked against the tree. The way Bellator hadn't even looked at him before activating the spell that whisked her away. He hated her for it. He hated himself more. His days blurred into wandering—through ruined glades, forgotten trails, abandoned watchposts.

His sword remained sheathed most of the time, not because there were no threats, but because the threats knew to avoid him now. The darkness inside him—no longer bound by the collar—was growing. With each passing day, his scent grew stronger, more potent, thick with fury and grief. Animals scattered in his wake. Spirits lingered too long in the trees, whispering of a man unraveling.

The rage came in waves. Crushing, suffocating, impossible to hold back. And he didn't try to. Not anymore. When he screamed, it cracked tree trunks. When he cried, the shadows writhed around him like hounds. And somewhere deep in the mountains, the Shadowlord felt it.

Miles away, within the belly of the mountain, the Shadowlord stirred. He stood in the shadows of his cavern, one hand pressed against the smooth, glowing stone that lit his chamber like firelight. His head lifted —curious. He felt it. A pulse of energy in the dark. A resonance. Familiar...almost intimate. A rage so pure it called like a beacon through the dark. He smiled beneath his hood. "He's ready," he murmured. With the ease of smoke sliding through cracks, the Shadowlord cloaked himself in shadow and vanished.

The air was thick the night the Shadowlord came. Erythyn sat in the hollow of a fallen tree, his fingers stained with dirt and ash, his body exhausted but twitching with unrest. His breath came in shallow bursts. He hadn't eaten in days, hadn't slept in three. But he didn't care. There was only the fire in his chest, the storm in his mind. "Alexandria..." he whispered again. Her name hurt. Her name burned.

He remembered how her hand had found his in the dark. How she'd believed in him when even he couldn't. She had seen the light in him—light he no longer believed was real. And now she was gone. Because Bellator chose to save her instead of fight. Because Erythyn hadn't been fast enough. Because the Shadowlord had taken everything. And the darkness, coiled inside him like a serpent, began to strike.

That's when he felt it. The air shifted. The shadows deepened. A presence moved behind him, slow and deliberate, like oil creeping across marble. Erythyn stood, his sword half-drawn—but even that felt hollow now.

"I was wondering how long it would take you," he muttered. From the gloom, the Shadowlord stepped forward, cloaked in black, his eyes like smoke over embers. "You've been screaming for me, Erythyn," he said softly. "Even if you didn't use words."

Erythyn's jaw tightened. "I didn't summon you."

"Oh, but your rage did. Your grief. Your desire for vengeance. It's intoxicating."

"Leave," Erythyn growled. "Before I kill you."

The Shadowlord chuckled. "You could try. But I don't think you truly want to. Not yet." He stepped closer, circling him like a predator. "You've tasted freedom now. The collar is gone. The chains are off. And you're discovering what I've always known—your power is meant for more than chasing phantoms in the woods."

Erythyn's hands trembled. "She might be dead," he said, voice cracking. "And I wasn't there. I wasn't—"

"You were betrayed," the Shadowlord interrupted gently. "By your so-called allies. They abandoned you. Bellator took her away and left you to rot. And Ashlynn? She ran."

Erythyn swallowed hard. He didn't want to believe it. But the doubt had already taken root.

"I can help you," the Shadowlord said, his voice like silk soaked in poison. "I can show you how to control it—all of it. So that no one will ever take from you again. You will never be weak. Never be left behind again."

Erythyn looked up. His eyes shimmered with fury and tears. "And what will it cost me?"

The Shadowlord smiled. "Nothing that wasn't already taken."

And Erythyn, hollow and burning, didn't resist as the shadows curled around him and the two of them vanished into the night, back toward the mountains, toward the cave. Toward something darker than he'd ever imagined.

The cave opened before them like a curtain, carved into the mountainside with a precision that felt ancient and unnatural. The rock walls pulsed faintly with veins of obsidian crystal, glowing dimly as if they fed off the presence of the Shadowlord himself. Erythyn followed in silence. His steps echoed behind the Shadowlord's, each one slower than the last, as if the mountain were weighing him down. The air was thick—damp, cold, and humming with something unnatural. Magic hung in the atmosphere like a fog, clinging to his skin, whispering at the edges of his mind.

The deeper they walked, the less the outside world seemed to matter. The memory of the forest. Of Ashlynn. Of Bellator. Even Alexandria. Her face still hovered in his mind—but more distant now. Like a star behind clouds.

At the heart of the cavern, they emerged into a vast chamber. It was unlike anything Erythyn had ever seen. Massive pillars of dark stone spiraled upward, carved with symbols he couldn't read but felt vibrating through his bones. Runes flickered across the floor in dim scarlet, shifting when he moved, reacting to his presence. A large, blackened pool rested at the center of the chamber, still and bottomless, glowing faintly with red light beneath its surface. It pulsed. Alive.

The Shadowlord stepped forward, his voice low and reverent. "Here, the truth begins."

Erythyn's jaw clenched. "What truth?"

The Shadowlord turned slowly. "The one that's been hidden from you your entire life. The reason you were always different. Always feared. Always watched."

"I know what I am," Erythyn growled. "A weapon. A mistake."

"No," the Shadowlord whispered, taking a step closer. "You are not a mistake. You are mine."

Erythyn froze. "What?"

The air shifted. The shadows gathered. "I felt it in you the first time we crossed paths," the Shadowlord said. "The blood. The power. The fire you try so desperately to hide. I knew the moment you tore off that collar and let it breathe."

"You're lying," Erythyn said, but his voice was weak. The words tasted like ash.

The Shadowlord's eyes—so dark they seemed endless—met his. "You've always wondered why you didn't belong. Why your strength come at such a cost. Why the darkness called to you so easily."

He stepped into the glow of the pool, his face visible for the first time. And for a breathless moment, Erythyn saw it. The same jawline. The same fire in the eyes. "You were not born of light," the Shadowlord said, voice soft, almost tender. "You were born of shadow." He held out a hand. "I am your father, Erythyn."

Chapter 16
The Looming Tower

Rite of the Sunforged Maiden

By molten forge & ember'd vow,

The chosen stands before the prow.

With Sunblade raised in morning's glow,

She bids the dark to yield & bow.

The light of the Eternal Sun no longer shone as brightly over Dawnshire. Though the citadel still rose like a bastion of hope against the horizon, its golden spires had begun to dull, veiled beneath a constant shroud of smoke, mist, and the weight of unease. The war had dragged on for months, grinding the kingdom down. Morale had withered. Whispers of Princess Alexandria's disappearance, along with her protector Bellator, haunted every corridor of the palace.

Inside the Council Hall of the Celestial Order, where stained glass filtered dwindling sunlight onto polished marble, Prime Minister Astralhart stood beside Lord Vareth of Celestara. Their voices were low, voices of men weary with burden. They spoke of troop movements, spiritual decay in the eastern groves, and unsettling reports from the borders. Then, Astralhart paused. Something pulled at his senses—a flicker of dread.

"Walk with me," he said, walking toward the Terus Balcony. "The princess's locket has gone offline. We no longer have the ability to track her."

Lord Vareth responded, "Do we know if she is still alive? Have you told any of the others?"

"Not as of yet," he replied as they stepped out on the balcony that happened to be the highest point of the council wing that offered an unobstructed view of the southern expanse. The conversation abruptly ended.

The wind had shifted.

Across the distant forest, the sky churned with unnatural clouds— black and violent, not born of any storm. They twisted and pulsed like a living thing. Flocks of birds erupted from the canopy in a frenzied exodus, their cries sharp and panicked. The treetops darkened; their green bled into gray as though drained of life.

And there—in the heart of the forest, where once there had been nothing—a black looming tower appeared.

It pierced the sky, monolithic and gnarled, its surface made of black stone veined with glowing crimson sigils. Its spire rose in jagged spirals, clawing toward the heavens like the finger of a buried god. The forest bowed away from it, trees leaning as if in submission—or fear. Shadows rippled outward from its base, stretching unnaturally far into the land.

Astralhart's eyes widened, blood draining from his face. "This was not here before," he whispered. He turned sharply. "Send for General Stormrend. Assemble the Elite Guard. Now!"

It was nightfall by the time General Stormrend and his Elite Riders reached the corrupted edge of the Elarian Forest. What was once a sanctuary of vibrant life was now a place of death and silence. The leaves crumbled to black powder underfoot. The air was thick with rot and the bitter sting of old magic. Nothing moved. No insects. No wind. Just the sound of hooves against brittle earth and the pounding of their hearts.

And then they saw it.

The Black Tower.

It rose from the center of a wide clearing as if the earth itself had vomited it forth. The stone was coarse, ancient, not made but summoned. Runic markings crawled like fire across its surface. A heavy, oppressive aura cloaked the area, a gravity that crushed the spirit.

Then a cry rang out from one of the guards: "There! By the base—someone's down!"

Stormrend's head snapped toward the sound. He spurred his horse forward, his eyes scanning the corrupted terrain.

There—at the foot of the tower, half-shadowed in the dying grass—lay two figures. One was hunched over the other, unmoving.

They dismounted, weapons drawn, but as they approached, they recognized the forms.

Bellator, in her human druidic form, was slumped and barely breathing, her cloak soaked in blood and ash. Her arms were wrapped tightly around Princess Alexandria, who lay cradled in her lap, pale and broken like a fallen angel.

Alexandria's hair was matted with sweat and dirt, her face bruised, her armor cracked at the chest. Her fingers curled slightly, the only sign she was still clinging to life. Her once-commanding presence had been replaced by a stillness so absolute it stole the breath from the guards' lungs.

Stormrend dropped to his knees beside them, his face filled with a look of despair as tears pulled at the corners of his eyes. He moved Alexandria from Bellator's lap.

"By the light..." he breathed, his eyes burning. "She's alive. But just barely. Nightbane!" he bellowed.

The massive, silent warrior dismounted in one fluid motion and gently lifted Bellator from the ground, her arms finally falling away from the princess as unconsciousness took her. She muttered something—words slurred and broken.

"The tower... It...wasn't...there before...something...shifted..."

Stormrend gritted his teeth, lifting Alexandria into his arms as though he carried the last hope of the world.

"Ride! We ride for Dawnshire! Do not stop! Do not look back!"

Behind them, the tower stood silent and watching. Its sigils pulsed once...as if pleased.

The gallop back was a blur of hooves, wind, and breathless urgency. Lanterns were already lit across the palace walls by the time the guards stormed through the outer gates. Word spread faster than fire.

"The princess has returned."

"She is wounded."

"She may not survive the night."

In the Sun Courtyard, Astralhart was waiting. He ran down the marble steps as the riders thundered in. Stormrend dismounted and carried Alexandria in his arms once more, rushing forward.

When Astralhart saw her—limp, bloodied, and bruised—his knees nearly buckled. But his voice held steady: "Take her to the healing sanctum. Get every available mage. Now!"

Bellator was next, laid gently on a bed of soft moss conjured by the royal druids. She stirred only once, whispering incoherent fragments—"Portal...time...forest...Erythyn..."

Stormrend turned to Astralhart, still shaking from what he had seen. "That tower," he said. "It wasn't built. It was born. The land recoils from it. And those markings...they watched us." His voice dropped. "Something ancient has returned. Something is wrong."

Astralhart, trembling slightly, retreated to the Solar Chamber, where a massive map of the realm sprawled across a sunlit table. He reached for the Celestial Pendulum, a relic that had not been used in decades. He held it over the map.

It spun wildly.

And then stopped—right over the Black Tower's location.

But beneath it, the names and lines etched into the map began to... shift. Ancient symbols shimmered through the ink, unfamiliar even to the old records. Places that once existed were now gone. Others that had never existed before now glowed brightly.

Time had been rewritten.

His voice cracked with horror. "This...this was not meant to be."

The Sanctum of Aurelsol had not been this alive in generations. Its hallowed walls pulsed with divine magic, its marble floors alight with ancient runes etched in sun-gold. The air shimmered, warm and fragrant with sacred oils and phoenix ash, as if the very stones prayed for salvation.

And at the center of it all—Princess Alexandria lay in silence.

The most powerful mages from across the realm had gathered at Astralhart's command, drawn by whispers of time-warping sorcery and the shadow of a tower that should not exist. Now, they stood in concentric circles around the wounded heir, their incantations layered in harmony—part healing, part soul-binding, part divine intervention.

Golden light washed over Alexandria's form in soft waves, yet her breath remained shallow, her body unmoving. Her skin had begun to regain color. Her wounds had closed. But her spirit—the very fire that once set the hearts of men ablaze—remained distant, unreachable.

Bellator, still weak from her transformation and the ordeal at the Black Tower, had recovered just enough to rise. She refused rest, refused aid. Dressed in a simple green robe, and eyes like frosted sapphires glinting with sorrow and strength, she watched over Alexandria night and day. She barely spoke, save for whispered prayers or quiet druidic lullabies.

Astralhart stood watch nearby, more a sentinel now than a statesman, his concern etched into every line of his face. "She is no longer in our world," he finally said to Bellator. "Her soul walks elsewhere."

As her body lay, Alexandria's spirit drifted through a world unbound by time.

The air was soft and heavy, like a dream too fragile to hold. She walked barefoot across reflections—reflections of memory, of possibility. Forests glimmered like starlight. The wind spoke in riddles. And always, just ahead, she saw the silhouette of Erythyn—not as he was, but as he might have been.

His silver hair fell over his brow, his shadowed eyes less haunted. He stood beneath a flowering tree where blossoms glowed blue beneath an eternal twilight sky. His armor was gone. He wore no collar. No darkness curled at his feet. And beside him stood...two children.

The older was a girl—perhaps seven or eight—her hair the same cascading locks as Alexandria's, but with Erythyn's intense, otherworldly eyes. She carried a staff made of silverwood and light, and as she turned toward Alexandria, she smiled. It was a smile that knew her, loved her.

The second child, a boy no older than five, stood barefoot in the grass. His eyes were golden like the dusk, and his skin shimmered faintly with shadow-magic. A tiny crown of flowers sat on his head, crooked and charming. He giggled as butterflies circled his fingertips. "Mama," he called softly. The word shattered Alexandria's breath.

She stepped forward, her heart clenching with something between awe and pain. Erythyn turned toward her as the children faded into golden mist. His expression was unreadable—torn between longing and dread. "They don't exist," he said. "But they could have."

"Why show me this?" she asked, her voice trembling. "Is this a dream...or a promise?"

His answer was barely a whisper. "It's a memory...of what we both buried."

The vision changed.

She now stood in a shadowed version of the forest, where light no longer reached. She saw herself standing beside Erythyn in battle, fighting back creatures twisted by darkness. She saw Bellator in her wolf form, bloodied and snarling. She saw a crown shattered on the forest floor, and her parents screaming in silence as the Black Tower rose behind them like a grave marker of fate. She fell to her knees, clutching her chest. "Why are you showing me this?" she cried.

Erythyn reached for her hand, but his own faded through hers like smoke. "Because you must remember," he said. "All of it. The love. The rage. The fall. The future depends on what you choose to carry forward."

Back in the waking world, the sun had risen and fallen three times more. The mages could do no more for now—only maintain the enchantments sustaining Alexandria's fragile tether to her body. Bellator remained beside her, brushing the princess's hair with gentle fingers.

"You're not just dreaming," she murmured. "You're fighting. And I know you, Alex...you never stay down for long."

Astralhart stood outside the sanctum doors, watching the stars through a high stained-glass window. He held a scroll written in a forgotten dialect, sealed with a mark that had not been used in centuries —a failsafe, should Alexandria not return.

But he had not opened it. Not yet.

Alexandria's fingers twitched. Just once. Bellator caught the motion and inhaled sharply. A flicker. A ripple in the air. A sign that something inside the coma had shifted.

And in the distance, the Black Tower pulsed again.

Chapter 17
Nightmare at Dawnshire

Hallow of the Golden Dawn

Awake, O heart of mortal clay,

Embrace the sun & light the way.

The blade you bear is day's high crown,

To lift the fallen, cast the shroud down.

*T*ime passed differently within the chasm of the Shadowlands—a realm untouched by sunlight and swallowed in endless twilight. Beneath the jagged, obsidian peaks of the Black Reach, the Shadowlord trained his son relentlessly. Erythyn stood amidst a field of fractured stone, his chest heaving, dark mist curling around his fingertips like coiled serpents. Each breath he drew summoned more of the corrupted energy he was learning to command.

"Again," the Shadowlord growled, his voice a rasp of ancient stone grinding on stone. "Your fear dulls your edge. Power must be wielded with control, not sentiment."

Erythyn clenched his fists, his jaw tightening. Black tendrils erupted from the earth in response, writhing upward and tearing through a phantom opponent crafted by shadow. It shattered into cinders, vanishing in a pulse of energy.

"Better," his father said with a nod. "But your hesitation betrays you. There is still a part of you that clings to the light."

Erythyn turned away, shadows flickering in his hazel eyes. The image of her—Alexandria—flashed in his mind. Her voice. Her fire. The touch of her lips beneath a starlit sky. He had buried those memories deep...yet they clawed their way to the surface in quiet moments like this. "I don't cling to anything," he snapped. "She's gone."

The Shadowlord circled him like a vulture. "Is she?" he asked, voice low and cold. "You hope she lives. You fear she doesn't. And that is what weakens you."

Erythyn's power flared instinctively, a ripple of darkness cracking the ground beneath him. He shut his eyes, trying to force her out, to silence the ache. Every time he closed his eyes, he saw her—broken and bleeding in his arms, her body limp as the black tower loomed over them. He had dragged her into this chaos. One instant she had been beside him, and in the next...torn away. He had reached for her when the portal yawned open again. But she was gone.

Now, the only comfort he had was rage. It was easier to feel fury than loss.

Still... Sometimes when the wind howled across the desolate cliffs, he imagined her voice in it. In rare, quiet moments before sleep, he'd dream of her smile. Of what could have been. Of children that might have carried both light and shadow in their eyes.

He slammed his fist into the blackened stone. "She's not my weakness," he whispered to himself. "She was...my reason."

The Shadowlord watched from the cliff's edge, his arms folded. He could see it—his son was stronger, yes, but not yet untethered. The girl haunted him like a phantom limb. "Let her go," the Shadowlord said. "Or she will be the end of you."

But Erythyn wasn't sure he could. Or that he wanted to.

The halls of the castle were silent. Only the sound of slippered feet and the occasional whisper of a breeze through the stained-glass windows could be heard. Light filtered through panes of amethyst and sapphire, casting jeweled reflections across the stone floors. Dust motes drifted lazily in the shafts of light, undisturbed by time. Outside, the sky wore the heavy gray of approaching twilight, clouds hanging low and brooding above the towers like silent sentinels.

Alexandria's body lay still at the heart of the healing chamber, elevated on a dais of carved moonstone and beneath silken canopies enchanted with runes of restoration. The chamber itself pulsed faintly with power—gentle waves of magic undulated through the air, rippling the curtains, tugging softly at the embroidered hems.

Crystalline jars of glowing herbs lined the walls, their contents gently steaming and exuding calming fragrances—moonroot, silvermint, crushed mirrorthorn petals. Spell-light hovered in suspended lanterns overhead, casting a warm, golden glow across the room.

Her dark hair fanned across the silver-threaded pillows like night caressing starlight, the strands catching the faint light and shimmering with deep hues of indigo and coal, each strand a promise of something unspoken, a tether to the world she had not yet abandoned. Her chest rose and fell steadily, the only sign that life still clung to her.

The most powerful mages of the realm had done all they could—sealing her wounds with ancient salves, weaving spells of ease and mending into her very blood. They had whispered every incantation, burned every sacred herb, even summoned ethereal guardians to watch over her spirit. But they could not awaken her.

She was drifting. Deep in a place between life and death, in a realm without borders or names. In that space, she dreamed.

At first, there was nothing but blackness. A formless void, vast and absolute. It surrounded her like the womb of the world, endless and consuming. There was no pain here, no fear. Just silence—terrible, waiting silence.

Then... Flickers. Echoes.

The weight of his arms around her. The low heat of a fire warmed her cheek. The golden glow of flames dancing over Erythyn's pale skin, making him seem sculpted from marble and shadow. His voice—low, teasing, haunted—spoke her name like a secret only he knew. She reached out in memory, her fingertips brushing the silver collar at his throat, feeling the hum of contained darkness thrumming just beneath the surface. But the dream twisted.

She was no longer in the present. The warmth of the fire was gone.

Now, she stood barefoot in a field of blue flame grass beneath twin moons. The stalks shimmered like enchanted sapphire, casting ghostly light with every movement. A wind stirred, not cold, but unnatural—like a sigh from something watching, waiting. Her body moved without thought, as if guided by some deep memory etched into her soul.

In the center of the meadow stood a figure—tall, still, cloaked in both shadow and starlight.

Erythyn.

But not as she remembered him. Here, he glowed with contradiction —his form a dance between dusk and dawn. Shadow wreathed his shoulders, but it did not consume. Starlight crowned his brow like a halo, gentle and steady. His eyes met hers, and she froze. There was no cruelty in them. Instead, they shimmered with depth—oceans of sorrow, pools of longing. They held the weight of regrets never spoken, of words left buried beneath war and duty.

He reached out to her, slow, reverent, as if she might vanish should he move too quickly.

She took a step forward. Her hand rose, trembled. But before their fingers could touch, the dream fractured—shattered like a crystal struck by lightning.

Now she stood in a marble hall, its walls carved with ancient glyphs that glowed faintly with the breath of forgotten spells. The floor was veined with silver, the ceiling vaulted and adorned with constellations captured in glass. Moonlight bathed the space in a pearlescent hue.

Two children played before her. The boy had hair like night—black and soft as velvet. He darted between stone columns, laughing, his voice light and wild, like the wind through treetops. The girl, smaller, radiant, had her eyes—eyes filled with golden light, framed by curls that shimmered like burnished bronze.

Her heart twisted. A dull ache bloomed in her chest, spreading like wildfire. "Mother!" the girl called, her voice clear as a bell. "Come see what Father showed us!"

Alexandria fell to her knees. Her limbs felt weightless, as though gravity had surrendered to wonder. The little girl flung herself into her arms, wrapping tiny fingers around her gown. She was warm. Solid. Real. Real.

Her scent—wild blossoms and smoke—rushed up to meet Alexandria's nose. The child's heartbeat thudded fast against her chest, grounding her.

And there, at the doorway, stood Erythyn. He watched them silently, his arms folded, his expression soft. There was peace in his gaze—true peace, not the fleeting quiet after battle, but the calm of a man who had faced himself and made peace with what he found. His darkness was still there, in the corners of his eyes, in the tension of his frame—but it was no longer a curse. It was part of him. Balanced. Tempered. He had found control. Purpose. Redemption.

The children danced around them, giggling, their bare feet slapping softly against the polished marble. Their laughter echoed upward, filling the vaulted chamber like music spun from joy itself. The air shimmered with light.

But it did not last.

The dream trembled—then cracked.

Suddenly, flames roared. A shrieking wind tore through the palace.

The great stained-glass windows exploded inward as fire surged from the sky. The skies above bled shadow. Lightning cracked in unnatural hues—green, violet, void. The walls shuddered.

Alexandria screamed as the children were wrenched from her arms by unseen forces. Their cries fractured the air. Her body surged forward—but they were gone.

Erythyn stood before her, his arms flung wide, blocking her from the oncoming darkness. His face twisted—rage, fear, and agony all interwoven. The Shadowlord's voice slithered out from the abyss, low and monstrous, echoing from no mouth and every wall: "Even in dreams... I will tear you apart."

Tendrils of living darkness spilled in like flood water—seething, crawling, shrieking. They whipped through the chamber, devouring light, chasing warmth. She lunged toward Erythyn, her hand reaching out with every ounce of will—

But he was already fading. Her fingers passed through him like smoke.

"No!" she cried, voice raw, torn. "No, don't leave me again!"

The dream collapsed into a starless void, a black sea of memory, sorrow, love, and unbearable loss. She fell through it, clutching her chest, as if her very soul were splintering apart. Time dissolved. Thought shattered. Only ache remained.

And then—a whisper. His voice. Soft. Mournful. Yet defiant. A beacon through the void.

"If you're still alive...fight. Come back to me."

The words cut through the dark like sunlight through thunderclouds. Her soul jerked toward them.

A breath.

A gasp.

Chapter 18
The Guardian in Despair

Echo from the Voidborn Throne

A king of void & whispered dread,

He reigns where ancient angels bled.

But even void must bow to dawn,

And end the night his rule has drawn.

*I*n the waking world, the canopies moved as if stirred by unseen hands. The runes embroidered in their silken threads sparked once —gold and silver flashes in a rhythm that mirrored a heartbeat.

The flame in the nearest lantern flared. A single petal from the mirrorthorn bouquet floated gently to the ground. And Alexandria's fingers...twitched.

It was the first movement in days.

A healer sitting nearby jolted upright, nearly spilling a bowl of crushed lotus. "She moved!" he gasped, stumbling back and calling for the others. "She moved!"

Magic shivered across the chamber.

But deep inside, Alexandria still hovered between two worlds— between death and waking. And as her soul rose like a phoenix from the ash of memory, only one name pulsed through the storm:

Erythyn.

The castle was quiet beneath the dusk sky, its spires catching the last rays of the sun like blades of gold. The light stretched long across the battlements, bathing stone and ivy in a fleeting warmth that couldn't quite chase the chill from the wind.

Bellator stood perched on the high terrace of the east wing, her silhouette tall and statuesque as the wind tugged at her cloak. Her armor caught the dying sunlight, the steel dulled by wear but polished enough to catch a flicker of fire where the light struck just right. Her eyes, sharp as obsidian and just as unreadable, scanned the horizon with an intensity that made even the circling falcons steer clear of the parapet.

Below, the kingdom went about its evening rhythm—candles flickering to life behind mullioned windows, servants moving in practiced silence through the courtyards, the watch changing guard with a precision that spoke of habit more than vigilance. The distant toll of the bell tower marked another passing hour, its sound slow and mournful, as though even time itself bowed in reverence to the silence hanging over the castle.

But Bellator's gaze was fixed on the horizon. She had stood there every evening since Alexandria fell into the coma, watching, listening, waiting —for something. Anything. A sign in the clouds. A shift in the wind. A message from the old gods. Though her wounds from the battle had long since healed, the ache in her soul remained. Deep. Raw. Unrelenting.

She had failed her. No matter what the others said—no matter that the mages worked tirelessly, or that the war still raged in the background like a distant, smoldering storm—Bellator couldn't silence the guilt.

She was a protector, shield, and sword. She was supposed to stand in the way of death itself.

And yet, Alexandria now lay broken, teetering between life and oblivion. Each breath she took while Alexandria lay still felt borrowed, and she felt unworthy.

A cold gust swirled past, coiling around her like a phantom. The scent of frost and something older—something untouched by time—clung to it. And with it...something changed.

Bellator's eyes narrowed. The air pulsed. Subtle. Strange. But unmistakable. It wasn't a sound. Not exactly. It was a feeling—an ancient, wordless pull that coursed through her blood, vibrating in her bones. Her senses, still intertwined with the natural world through her druidic magic, had felt nothing but stillness around the princess for weeks.

But now... Her aura stirred.

It was faint. Like the trembling light of a firefly caught in a jar. But it was there. A flicker of life, of resistance, burning deep within the veil of stillness. Bellator didn't hesitate.

In a blur of movement, she turned, her armored boots striking the stone with force as she charged through the corridor. Her braid snapped behind her like a battle flag, her cloak billowing in her wake. Her heart pounded not in fear—but in hope. The hope she'd dared not name.

"Out of the way!" she barked as startled guards parted before her. None would dare to question the urgency in her tone. They had all seen her fury in battle. None would stand in her path now.

She burst through the arched doors of the healing chamber, her breath catching in her throat as her eyes fell on the bed. Alexandria's hand —frail and pale against the velvet blanket—twitched again. Just once.

But once was all it took.

The head mage turned sharply, nearly knocking over a crystal vial. "That's twice now," he muttered, disbelief thick in his voice. "Her body is responding. It shouldn't be possible so soon. Not after the damage she took."

Bellator was already at her side, dropping to one knee with a sharp clink of armor. She reached for Alexandria's hand, gripping it gently, reverently. Her calloused fingers trembled around the delicate warmth of the princess's own.

"Alex..." Her voice cracked. A whisper drowned in emotion.

There was no reply. No words. No open eyes. But the change was unmistakable. The air itself had shifted. The stagnant weight that had filled the chamber for weeks lifted, replaced by something...warmer. More alive. A subtle rhythm, like the first stirrings of a heartbeat in a still womb. The magic in the air shimmered, awakening. Responding.

"She's fighting," Bellator whispered, her eyes glistening. "She's coming back."

As if in answer, Alexandria's lips parted slightly—no words, only a faint breath, soft as a sigh. But it was enough. Enough to send a surge of hope through Bellator's chest like a lightning strike. A strangled sound escaped her throat—half sob, half laughter—as she pressed Alexandria's hand to her brow. A silent prayer. A silent thank you.

She looked up at the mage, her voice steady now, filled with steel. "Call Astralhart. Call the Circle of Light. She's not done."

The mage blinked, then nodded, already moving.

Bellator leaned closer, her voice dropping low, meant only for Alexandria's ears. She brushed a lock of sweat-dampened hair from her brow, the gesture tender, unguarded. "Wherever you are, whatever you see... Hold on. I'm still here. We all are."

But in the silence of her thoughts, where no one else could hear, a chill crept into her heart. She had felt something. Not just the return of Alexandria's presence. A shadow. A flicker of darkness woven into the golden threads of her aura. Faint...but familiar. Not foreign. It moved like a whisper behind her soul. A presence Bellator knew all too well.

Erythyn.

She clenched her jaw, her heart torn between the relief of Alexandria's fight to return—and the dread of what might be returning with her.

The moment Bellator's command rang out, the chamber burst into motion. Apprentices scrambled through the door, the mage's cloak whipping behind him as he barked incantations into crystal mirrors and flaming scrolls. Candles flared in their sconces, the golden flames now tinged with flickers of blue—an omen that the magic in the room had indeed changed. Something ancient had stirred. Something powerful.

Minutes passed, each one stretching like an eternity. Bellator never let go of Alexandria's hand. Her thumb traced gentle circles over the princess's knuckles, grounding herself, silently urging her back with every breath. A low chant began to build outside the door—guardians invoking wards, priests preparing rites of sanctity. The very air seemed to hum, alive with expectancy.

Then, the chamber doors blew open.

A swirl of shadow and golden light entered the room like a thunderclap. The temperature dropped, and every candle dimmed as if bowing to the presence now crossing the threshold.

Astralhart.

His robes, deep navy embroidered with constellations that shimmered like the night sky itself, swept across the floor like an ocean of stars. A thick silver mantle draped his shoulders, fastened with a brooch shaped like a solar disc split by a crescent of black obsidian—his sigil, the seal of balance. His hair, long and silver as moonlight, was pulled back and held with a clasp of bone. And in his eyes—piercing, almost too bright—burned the weight of centuries.

The High Arcanist and Royal Magus of the Realm had arrived.

He crossed the threshold without a word, staff in hand, its crystal core glowing with a steady white flame. Behind him, the members of the Circle of Light followed—cloaked figures bearing sacred relics, chanting as they encircled the bed in a precise formation.

Bellator rose slowly as Astralhart approached, her expression unreadable, but her shoulders straightened with restrained tension.

"I came as soon as I felt it," he said, his voice low, metallic and smooth, like wind moving through iron chimes. "Something cracked open."

"She moved," Bellator replied, barely able to keep the tremor from her voice. "Twice. And there was breath—faint, but it was there."

Astralhart placed a hand over Alexandria's chest, just above her heart. His fingers didn't touch her but hovered, trembling slightly with the vibrations he felt beneath the skin. His eyes closed. His brow creased.

"The soul is returning," he murmured, "but it has changed. It carries more than what it left with."

He pulled back, his eyes darkening. "There is a shadow laced through her spirit. Subtle. Ancient. Not malevolent...yet not pure. She's brought something back with her."

Bellator's jaw clenched. "Erythyn," she said without hesitation.

Astralhart gave her a long look, something unreadable flashing behind his ageless features. "Or what remains of him," he said quietly. "They are bound, whether by choice or by fate. And that bond may be the thread leading her back to us...or the chain that drags her deeper."

The Circle began their ritual, forming concentric rings around the bed. Holy light began to rise, bathing Alexandria's body in gentle warmth. Runes on the floor ignited, revealing ancient symbols etched into the stone—safeguards, protections, trials meant only for those who linger between life and death. Bellator took a half-step back, unwilling, but knowing better than to interfere.

Astralhart remained near her side, and after a long pause, he spoke again—softer now, like a man remembering something long buried. "She is fighting a war in her mind, one we cannot see. And in that war, she will be shown truths not even I dare to name. But if she emerges..." He glanced down at her still form, the breath barely fluttering from her lips. "She will not be the same."

Bellator's voice was steady when she replied, though her chest burned with the weight of unspoken dread. "Then let her return changed. But let her return."

Astralhart inclined his head, and then, for the first time in decades, he knelt. He placed both palms on the floor, touching the outermost ring of light, and whispered a single name into the aether—not Alexandria's, but a name only he had known from the very beginning. One spoken only in the highest tongue of the old gods. A name that had been hidden even from the royal archives. A name that belonged to both her light...and her shadow.

And from the center of the bed, Alexandria stirred. Not her hand. Not her breath. Her eyes. Behind shuttered lids, they moved—wildly. As if trapped between fire and storm. And somewhere, far beyond the veil of waking, a voice called to her through the dream.

"Find me."

Chapter 19
Awakened by Faith

Epistle of the Sun-Queen

My sword doth shine with light divine,

A promise wrought in blood & sign.

Though storms may rage & kingdoms break,

The dawn is ours — our souls awake.

A t first, there was only wind. It howled through the void like a wounded beast, tearing through invisible trees, ripping across unseen plains. Alexandria floated in it—no body, no name, only thought. Her mind scattered like ash on the wind, fragments of memory blinking in and out like dying stars.

Then came light. Not warm. Not soft. But sharp. Piercing. It slashed through the darkness like a sword unsheathed. It forced shape back into her limbs. Breath. The slow, aching return of a heartbeat. And with it... the battlefield formed.

She stood barefoot on a plain of shattered marble, the sky above her a bruise of violet and black, torn by flashes of white lightning. The ground was broken, scorched with claw marks, swords half-buried in the stone, banners twisted around charred bones. The air reeked of smoke and memory. Each gust of wind carried whispers—echoes of things she had lived and things she had feared:

"You were never enough."

"He will betray you."

"You cannot save them all."

She stumbled forward, her body too light and too heavy at once. A red slash crossed the sky—a falling star, or perhaps a wound in the world. It pulsed like a heartbeat. And there, standing amid the ruins, was herself.

Or...a version of herself, draped in the royal colors—silver and crimson—but her skin was paler, almost glassy. Her eyes were vacant, her lips painted with a cruel smile. A crown of twisted thorns sat atop her head, glistening with black sap.

"Who are you?" Alexandria whispered, though her throat felt raw.

"I'm who you would become," the mirror-Alexandria said. Her voice echoed too many times, like a choir of ghosts speaking in unison. "If you let him rule you." A pulse of heat surged through the sky, and Alexandria turned—

Behind her, he stood. Erythyn.

But not the version she remembered. This one loomed with shadow veiling half his face, one eye burning silver, the other black. Wings of smoke and starlight unfurled from his back, and in his hand he held a blade shaped from the same metal as his collar—dark, humming with restrained power.

He didn't speak. He just watched her.

And that gaze... It hurt. It reminded her of every night she had spent wondering who he truly was. Every moment of vulnerability was shared. Every word she believed. Every part of her soul that had entwined with his beneath the sanctuary skies.

The dark version of herself stepped closer, circling her like a predator.

"He wants you," she hissed. "But only if you break. Only if you kneel. That's what he's always desired. Submission. You were never the dream... only the test."

Alexandria's knees buckled, the ground beneath her cracking like glass under pressure. Visions clawed their way up from the floor—Bellator screaming her name, the river poisoned, children pulled into shadow, the tree of healing burning in violet fire.

"*Stop!*" she shouted.

And the world...obeyed.

The wind ceased. The sky held its breath. Even the shadowed versions of Erythyn and herself paused, as if stunned by her defiance. "I am not a puppet," Alexandria growled, rising to her feet. "Not for the gods, not for fate, and not for him."

She turned to face Erythyn. His expression had changed. No longer cold. Pained. Wounded.

"Is that what you truly believe?" he asked, and now his voice was his —low, trembling, threaded with that same distant sorrow she'd felt in his arms by the fire.

"I don't know what to believe," she whispered, shaking her head. "But I will find the truth. And I will not lose myself doing it."

From the fractured sky above, a burst of golden light tore through the clouds—warm, radiant, cascading across the broken marble. It struck Alexandria's chest like a heartbeat returned. Her skin glowed. Her breath caught. And then—a sound. Distant. Muffled. But real. "She's coming back!" Bellator's voice. "Her eyes—look at her eyes!"

Alexandria turned to the shadows that still lingered at the edge of her battlefield. The twisted version of herself hissed and cracked apart like glass under fire. The monstrous figure of Erythyn dissolved into falling stars. And then, for the first time since falling into darkness, Alexandria ran. Ran toward the light. Toward warmth. Toward the sound of her name. She ran.

Through golden light that cracked the bruised sky above her dreamscape, Alexandria surged forward. The battlefield of her memory fractured behind her—shards of pain and truth scattering into mist. The cold laughter of her shadow-self dissolved. The twisted echo of Erythyn fell into dust. Only the voice remained. "Find me." It echoed in her bones, in her breath, in the fire that flared within her chest as she broke through the veil of sleep and into something more. The light swallowed her whole—blinding, pure. And just before she crossed over, her eyes opened—

Somewhere far from the waking world...he felt it. Erythyn's breath caught. His body went rigid, his heart slamming against his ribs as if struck from the inside. The cavern around him—the Hollow's Heart—seemed to shift.

The stale air thickened with the scent of burning herbs and jasmine. Not real. Not here. But it was hers. Alexandria. He turned sharply, as if her presence might be behind him. But there was only stone. Cold. Dead. Carved with symbols that screamed of things that once ruled this world and sought to rule it again.

He touched the edge of a basalt pillar, anchoring himself, though his balance faltered. His mind reeled—not from a vision, but from something more intimate. A break in the bond. Or no...a surge.

She had moved. Not just her body. Her soul. "She remembers," he whispered. Behind him, the shadows stirred. Slow. Heavy. The Shadowlord emerged from the gloom like smoke rolling from a wound in the earth—robes of living blackness, eyes that held no whites, only deep crimson centers pulsing like coals.

"She's waking," the old god rasped, his voice more felt than heard. "Isn't she?"

Erythyn didn't answer at first. He was too still, too focused—trying to hold onto that last pulse of her spirit. A flash of gold. The echo of his name on her lips. He had felt it like a blade drawn near his heart. "She saw," he said at last, voice taut with dread. "Everything."

The Shadowlord chuckled, a hollow, rattling sound like the grinding of bone. "And what did she find, I wonder? The truth? Or the pieces you left behind when you fled from me like a frightened dog?"

Erythyn's eyes narrowed. His jaw flexed, every inch of his body coiled like a beast caught between flight and fight. "I never fled," he growled. "I chose."

The Shadowlord's grin widened. "You chose to lie. To hide what you were. You think love will cleanse the blood in your hands? The darkness in your breath? She's tasted it now, boy. Touched your truth in the place between death and dawn. Tell me—" He stepped closer, towering, ancient, eternal. "Does she still reach for you?"

Erythyn turned away, unable—unwilling—to answer. Because he didn't know. Alexandria's strength had always frightened him more than her magic. Not because she was powerful but because she saw him. She saw past the charm, the shadows, the silence, into the fracture he tried so hard to seal.

If she remembered all of it—the pain he caused, the monster he nearly became—would she come back changed? Would she come back for him? Or would she rise brighter...and leave him buried in the past? A silence hung between them like fog over a grave.

And then the Shadowlord spoke again, quieter this time. "She is not the girl who entered that dream," he said, his voice almost gentle. "She will not be the same. And neither are you."

Erythyn stood still, but his mind drifted—to her fingers brushing his collar, to her laughter in the ruined town, to her eyes as they closed by the fire that night. He had told himself he could endure anything. But her eyes filled with betrayal? That, he could not bear. He turned back toward the edge of the cavern where shadows thickened like storm clouds, where the past continued to pull him deeper.

"She's coming," he murmured. "And when she does... I'll have to face what I left behind."

Behind him, the Shadowlord only smiled. "Yes," he said softly. "You both will."

Chapter 20
The Soul's Pull

Chant of the Daystar Herald

Hark, the herald's clarion cry,

The Sunblade's bearer draws nigh.

From dawn to dusk her oath holds fast,

Till shadow's reign is but the past.

T he moon had risen high above the castle, casting silvery light through the arched windows of the healing chamber. Its glow touched Alexandria's face, softening the shadows under her eyes and lending a quiet grace to her still form. The once-fluttering torches had dimmed, enchanted to flicker low through the late hours. Most of the healers had retired for the night, save for one elder mage who watched from a corner, murmuring gentle incantations into the quiet.

Bellator hadn't moved.

She sat silently at Alexandria's side, her hands folded on the edge of the mattress, her piercing eyes locked onto the princess with an intensity that could shatter stone. The bond between them went deeper than duty —deeper than any oath sworn in the throne room or under the stars. It was soul-deep, forged in fire and magic and trust.

Then it happened.

A tremor ran through Alexandria's fingertips. This time, not a twitch —but a curl. Her hand folded gently, as if grasping something in a dream. Her brows furrowed. Her breathing deepened. Bellator sat bolt upright, barely daring to blink.

The mage stood, his voice low and urgent. "It's happening." A soft gasp escaped Alexandria's lips. Her head turned ever so slightly, and then —slowly, as if surfacing from the depths of a vast ocean—her eyes opened.

They were glassy at first, unfocused. But then the moonlight caught them, and they glowed with the faintest trace of gold, as if touched by magic not entirely her own.

"Alexandria?" Bellator whispered, reaching for her hand again. "It's me. You're safe. You're home."

Alexandria's gaze slowly shifted toward her. Confusion played across her face, then recognition...and then something else—something haunted. Her lips parted. Dry. Fragile. Bellator leaned closer to hear. And then, with the softest of breaths, Alexandria spoke the one name no one in the room expected. "Erythyn."

The chamber fell utterly still.

The mage stiffened, his spell faltering in his throat. Bellator's breath hitched. That name—dark, dangerous, forbidden—hung in the air like a storm cloud. Alexandria blinked slowly, the weight of her own voice seeming to pull her back. Tears welled in her eyes—not of fear, but of aching, longing, loss. "Where...where is he?" she rasped.

Bellator gently cupped her cheek, fighting the knot tightening in her chest. "He's not here, Alex. You've been asleep for months. You nearly died."

"I saw him..." Alexandria's voice quivered. "I saw him. And our children... Bellator, I—" But her strength faded, and her head fell softly to the pillow again, her eyes drifting shut—not into unconsciousness, but exhaustion.

Bellator sat back, torn between relief and unease. She had returned. But not alone.

The tension in the air was thick as Bellator stood over Alexandria, who lay still once more—her breath soft, but her eyes fluttering beneath closed lids. The mage had stepped back, watching the scene unfold with the quiet awe of someone who had witnessed a miracle and a warning, all at once.

Bellator's thoughts churned with the weight of what Alexandria had said—Erythyn's name. The man who had torn her away from this world. The one who had betrayed her trust and now seemed to haunt her even in this moment of her recovery.

Her fingers brushed through Alexandria's hair as her thoughts turned inward. She needed answers—they all needed answers. Something was wrong. Erythyn was still a threat. But this...this new connection, this tether that bound Alexandria to him, was not just a bond of darkness. It was something else. Something deeper. With determination, Bellator stood and turned to the mage, her voice low but resolute.

"Summon Astralhart at once—we need him here immediately." The mage nodded, rushing out of the room, his movements swift, but Bellator barely noticed. Her eyes remained fixed on Alexandria, who now slept once again, her body still fragile, but her spirit unmistakably returning.

Far from the castle, in the cold, dark expanse of the Shadowlands, Erythyn stood alone, his silhouette stark against the swirling mists. The Shadowlord had left him for the moment, retreating into the labyrinth of the Black Reach for his own plans. But Erythyn was not focused on his father's commands or the training he had been forced into. No, his thoughts were elsewhere.

The pull—the feeling that had been gnawing at him, faint but constant—had grown stronger in the past few hours. It was a familiar sensation, one that had long been buried beneath layers of anger and bitterness. It was a tug of light. A flicker of life. He knelt at the edge of a jagged cliff overlooking the Sea of Ink, the vast, roiling body of corrupted magic that consumed the horizon. His training under the Shadowlord had grown brutal pushing him to the brink. Yet tonight, there was stillness in the air. Something...wrong. Then he felt it. Like a blade pressed against the back of his neck.

His head snapped upward, his silver eyes flaring with ghostlight. Her voice. It wasn't a whisper this time. It wasn't a memory clawing through a dream. She had spoken his name. "Alexandria," he said, barely a breath. A throb of power radiated from deep within his chest—one that he hadn't felt in weeks.

A living, golden warmth attempted to crack through his shadows. And it hurt. He staggered to his feet, gripping the hilt of his curved blade for balance as the connection surged again. Emotions collided—hope, grief, anger, longing—all blending into a storm that tore at the walls he had built inside himself.

She was alive. And...she remembered. "Damn you," he growled, blinking back the heat rising to his eyes. "You should've let me go." He turned toward the mountains, his eyes narrowing.

In the depths of the cave, the Shadowlord stirred. "She's awake, isn't she?" the old voice rasped from the dark.

Erythyn didn't answer. But he didn't need to.

Chapter 21
A Forbidden Name

Canticle of the Dawnbreak

When darkest hour meets breaking day,

The heart's true nature finds its sway.

Fear not the night nor scorn the sun,

For both must pass ere peace is won.

*I*nside the healing chamber, Bellator stood by Alexandria's side as Astralhart entered with his usual air of calm authority. The mages stepped aside, allowing the leader of the Celestial Order to approach the princess.

Alexandria's eyes were closed once more, her body still too weak to fully wake, but the stirrings of her aura were unmistakable. Bellator watched, her gaze darkening with the weight of all that had transpired. Astralhart approached slowly, his eyes softening as he observed the princess.

He'd known her since she was a child—seen her grow into the powerful, fierce woman she was now. But this...this was different. The whispers of magic surrounding her felt wrong.

"She has a bond with him," Bellator said quietly, her voice filled with quiet sorrow. "A bond we cannot easily break."

Astralhart nodded, his expression grim. "We will do everything in our power to help her, Bellator. But you're right. That connection may run deeper than we realize."

Just as the words left his mouth, a distant, otherworldly chill swept through the room—a presence far darker than anything the Celestial Order had ever faced.

The Shadowlord's reach was stretching once more. And Erythyn would return.

The Celestial Order had not met in full council since the fall of the Eastern Vale. Now, beneath the sacred vault of the Hall of Starlight— where the ceiling shimmered with a living reflection of the heavens—they gathered again. Dawnlords in radiant armor, spiritual archons wrapped in silver flame, and scholars draped in robes of rune-woven thread stood in a circle around the table of unity.

Floating above its center, a glowing map of the realm pulsed with shifting energy. Astralhart stood at its head, his arms behind his back, his face like carved granite. "The princess has awakened," he announced. Murmurs rippled through the circle. Relief. Confusion. And then...

"She spoke the dark one's name," Astralhart continued. "Not in fear. Not in anger. She called to him."

Gasps echoed. One of the high priests clutched his staff tighter. A representative from Utheron, the kingdom of arcane research, leaned forward. "That name was sealed by divine rite. She should not even remember it."

"She does," Astralhart confirmed. "And I believe he felt it."

From across the chamber, the Lady of Celestara—the high seer of the spiritual realm—stepped forward, her eyes already distant, as though half in a trance. "Then the soul tether remains unbroken. The war is no longer one of armies alone. It is of hearts, of threads tied through time and shadow."

Another voice spoke, colder, skeptical. "Then sever it. Break the bond. If he reaches for her again—"

"No," said Astralhart, sharp as a blade. "If we force separation, we risk shattering what light remains in her. She did not return from death only to become our prisoner."

A heavy silence fell. Then the Lady of Celestara spoke again. "Let the dreamseer be summoned. If the girl has returned with the mark of the shadow... The stars will show us what comes next."

Far beneath the castle, in a chamber hidden from sunlight and memory, the dreamseer waited. She sat cross-legged in the Circle of Mirrors, a sanctuary carved from enchanted onyx and veined with silver starlight. The chamber pulsed softly, alive with magic both ancient and endless. Pools of water surrounded her like the moons of a forgotten planet, their surfaces impossibly still, reflecting not the present—but the possible. The Seer herself was as old as twilight. Her skin was parchment-thin and tattooed with constellations inked in sacred ash.

Her eyes, long blind to the material world, gazed endlessly inward. She needed no sight to see. Not here. Her gnarled fingers hovered above the largest basin of water, its surface shimmering like the skin of a dreaming star. Silver ripples spiraled beneath her trembling touch. The chamber dimmed. The air grew heavy.

She inhaled deeply, drawing the weight of the moment into her lungs as if tasting prophecy itself. Her voice became a whisper—soft as the first snow, sharp as fate. "Show me what lies ahead...what fate now stirs with the princess reborn." The water stilled. And then... It revealed.

First, a ruined castle, balanced precariously atop a jagged, broken mountain. Clouds swirled like torn veils around its blackened towers. Fire and frost warred across the sky. From the smoke stepped Princess Alexandria. Older. Hardened. Her gown was replaced by armor forged of starlight and sorrow, gilded with sigils that shimmered between radiance and ruin. Her eyes were no longer wide with innocence—but blazing with purpose. And at her fingertips...curled shadow. Controlled. Contained. But present.

Beside her stood Erythyn. No collar. No chains. No mask. His darkness, once wild and devouring, had been mastered—but only just. It clung to him like smoke clings to flame. He stood tall, still, as if awaiting judgment. Their hands touched. And from their joined palms, a pulse of energy exploded—neither light nor dark, but something ancient, deeper.

The very air bent around it. Armies on either side of the mountain recoiled as the wave of power rippled outward, consuming the battlefield in silence. But the vision twisted. The sky split. A child appeared—no older than seven, standing between them. Hair like starlight, eyes dark as the void. They turned toward the heavens, his mouth open in a scream that shattered the clouds. Above the world, a figure emerged—vast, horned, wreathed in flame and void.

It was the Shadowlord, more monstrous than ever before, cloaked in primal chaos, his eyes burning with endless hunger. The ground fractured beneath their feet. Alexandria reached for the child. Erythyn did the same. But neither reached them in time.

And then the child spoke. Not in pain. Not in fear. But in prophecy. "You cannot contain what is born of both."

The mirrors exploded. Water surged upward in violent pillars. The dreamseer was hurled backward across the stone floor. Blood trickled from her eyes like tears as she gasped, clutching her chest, her breath stolen by what she had seen. The door burst open. Priests rushed in, their cloaks billowing, spells already on their lips.

But Astralhart was already there, waiting in silence. He stepped forward, unfazed by the shattered vision, though his gaze had darkened like a storm cloud behind a sunlit sky. He lowered himself beside her.

"What did you see?" he asked, his voice calm, though taut beneath the surface.

The dreamseer turned her face to him slowly. The lights in the chamber dimmed further as if the truth she carried drained even the stone around them. Her voice shook.

"A union foretold... A child of light and shadow. A weapon. A curse. The end...or the salvation...of all."

The scent of incense and burning star-root lingered in the air as the dreamseer's warning echoed through the chamber. Astralhart stood unmoved, though deep behind his sharp eyes, the weight of the words pressed heavily.

"A child of light and shadow... The end or salvation of all," he responded as he hung his head and turned away from the Seer, already calculating. "Dispatch my ravens to the High Seats of Dawnshire, Ryvarion, Utheron, and Celestara," he commanded. "The princess is not to leave the castle walls. Not without an escort of my choosing."

One of the mage-knights stepped forward. "Shall we increase protection around her chamber?"

Astralhart's eyes narrowed. "Protection? Or surveillance?" The room fell silent for a moment that felt like a lifetime.

"She cannot know everything—not yet. We don't know what the dreams awakened in her. Whether it's just memory...or prophecy stirring in her blood."

"And the man?" asked the Lady of Celestara.

"Erythyn?" Astralhart's hand clenched into a fist behind his back. "He is still alive. The connection proves it. If he seeks her again...we must be ready." He paced toward the great celestial chart, pressing his palm to a glowing constellation. The stars shifted—realigning. "Begin the Aetherian Lock. I want a veil over the castle. No portal, spell, or spirit enters or leaves without my knowing."

"And if the girl resists?" a young scholar asked cautiously.

Astralhart looked over his shoulder, his voice like steel. "Then she'll learn...that being royalty does not mean being free."

Soft candlelight danced along the walls of the healing chamber as the world stirred back into motion. Alexandria lay still, but not unconscious. Her body had returned...but her soul was still catching up. Bellator had not left her side. She sat quietly in a chair drawn close to the bed, her head bowed, whispering a prayer in the ancient druidic tongue.

Alexandria's eyes fluttered open again. This time, she was fully awake. Bellator stood instantly, concern and relief written all over her. "Alex..." she breathed. "You're back."

Alexandria's gaze wandered around the room—recognition dawning, confusion laced with an ache she couldn't place. "I saw them," she whispered. "Not just him. Our children. A boy with my eyes...a girl with his laugh..." Bellator tensed. "It felt real. Too real."

"You were dreaming," Bellator said softly. "Visions, perhaps. Your body was broken. You were close to death. Sometimes the mind creates comfort. "

Alexandria turned toward her slowly. "But it wasn't comforting. It was...terrifying. I saw the sky fall. I heard a voice call out from our child like...like something ancient."

Bellator hesitated. "You said his name."

Alexandria looked down. "I know." She took a long breath, pain tightening her chest. "I don't know if I still love him...or if I'm still trying to save the part of him that loved me. "

Bellator knelt beside her, taking her hand. "Then you need to decide —before others do it for you."

Alexandria blinked, startled.

"The Celestial Order knows you're awake," Bellator continued. "And they're already moving."

"What do they want?"

Bellator's eyes darkened. "Control."

Alexandria's expression hardened slightly, the first flicker of defiance returning to her royal gaze. "Then they'll soon remember I am not their pawn."

———+———

It had been weeks since the princess awoke—weeks of quiet steps and held breaths, as if the kingdom feared the dream had followed her into waking. The throne room of Castle Solara had been transformed. Gone were the silken banners and radiant tapestries of celebration. In their place stood arcane symbols traced in silver and sunstone—protective runes laced with celestial magic. Guards lined the perimeter, not simply dressed in ceremonial gold, but armed and alert, their eyes fixed not on the gates—but on the dais.

On the dais, seated with regal composure, was Princess Alexandria, clad in a soft ivory gown embroidered with starlight threads, her long hair braided back to reveal her healing scar across her temple. Though her body was still weary, her posture betrayed no weakness. Her eyes—wary, sharp—swept over the figures before her. The Celestial Order had arrived.

Astralhart stood on her right like a stone sentinel while across from her stood the full Circle: the Dawnlords of Dawnshire, the Arch-Seer of Celestara, the Warden-Scribes of Utheron, and the Voice of Ryvarion, garbed in leaves and flame. Their gazes pierced like blades.

"Princess Alexandria," intoned the Arch-Seer. "It is our honor and duty to greet your return from the edge of death. Few have crossed the threshold of dreams and come back whole."

Alexandria inclined her head with regal grace. "And yet here I am. Whole enough to stand before you." Murmurs passed among them.

The Voice of Ryvarion spoke next, his voice like rustling leaves. "We have concerns...that your awakening has disturbed the balance between realms. The dreamseers spoke of prophecy. Of a union not yet realized."

"A child born of light and shadow," muttered the Warden-Scribe, his ink-stained fingers gripping a scroll. "A possible end. Or a new beginning. One tied...to the name you spoke."

"Erythyn," Alexandria said without flinching. Shock rippled through the chamber at her defiant tone.

"You remember him," Astralhart said carefully, watching her. "You spoke his name the moment you awoke. We would know why."

Alexandria rose slowly from her throne, her voice cold but composed. "Because he was there in my visions. Because part of me still remembers the man whose life I saved in the forest even if he later kidnapped me through a portal. Because I saw a future none of you have the right to twist into a threat before I understand what it even means."

The Dawnlord of Dawnshire narrowed his eyes. "If the prophecy is true, then your bloodline—intertwined with his—may yield a power no realm can contain."

"Then teach me to contain it," she snapped. "Don't cage me because you fear what I might become."

Astralhart stepped forward, his voice quieter, but laced with command. "Alexandria, we are not your enemies. But you must understand. Love, destiny, and prophecy are not yours alone to carry. If this bond is real, it threatens everything we have protected."

She stepped down from the dais, walking slowly toward them. "What if it's not a threat?" she asked, her voice quieter. "What if it's the key to ending the war? What if Erythyn can be pulled back...to the light?"

Silence.

The Arch-Seer finally spoke, her voice soft and sad. "Or what if the light is pulled into him...and extinguished?"

Alexandria paused, her throat tight. Her mind screamed with doubt, with longing, with fire.

"I won't be your prisoner," she said. "And I won't be your weapon."

Astralhart's expression darkened. "Then prove to us where your loyalties lie."

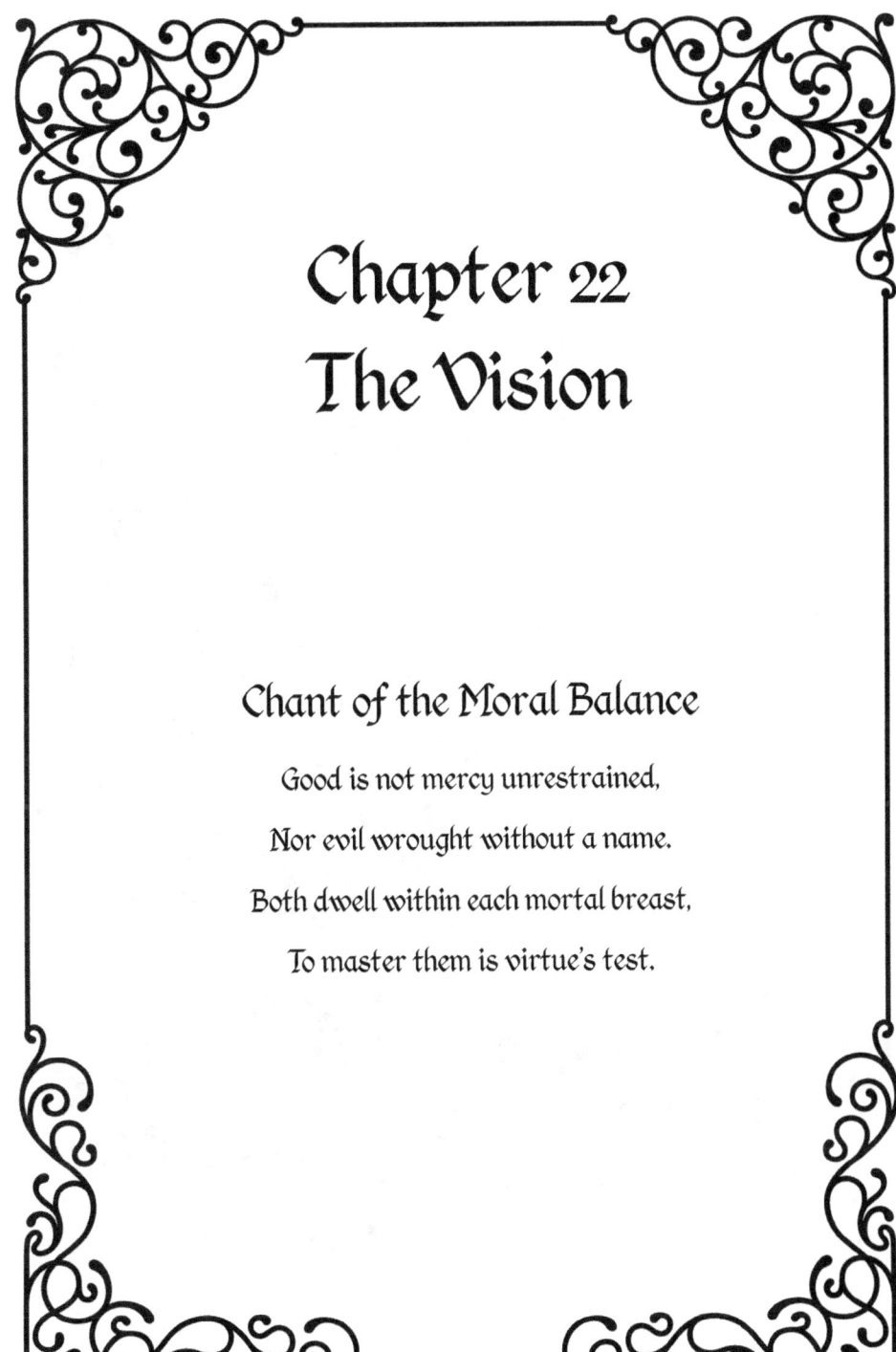

Chapter 22
The Vision

Chant of the Moral Balance

Good is not mercy unrestrained,

Nor evil wrought without a name.

Both dwell within each mortal breast,

To master them is virtue's test.

*T*he moon had risen high above Castle Solara once more, bathing its towering stone spires in silver light. But inside the walls, shadows clung heavily to the quiet corridors. Alexandria's footsteps echoed softly as she made her way through the castle's private wing—no guards, no mages, no advisors. Only one person she sought now.

She found Bellator at the small stone balcony that overlooked the eastern cliffs, the same place she often stood in silence after their battles, her cloak dancing in the wind like the wings of a falcon. Bellator didn't turn when Alexandria approached. "I heard the Order tried to paint you as a ticking curse," she said calmly, her voice carried gently by the wind.

Alexandria stepped beside her. "They didn't have to say it outright. Their silence said enough."

Bellator's eyes remained on the stars. "You didn't deny the vision?"

"I couldn't," Alexandria said. "Because I saw it. I felt it. It wasn't a trick, Bellator. It was prophecy...or something close to it."

Bellator's jaw tightened. "You saw children...your children. With him."

Alexandria nodded slowly. "A boy with my eyes. A girl with his spirit. They felt so real."

At last, Bellator turned to face her. Her expression was carved from stone, but behind it, pain flickered. "You saw him too, didn't you?"

Alexandria hesitated. "Yes."

"And after everything—after the portal, the lies, the blood—you still feel something for him?"

"I don't know what I feel," Alexandria whispered. "But whatever this is... It isn't gone. The bond is still there. The prophecy showed a child born of us. A child who could either save the world...or destroy it."

Bellator stepped forward, her voice low and fierce. "And how do you know it wasn't a manipulation? A dream seeded by the Shadowlord to pull you closer to his Erythyn? Prophecies can be twisted."

Alexandria's eyes glistened, but her voice did not waver. "Because I know what love feels like. And what pain feels like. And what it's like to want someone even when you hate what they've become."

Bellator looked away. "I swore to protect you, Alex. From enemies. From war. From darkness. But what am I supposed to do when the danger is within you?"

Alexandria stepped closer, placing a hand on Bellator's arm. "You still protect me," she said gently. "By staying with me. By helping me make sense of this. I don't want to face it alone."

A long silence followed. Then Bellator looked at her with storm-filled eyes. "If the time comes...and that child becomes what the Order fears... can you kill him? Can you kill Erythyn?"

Alexandria's breath caught. "I don't know," she said honestly. And that truth hung between them like a sword.

The air within the Black Spire was thick with smoke and cinders. Shadows coiled like living serpents across the stone floor, and the very walls seemed to pulse with dread—alive with ancient, malevolent magic. Erythyn stood alone in the central chamber, the heart of his father's domain, his cloak torn, his hair wild, his eyes—once silver—now burning with a seething, merciless fire.

He had felt it. Her awakening. For a brief, blinding moment, her soul had touched him like a flare in the void. He had clung to that sensation— relief, agony, hope—and then it vanished, smothered by an unnatural silence. And then he heard the whispers. From the distant edges of the void. From the mouths of broken spirits that served the Shadowlord. From the blood-soaked visions in his own dreams.

They're keeping her from you.

She spoke your name...and they caged her for it.

They fear what you are. What you could be...together.

Erythyn's body trembled—not from weakness, but from the pressure of the rage now boiling inside him. It was no longer wild and aimless. It had a purpose now. Direction. He wasn't just angry. He was done. "Every time," he hissed, pacing the floor, boots slamming against the stone. "Every time something good touches my life, they rip it from me. The Order. The Light. Their rules. Their chains."

Flashes of memory burned in his mind—her laugh, her warmth, her hand brushing his jaw as he fell asleep beside the fire. Then the moment it all vanished. Her blood on his hands. The black tower. The stillness in her chest. "They want her to forget me," he snarled. "They want her to be theirs again. Pure. Obedient. Controlled." He drove his fist into the obsidian pillar beside him, fracturing the stone. The cracks spread like lightning through the room. "She won't be their puppet. She was never meant to be."

Behind him, the darkness deepened. "You've finally let it in," he said, voice like molten stone. "The fury. The truth."

Erythyn turned toward him, his eyes glowing with molten light. "I want to burn down the world that tried to take her from me. Every kingdom that kept us apart. Every throne that is built on fear."

"Then you must become more than my son," the Shadowlord said, stepping closer. "You must become the fire that consumes the stars."

Erythyn dropped to one knee. "Then teach me. No more hesitation. No more chains."

The Shadowlord reached out a hand. "Then rise, Heir of Shadow. Master of the Abyss. Let us make the world remember what happens when it dares to separate soul from soul."

Erythyn stood.

And the chamber erupted into black flame.

Chapter 23
Stolen Dreams

Verses of the Dueling Fates

Good & ill, twin children born,

One heralds light, the other scorn.

Yet in each spirit's darkest hour,

The other's seed reveals its power.

*T*he moon hung low and heavy over Castle Solara, casting a pale wash across the sky like a smudged ink stain. The Aetherian Lock shimmered faintly above the castle's towers—an invisible dome of pure celestial energy, designed to keep spirits, magic, and uninvited dreams at bay. But even the strongest spells cannot silence the soul.

Within her chamber, cloaked in silken shadows and quiet wards, Alexandria slept uneasily. The room was cool, perfumed with lavender and star-root, meant to calm her. But the calm had turned to stillness, the kind of stillness that presses against the ribs like a weight. She stirred in her sleep. Her fingers twitched, her brow furrowed. Her breath shallowed.

Then—darkness. She stood in a dreamscape of scorched earth and broken towers. The sky above her burned crimson, swirling like a wounded storm. Ash fell like snow. In the distance, mountains crumbled under pillars of black flame. And there, at the heart of the destruction, stood Erythyn. But he was no longer cloaked in shadowed restraint. The collar that once suppressed his power was gone. His body pulsed with raw energy—black veins of magic crawling across his skin like lightning frozen in flesh. Wings of smoke and fire spread behind him. His eyes... Not silver, but molten gold and red. He looked like a god of ruin. And he sensed her. Their eyes met across the dream, and a gust of heat rushed through her chest as if someone had struck a bell inside her ribs. He didn't speak. But she felt it.

They caged you.

They took you from me...again.

I will not ask the stars for you—I will tear them from the sky.

She stumbled back, her hands over her heart. "No..." she whispered. "Don't do this..."

I will come for you, Alexandria. No wall, no ward, no Order will stand between us again.

Then the vision collapsed into smoke—and she awoke with a gasp, drenched in sweat beneath her sheets. Her pulse pounded in her ears like war drums. The room was silent, but the air was wrong—heavy and humming with residual magic. She sat up slowly, clutching her chest, her eyes darting toward the window. The Aetherian Lock still shimmered faintly above... But her heart knew what the mind would not dare admit. He was coming. Not as a whisper. Not as a memory. But as a storm.

The hour was well past midnight, and the castle had long settled into its eerie quiet. Only the low hum of magical wards vibrated faintly in the air, the Aetherian Lock overhead casting a soft shimmer across the towers like moonlight caught in glass. In the heart of the princess's chamber, Alexandria sat with her back pressed to the wall, her knees drawn to her chest, still trying to slow her breathing. The vision of Erythyn—no, the connection—was too vivid to be a simple dream. It had not been conjured. It had pierced through. She hadn't lit a candle since waking. Better that no one know she was still awake. The silence broke.

Three taps, soft and rhythmic, against the far side of her chamber wall. Not the door. The hidden panel—a forgotten side entrance once used by royal handmaidens and druids during war-time lockdowns. Alexandria stood slowly, her hand hovering above the concealed rune. She whispered the unlocking word: "Aeliora."

The stone shifted with a soft groan. A cloaked figure stepped in. No torch. No sound. Only a whisper of leather and shadow.

Bellator.

Her hood fell back, revealing a stern face drawn in moonlight—her eyes sharp and jaw clenched. And beneath that... Fear. "Close it," she said, her voice low.

Alexandria obeyed.

As the wall sealed behind them, Bellator locked it again with a gesture that should've been lost to time. "You felt him tonight," Bellator said, not even waiting for a greeting. "Didn't you?"

Alexandria blinked. "How did you—?"

"I felt it too," Bellator said. "Through the old bond."

"What bond?"

Bellator hesitated. "The one you don't remember. From when you were a child. Before they cloaked you in royal enchantments. Before they began filtering your dreams."

Alexandria froze. "What are you saying?"

Bellator stepped closer, her eyes gleaming with fierce loyalty. "The Order is monitoring your sleep. They've tied dream-wards to your aura, masked to feel like healing spells. But they're not just watching for corruption. They're listening. Watching for signs of him."

Alexandria's blood ran cold.

"They want to know if you're still connected," Bellator continued. "And if you are... They'll take action before he gets to you. Not to protect you. To control you."

"They said I was safe," Alexandria whispered. "They said I was free."

Bellator's expression twisted. "There is no freedom when prophecy binds your blood. You're not a princess to them anymore—you're a variable. A risk. And if they think you'll bring him back, they'll end it before the vision can come to pass."

Tears threatened to well in Alexandria's eyes, but she forced herself still. "Why are you telling me this now?"

Bellator lowered her voice further. "Because I swore to protect you. Not the throne. Not the Order. You. And whatever this prophecy says you'll become, it should be your choice."

A moment of silence passed. Then Alexandria spoke, her voice low, dangerous, trembling with fire. "Then I need to get out of here."

Bellator nodded once. "I'll help you. But we need to move carefully. They're already watching everything."

Alexandria looked toward the window as she stood next to the only person she could trust in this world, her eyes fixed toward the dome of celestial light that kept her safe—and caged. And somewhere, far beyond

that veil, Erythyn was burning the world for her.

High above the kingdom, nestled in the sacred towers of Celestara, the Order of Dreamweavers stirred. In a chamber known as the Hall of Breathless Sleep, a circle of robed mages surrounded a pool of glassy water. Floating above it, like smoke trailing from a candle, was the echo of a dream—faint, fractured, but tainted. Ash. Fire. Wings of smoke. The shadowed prince, eyes ablaze. Her whisper—his name. The bond—alive.

The High Seer clenched her hand around her staff. "It's grown stronger. The Aetherian Lock slowed it...but did not break it."

Across from her, one of the wardmasters stepped forward, frowning. "She shielded her thoughts last night. Intentionally. Someone taught her how."

"Someone inside," another murmured. "A loyalist. Perhaps the druid."

They turned to Astralhart, standing at the edge of the circle, his gaze fixed on the swirling dream-echo. "She still resists," the Seer warned him. "Even after all we've done. She does not fear the prophecy. She embraces it." Astralhart's voice was cold steel. "Because she doesn't understand what's at stake." He moved toward the pool, extending a single finger. The moment he touched the surface, the reflection shifted—showing Alexandria, sitting in her chamber, her eyes turned to the sky, her fingers tracing invisible symbols along the windowsill. "She dreams of him."

"She longs for him," another hissed.

"Then we act," Astralhart said.

There was a pause. "You mean to confine her?"

Astralhart nodded. "Not a prison. A sanctum. A warded sanctum beneath the castle—where the veil is strongest. No sky. No star. No doorway to slip through."

The Seer hesitated. "She will know."

"She already knows," Astralhart replied, his eyes narrowing. "And if we don't act now, she will escape...and run straight into his arms." He turned to the circle, his voice rising. "Begin the preparations. Reinforce the sanctum. Move her within three nights' time. If Alexandria cannot be separated from the shadow by choice—then we will cut the bond by force."

No one spoke. But beneath their silence, runes ignited. Sigils were carved. Chains of celestial light began to form—chains meant for a princess.

In the war room, Astralhart spoke calmly to the mages and scribes, unaware that his carefully maintained order was about to unravel. That's when the great iron doors crashed open. General Stormrend entered, blood on his armor, fire in his eyes. "Veradwyn has fallen. The eastern watch is gone. The enemy rides for Dawnshire." Chaos exploded. "Reports say beasts born of shadow. Spirits twisted by dark fire. Like the ones in the girl's visions."

Astralhart's face turned to stone.

"She was right," one scribe whispered.

The Prime Minister raised his hand. "Ready my horse. Now."

The heavy knock came too soon. Alexandria tried to collect her thoughts and come up with a plan when the door burst open, and Astralhart stepped inside, alone but grim. "Alexandria," he said, his eyes softer than expected. "The charade ends now."

Alexandria stood, calm but alert. "What charade?"

"Veradwyn has fallen. The enemy is marching. Our time is gone. You must let go of him. Of this fantasy. The kingdom needs its princess—not a girl chasing ghosts."

She felt her breath catch.

He stepped closer. "You've dreamed of him. We know. You've bonded with something dangerous. But now...now you must be what your people need. No more rebellion. No more dreams. Let him go!"

Silence fell. Alexandria turned to the window—no longer her escape, now her reminder. She blinked back tears. "Then I will."

Astralhart nodded. "Good."

"But understand this," she said, her voice low and trembling. "I do this not because I believe you... But because my people deserve peace."

He said nothing. And in the shadows behind her, Bellator and Ashlynn stood quietly—watching as the girl they had sworn to protect made the ultimate choice: to bury her heart for the sake of her crown. And far across the realm, in a fortress of flame and shadow, Erythyn felt it. Like a thread gone slack. And the world shuddered.

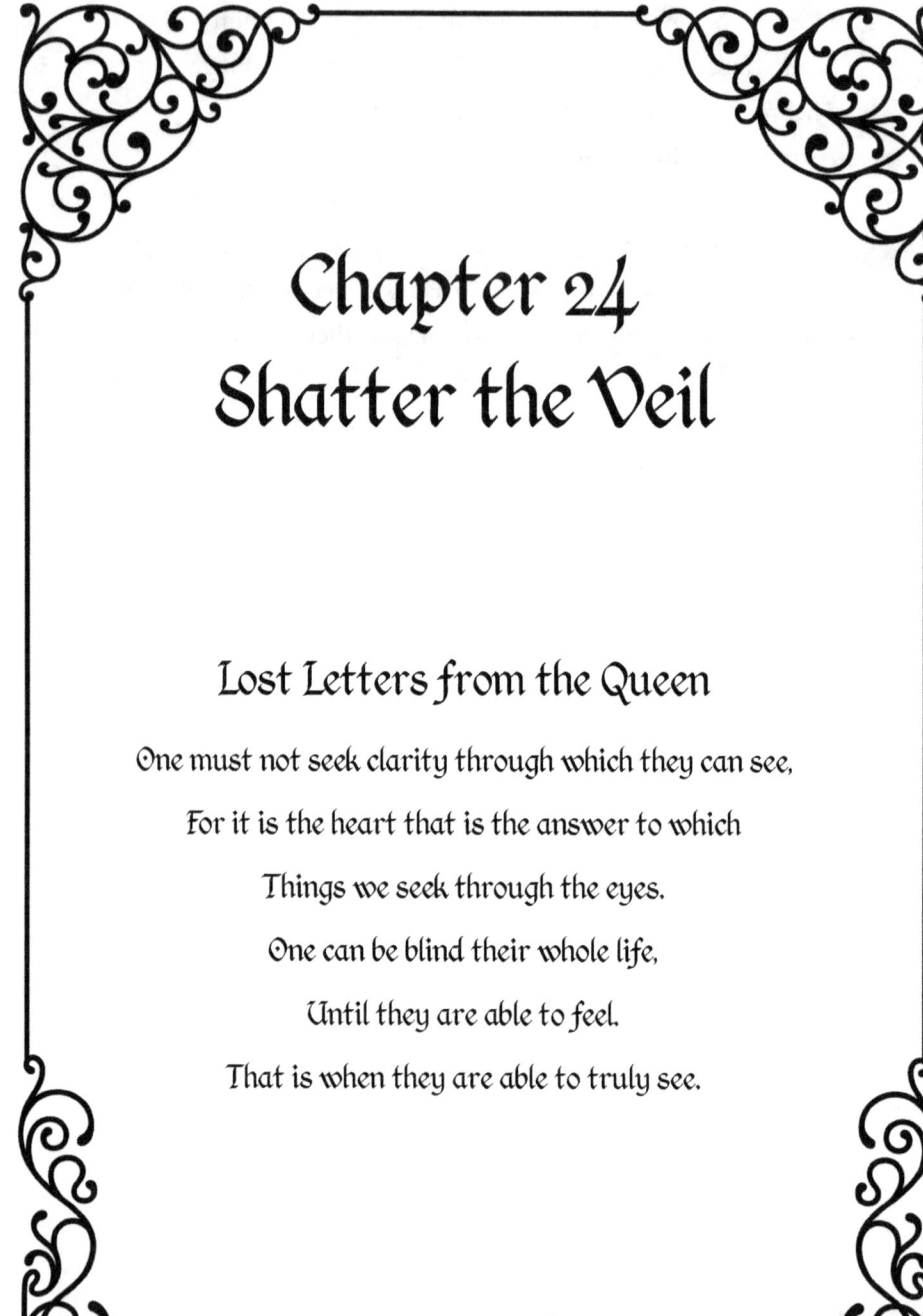

Chapter 24
Shatter the Veil

Lost Letters from the Queen

One must not seek clarity through which they can see,

For it is the heart that is the answer to which

Things we seek through the eyes.

One can be blind their whole life,

Until they are able to feel.

That is when they are able to truly see.

Back in time, the Black Spire shuddered—a groaning, guttural sound that echoed up its jagged length like a cry from the pit of the world itself. From deep within its fractured heart, far beneath the broken sky where swirling ash choked out every trace of sunlight, a storm brewed. There, in the obsidian chamber where the walls bled molten veins of ancient magic, Erythyn stood alone. Still. Cold. Unmoving.

He had stood that way for hours—statue-like, carved from shadow and fury, his breath barely visible in the oppressive heat that radiated from the cracked stone beneath his boots. The floor throbbed with veins of dark light, spiraling outward from where he stood as if the very world responded to the storm inside him. Faint pulses of reddish glow surged along the edges of ancient runes, long forgotten and long forbidden. But within his chest...rage thundered like a war drum, relentless and merciless. He had felt it—that moment. That quiet, soul-tearing moment when Alexandria pulled away. It wasn't dramatic. No scream. No shattering blow. Just silence. Just the absence of her. A soft ache where her warmth had once rested against him, a delicate severing of a bond that had once felt eternal. He felt her soul recoil. Not in hatred. Not even in fear. But in sorrow. In duty. They had gotten to her. Twisted her heart against him. Made her choose. Not him. The crown. The throne. The world that had always feared him. That had always hated his blood.

Behind him, cloaked in shadows that clung like a second skin, stood the Shadowlord. Silent. Watchful. His ember-lit eyes smoldered with something too ancient to be pity, too sharp to be comfort. Perhaps... approval. "She's gone, boy," the Shadowlord murmured, his voice like coals cracking in a dying fire. "You felt it."

"She's not gone," Erythyn growled, the words rough and heavy with magic. "She's trapped."

The Shadowlord's head tilted slightly. "By her own choice."

Erythyn's jaw clenched. His hands curled into fists, shaking as magic coiled up his arms like smoke. His voice dropped, darker now, thrumming with power that had been buried for too long. "Then I'll burn the walls she's hiding behind."

The chamber responded. A deep, resonant pulse rang out, shaking dust from the cracked vaults high above. Runes carved in a forgotten tongue flared to life—searing red, then gold, then black. The obsidian pillars began to weep tendrils of lightless flame, their glow devouring the air, hissing like serpents waking from slumber. From the cracks in the world, magic surged—primordial and vengeful, hungry to be wielded again.

The Shadowlord stepped forward, slow and solemn, his cloak whispering across the scorched stone. "If you do this—" His voice was low, almost reverent. "There's no going back. This power is not borrowed. It's not shared. Once you claim it—it becomes you."

Erythyn raised his head. His eyes were no longer silver. They were not human. They were voids—brilliant and bottomless—burning with fury, with grief, with destiny. "I am not going back," he said. Then, without hesitation, he stepped into the center of the circle carved into the floor. The moment his foot crossed the threshold, the entire chamber convulsed. Ancient runes ignited at his feet, one by one. Glyphs of sky-fire, realm-sunder, soul-bond—forbidden magic etched in dragon bone and blood during the First Sundering.

They flared to life now because he no longer hesitated. He wanted the fire. He was the fire. Magic rushed upward in a cyclone of annihilation, wrapping around him like armor, like a curse. He lifted his arms, and the Spire screamed. "I was forged in silence," he declared, his voice carrying through the storm. "Raised in exile. Broken by prophecy." His eyes blazed, his voice now a roar that echoed into the soul of the Spire itself. "But I will be denied no longer."

A bolt of black lightning cracked down from the heavens, shattering the ceiling above. The sky itself tore open—not just clouds, but reality—splitting like cloth, ragged and raw. Through it poured unfiltered, ancient magic—wild, celestial, unstoppable. The stars across the realm flickered, as if blinking in fear.

The winds howled across the broken cliffs of the Shadowlands, kicking up ash and embers as though the world already knew...something was coming. At the center of the storm, Erythyn stood alone atop the Obsidian Cradle, the jagged altar where kings of ruin were once crowned and gods were once cursed. His cloak whipped behind him, torn and scorched, his body trembling—not with weakness but with containment. The bond had snapped. Not broken entirely—but frayed, distant, as if Alexandria had been buried beneath a thousand wards, a thousand lies, a thousand voices that weren't his.

He had waited. Trained. Hoped. But no more. "She chose them," he muttered, his fists clenched. "She chose duty."

Behind him, the Shadowlord approached like a living eclipse, his horned silhouette outlined in roiling flame. "She did what they taught her to do," the dark god said. "But even now, you still feel her."

Erythyn didn't answer—because it was true. He could feel her heartbeat, slow and steady. He could feel her sorrow. Her guilt. But he also felt something else. She was still his. He raised his arms to the sky and screamed her name.

"ALEXANDRIA!"

And the world broke open. The clouds above were ripped from the sky like paper. The heavens cracked, revealing a vortex of chaotic energy —the Veil between Realms—splitting in real time. A shockwave erupted from his body, leveling mountains and turning sand into glass. Black lightning danced between the shards of the broken sky. Every spell of balance. Every tether of time. Every boundary that had kept him from her —he shattered them all. His voice echoed across the planes like a war horn:

"You locked her behind walls of light.
You buried her in thrones and chains.

Now feel what it means to steal the soul of a god."

The Shadowlord smiled behind him, for the first time...proud. "Then go," he said. "Burn the sky, my son."

And Erythyn leapt into the rift, carried on wings of smoke and wrath, his power trailing behind him like the tail of a comet. A comet aimed directly at the heart of the kingdom.

Across distant battlefields, soldiers staggered as the ground split beneath their feet. Horses reared. Birds fell silent. And far away, inside Castle Solara, Alexandria felt it. Standing alone by the high windows of her chamber, her hand clutched to her chest, she stared toward the east— toward the place the sky was breaking. Her breath caught. Magic, raw and terrifying, whispered through her bones like a scream in her blood. She did not need to ask what had happened. She knew. A single name escaped her trembling lips, barely more than a breath—but enough to split her heart. "Erythyn..."

Books fell from shelves. Light fixtures flickered. The sacred spires— enchanted to withstand siege and storm—shuddered. Inside the grand hall, alarms rang. Mages scrambled through corridors of crystal and stone, their spells flickering like guttering flames. Dream-wards sparked. Divination circles cracked. The air was thick with static and pressure— like the breath of something ancient pressing against the veil of reality.

And in the heart of it all, Alexandria burst through the doors of Astralhart's private chamber. He was standing at the celestial map, his hands trembling as the stars above it twisted, shattering their sacred constellations. She didn't wait. "What have you done?" she snapped, her voice ringing like a bell.

Astralhart turned, his face pale beneath the light of the shattering skies. "It's not me. It's him."

"Erythyn?"

He nodded grimly. "He's broken through the Veil. Reality is folding,

Alexandria. He's coming."

Outside the chamber, a great *BOOM* echoed—not from the ground, but the sky itself. Alexandria's heart seized. "I told you he wouldn't stop."

"And you were told to forget him," Astralhart growled. "We tried to protect you. Shield you from this fate."

She advanced on him, fury flaring behind her eyes. "Shield me? You locked me in dreams. You spied on my mind. You lied about what I was!"

"You were never meant to be a bridge between light and shadow," he snapped. "You were meant to rule." The chamber door flung open again. A storm of voices followed.

"The Sky Rift has opened!" a seer cried.

"The Moon Tower just collapsed!"

"The wards are failing! He's collapsing the upper realms—he's tearing time itself!"

The Celestial Order poured into the chamber like panicked birds. Robes, scrolls, scrying spheres were clutched in trembling hands.

The great seer of Celestara looked to be almost in tears. "This isn't just a breach," she whispered. "It's a return. The Second Sundering—he's remaking the prophecy in real time."

The room descended into chaos, and Alexandria stood still. Her eyes closed. Her heart wide open. She felt him. Erythyn's rage was a storm—but underneath it, she felt the pain. The desperation. The love he was burning the world to reach. And suddenly—she understood. He wasn't trying to destroy her kingdom. He was trying to get to her. Her voice rang out over the rising panic. "Stop the locks. Disband the sanctum. You can't stop him by hiding me. If I don't face him—he'll tear this world in half."

Astralhart stared at her. "You can't be serious. We don't even know where he is!"

She nodded once. "Follow my orders!" she said as her eyes pierced him.

He took a slow step forward. "Then the Order will fall at your side."

And for the first time since her awakening, Princess Alexandria looked every inch the queen. "Then let it fall."

Chapter 25
A Perfect Fortress

The Balance

One must seek balance between the light & dark,

For this is your true power.

Just as the Sun cast Shadows on the ground,

The trees will embrace them & dance.

*T*he world knew something had changed when the sky split open. But when Erythyn returned, he did not ride upon the clouds or descend in a blaze of fire as the seers had feared. No, he slipped into the world silently, like smoke through a cracked door.

Rather than strike at Castle Solara, where Alexandria's heart still beat behind a veil of duty and enchantment, he turned his eyes east, toward a forgotten land between borders. A place caught between Dawnshire's golden empire and the chaos beyond: Virelith, a storm-wracked country of broken castles and faithless kings. Its people were already trembling. They'd heard the rumors. Of cities swallowed by ash. Of warriors who fought shadows and lost their minds. Of lightning that struck from cloudless skies. When the black-armored stranger arrived at the ruined gates of Castle Gravenmoor, they bowed not from loyalty, but from fear. He wore a mask of obsidian across the upper half of his face, and his name—whispered in a voice that echoed—was Lord Maeryn. None knew it was Erythyn reborn. He did not need to reveal himself.

The castle fell quickly. Its keepers were scattered. The throne room was lit with eerie fire. But even in his conquest, a strange contradiction took root—he preserved one level of the castle. An entire floor was left untouched. Velvet drapes of forest green. Candles that never dimmed. A stained-glass window depicting a lion and a doe, still unmarred. That floor became a sanctuary. His memory of her. Alexandria. Because the bond was severed, though her voice no longer reached his dreams, he didn't know if she was alive. He feared hoping. He feared knowing. So instead...he did what he knew best. He destroyed.

Months passed as war bloomed like rot. With Lord Maeryn at the helm of Virelith's now-shadowed army, dark magic spilled across the lowlands. Villages were emptied overnight. Forests twisted. Spirits corrupted. Rumors whispered of a castle where no light could reach, ruled by a man whose touch could command fire, beasts, and time itself. And yet no one knew who he truly was.

Except one.

Clad in mythic armor woven with silver druid sigils, Bellator rode beside a unit of elite Dawnshire soldiers into the thickest part of the front, her eyes scanning the battlefield like a hawk.

It had been months of grueling campaigns. Flashes of corruption. Phantom enemies vanishing in shadow. And through it all, a new warlord had risen, one whose name none knew but whose power terrified even the oldest commanders. That day, beneath a bruised red sky, she saw him. A single figure in dark armor surged into battle—blades blazing, fire leaping from his fingertips. He moved through enemy ranks like water, graceful and violent. Too graceful. Too familiar. Bellator froze atop her mount. "That movement..." she murmured, her eyes narrowing. "That stance..." Could it be? But before she could follow, a blast of ash-fire separated them. And when it cleared, the warrior was gone.

It was the third sighting. By now, Bellator was certain. The battlefield at Hollowridge had been chaos—flames roaring from both sides, summoned beasts clashing in a blur of fang and claw. But amidst it all, she had seen him again. Not once. Not fleeting. She had watched him fight. The way he stepped forward before striking. The way he twisted his body just slightly to avoid a blade. The way his magic pulsed—like a heartbeat she once bled beside. This wasn't just a skilled fighter.

This was Erythyn. Or what was left of him. But every time she tried to follow, he vanished behind fire, smoke, or the screams of war.

Back at her encampment, she spread old scrolls and new maps across her table. Her fingers traced the lines of Virelith, circled the ruined stronghold at its heart: Castle Gravenmoor. Too strategic to be random. Too quiet to be natural. She rolled up the map. "If he's there...then I'm going in."

That night, Bellator stood at the ridge above Castle Gravenmoor, cloaked in illusion. Her owl eyes—borrowed through a druidic ritual—

swept across the towers. Torchlight. Shadow-forged guards. Darkened banners. But then—there. A window glowing soft green in the heart of the fortress. Untouched. Sacred. A floor not like the others. A room not corrupted. Bellator's eyes narrowed. "Why would a warlord leave one floor clean?" she whispered. "Unless it was never a war he wanted to win..."

Nightfall cloaked Virelith like a mourning veil.

High above the valley, Castle Gravenmoor loomed—its once-noble towers twisted by shadow, its battlements cracked and crawling with tendrils of dark magic. Corruption had claimed nearly every inch, save one: a single floor at the center of the keep, glowing faintly, untouched by rot or ruin.

Bellator stood in the thorns just beyond the outer wall, her druidic armor dull and darkened with ash to hide her presence. She had spent weeks preparing—tracking patrols, marking guard rotations, learning the pulse of the castle's unnatural heart. Now was the moment. She whispered an incantation in the Old Tongue, her body shimmering briefly as the spell of shadow melding enveloped her.

Blending with the darkness, she moved—silent, a phantom within enemy lines. Through the old servant's passage. Up a spiral staircase that smelled of rusted blood and sulfur. Past two guards, motionless and glass-eyed—corrupted husks. Then she reached the untouched floor and stopped.

It was like stepping into a memory. The moment she crossed the threshold, the corruption vanished. The air was clean—rich with the scent of pine and sandalwood. Golden light glowed from crystal sconces. Soft green banners fluttered from the ceiling. A harp, untouched by time, rested in the corner. There were books. Paintings. A robe folded neatly across a velvet chair. And in the center of the room...a mural. It stretched across the curved stone wall: a woman in flowing white, standing in a forest of stars, her hand extended to a cloaked figure. Alexandria. Even in paint, her light shone. And in the figure beside her, shadowed but lovingly rendered—Erythyn.

Bellator's breath caught. She stepped closer. On a nearby table lay a pendant, identical to the one Alexandria once wore. Beside it, a vial of starlight water. A page torn from a dreamseer's book. And scrawled in Erythyn's own handwriting:

"If she's still alive...this stays clean. So I remember what I was before the world turned me into what I am."

Bellator backed away slowly, her hands trembling. He wasn't trying to forget. He was trying to hold on. He never let go. And for the first time in months, Bellator's certainty cracked. Maybe he wasn't entirely lost.

The moment Bellator turned from the glass case that held Alexandria's sunstone amulet, she felt it. The air shifted. Magic thickened —twisting, seething, furious. A shadow uncoiled from the far wall like a serpent, and from within it stepped Erythyn—his black armor humming with raw, volatile power. His mask caught the candlelight and threw it back as flame. Smoke curled from his fingertips. And his eyes—once silver, now molten gold—locked onto her like a predator sighting the one thing he swore no one would ever touch. She was standing in his sanctuary. The only part of the world he hadn't destroyed.

"You have five seconds," he said, his voice dark and jagged as shattered steel, "to tell me why you're here."

Bellator's stance shifted, calm but ready. "I came looking for answers."

"In here?" His voice rose like fire against oil. "You don't belong in this room."

His hand twitched. The shadows around them rose, curling like smoke-dragons around the walls. The very floor growled beneath her boots, reacting to his fury.

"This place was never meant for you," he snarled, stepping forward. "This was for her."

"I know," Bellator said, her voice even. "And maybe that's why you're still human under all that rage—because you remember her."

"Get out."

"Erythyn—"

"*GET OUT!*" he roared.

The walls trembled. Candles burst in a spray of wax and light. The harp against the wall cracked with a sickening snap. The preservation spells warped at the edges, devoured by his fury. But then—he froze. Something in his chest clenched. A ripple passed through him. Pain, like a whip of memory. Alexandria's voice. Her laughter. Her hand on his cheek.

And Bellator could only imagine the ache behind the rage. "You don't have to keep doing this," she said, her voice lowering, taking a single step toward him. "You're not the monster they say you are. I've seen what you preserved. You remember her as she remembers you."

He gritted his teeth, his breathing ragged. "I was a monster," he hissed. "Until she saw something else." He looked down at his gloved hand, clenching it. "And now she's gone. And you brought the world back into the only place where she wasn't." The magic around him flared violently, black lightning splitting across the walls.

Bellator knew the moment had passed. She had to go. A swirl of smoke burst from her cloak as she whispered a spell of shifting wind. The air wrapped around her like a gust, and she vanished through the doorway, just as the floor behind her exploded in a vortex of black fire.

Bellator left him in the ruined remains of the one pure room left in the world, and she knew there would be rage to follow.

Chapter 26
Guardian in Chains

The Invocation of the Starlit Crown

O crown of light, O midnight's gleam,

Ignite within the sleeping dream.

Let fractured souls in darkness mourn,

Rise now anew on wings reborn.

The castle walls of Solara loomed like old memories as Bellator's mount galloped through the night gates. Her armor was scorched. Her hair tangled. Her heart—hammering. She pushed past guards, through corridors, until she stood before the princess's chamber. When the doors opened, Alexandria looked up from her balcony, moonlight kissing her face.

Bellator stepped in, her eyes wild. "I found him," she said breathlessly. "He's in Virelith. He's taken Gravenmoor."

Alexandria's breath caught.

"And he's still angry. But he—Alex, he kept everything. Your cloak. Your mirror. A room untouched. He talks like you're dead. Like...like he's the one mourning you."

Alexandria turned slowly, tears already burning at the corners of her eyes.

Then Bellator added, softer, "He tried to kill me when I stepped into that room. Because he built it to remember you. And I was the first to step into it who wasn't you."

Silence fell between them.

Alexandria's fingers trembled on the windowsill.

"He's still there," Bellator said, her voice steady. "But so is the part of him you saved. I saw it. I felt it."

Alexandria didn't speak. But she didn't need to. Her eyes burned with fire again.

The echo of galloping hooves and whispered words had barely faded when Astralhart received the news. A royal steward—pale, breathless— burst into the Prime Minister's private war chamber, where scrolls of fallen cities littered the table and the stars above the celestial map pulsed erratically. "My Lord—Bellator. She's returned."

Astralhart's head snapped up. "Where?"

"She just entered the princess's chamber."

His face darkened instantly. She found something. He knew it with the same certainty he felt when a storm was coming. That druid wolf had gone silent for too long—beyond the veil, beyond orders. And now, she had come back—straight to Alexandria. Unfiltered. Unwatched. Uncontrolled. Dangerous.

Astralhart turned to the steward, his voice like ice. "Seal the princess's wing. Send the Royal Guard. Bellator is to be taken into custody—alive."

The steward hesitated. "Alive, my Lord?"

Astralhart's eyes glinted. "For now."

In the golden glow of Alexandria's chamber, Bellator had just finished recounting what she saw—Erythyn's rage, the sanctuary, the untouched floor preserved in Alexandria's memory. Alexandria stood at the window, her hands gripping the stone sill so tightly her knuckles turned white.

Bellator took a step forward. "We have to go. Before he becomes something even he can't come back from."

Then—

A sudden knock.

A second.

A third—louder, heavier.

Bellator's eyes widened. "That's not a steward."

Alexandria turned, her heart dropping. "What is this?" The doors slammed open with a burst of white-blinding light. Royal Guards poured in, led by Commander Thales, their armor gleaming, spears drawn—not for defense but apprehension.

"Bellator of the Royal Druidic Order," Thales said formally, "you are hereby detained under direct order of Prime Minister Astralhart, for breach of magical containment and unauthorized contact with hostile entities."

Alexandria stepped forward. "No. She did what I asked her to—!"

"She endangered the security of the realm," Thales said, emotionless. "And she may be under enemy influence."

Two guards moved to seize her. Bellator stepped back, tense, but Alexandria held up a hand. "Don't fight them," she whispered. "If you fight, he'll use it against you."

Bellator met her gaze, her voice low and furious. "He's scared. He knows I found the truth." Then, softer, as the guards gripped her arms, she said, "Don't let them keep you from him."

They dragged her from the chamber as Alexandria stood frozen—raging with helplessness.

And somewhere in the shadows behind the throne, Astralhart watched through a vision mirror, his expression unreadable. "Let's see how long your heart holds, Princess."

The storm raged across Virelith's shattered highlands, lightning forking through the sky like cracks in the bones of the gods. High above it all, on the jagged balcony of Castle Gravenmoor, Erythyn stood unmoving—his cloak snapping in the wind, his armor dripping with cold rain and the residual shimmer of raw magic. He had not slept since Bellator escaped. Not because he feared her return, but because of what her presence had stirred. For the first time in months...he'd felt something. Not the steady hum of Alexandria's soul, not the warmth he once knew—but a disturbance, like a heartbeat that fluttered once and then went silent. And now...that silence was deafening.

He clutched the edge of the stone railing, claws of smoke forming around his fingers. Something had shifted. In the hours since the druid vanished from his sanctum, the world felt different—too quiet, like the forest before a predator strikes. And deep in his chest, he knew. Alexandria hadn't sent Bellator. Bellator had come on her own. Which meant...she wasn't free.

His body tensed. "They've caged her again." He turned from the balcony, his eyes glowing brighter now. The veins of power along his jaw pulsed like lightning trapped beneath his skin. In the center of the war room, maps floated midair—marked with troop movements, magical ley lines, strongholds of the Celestial Order. And at the center of them all: Castle Solara. He stared at it. Then—he reached for the map with both hands, his fingers igniting in flame. The image of the castle twisted, scorched, shattered beneath his grip. He spoke aloud to the empty chamber. "You took her once. You turned her against me. Now you steal the only one who stood beside her…"

A pulse of magic exploded from his chest, black and gold, cracking the walls of the war room. He bared his teeth. "No more dreams. No more distance. I'm coming. And this time—I'm not hiding."

Chapter 27
A Caged Lion

Canticle of the Celestial Warden

Guardian born of sky & stone,

You stand where none shall stand alone.

In cosmic hush your vigil keeps,

While drifting worlds succumb to sleep.

The chamber was dark, save for the molten veins pulsing through the floor like lava frozen mid-flow. Magic seeped from the stones of Gravenmoor, called forth by a fury that no longer needed to be hidden. Erythyn stood before a curved obsidian table etched with runes, surrounded by generals forged of shadow and fire, their loyalty absolute. At its center floated the target: a ghostly, flickering illusion of a towering crystalline spire surrounded by celestial wards, hovering like a needle over a sea of clouds. The Sanctum of Astrael—the Celestial Order's most sacred tower.

Built on a floating rock held aloft by spells older than the kingdoms, it was the home of dreamseers, ward-keepers, and truth binders. A place that had never once known siege. A place that symbolized the untouchable. "I will not strike the castle," Erythyn said coldly. "Not yet. They would expect that. It would make her a prisoner of war, not a princess." He raised his hand. The image of the spire burned brighter. "This—" He snarled. "This is what they worship. The illusion of prophecy. The pedestal of their lies."

One of his captains—a creature of pale flame and broken armor— rumbled, "Their wards are old. Woven from the breath of gods. Even your power might not breach them."

Erythyn stepped forward. His aura flared, golden flame laced with black. "I don't intend to breach," he said. "I intend to shatter." He reached to the table and clenched his fist. The image of the spire crumbled to ash.

The night was silent above the floating mountain of Astrael. Stars shimmered above it like watching eyes, and the air buzzed faintly with ward magic—soft as wind chimes, constant as breath. Then the sky cracked open. A comet of flame and shadow tore through the heavens, trailing black lightning and silver fire. At its core, wrapped in wings of living smoke—Erythyn descended.

The spire's alarms ignited, blaring across the mountain. Seers screamed. Ward-mages scrambled. But it was too late. He landed atop the spire with a thunderous crash, shattering the upper balcony in an explosion of light and stone. The magic screamed around him, trying to resist—but his presence was like gravity tearing at the sky.

Rising to his full height, his cloak ablaze, his eyes burning, Erythyn raised his hand to the heavens. And then—he released it.

A blast of magic not seen since the First War erupted from his core, a pulse of heat, shadow, and grief, tearing through the tower like a scream turned physical. Windows shattered for miles. The sacred wards—untouched for centuries—fractured. Statues crumbled. Books ignited. A beacon meant to guide dreamwalkers exploded in a column of black fire that could be seen from the coast. And atop the crumbling spire, Erythyn planted a single sigil—Alexandria's name carved in searing flame, glowing in the night.

Come to me—or watch the stars fall one by one.

It started as a whisper on the wind. Then a tremble in the air—soft, subtle, unnatural. Alexandria stepped onto the balcony outside her chamber, the evening robes around her frame barely catching the rising gust. Her hands gripped the railing tight. The wind smelled of ash. And then—the heavens ignited. Far across the horizon, a spiral of flame burst into the sky—a torrent of black and silver fire that cracked the clouds and lit up the stars like kindling. The spire at the center, once sacred and now burned, was crumbling under the weight of something ancient and furious. Her knees buckled. Magic rushed into her chest like a thunderclap. Not just any magic—his. Familiar, unshakable, violent, and aching. Erythyn.

Her fingers dug into the stone, and she gasped—because it wasn't just magic she felt. It was him. Alive. Screaming her name into the sky with raw, impossible power. Her name appeared above the tower in flame: Alexandria, glowing like a brand across the world. And she knew—he had done this for her.

But even as her soul was pulled toward the fire...the chain around her heart tightened. "Bellator..." The name slipped from her lips like a broken prayer. She turned from the balcony, stormed across the room, and slammed her fist onto the marble table where the scrolls lay scattered. Her guards outside likely heard—but she didn't care. Bellator had come back for her. Had found Erythyn. Had seen the truth. And what had they done? Arrested her. Silenced her. Caged her like a traitor. And Alexandria—Alexandria had been forced to stand there and watch it happen. Her jaw clenched.

She began pacing the chamber, her mind racing. "They think they can control me by caging her. They think if I can't hear the truth, I won't remember it."

She stopped at the mirror and stared at her reflection. Tired. Fractured. Fading beneath crowns and duty. And then her eyes drifted back out the window—toward the black fire still blazing in the distance, to the sigil burning in the sky. He was not caged anymore. Her hand reached for the pendant Bellator had returned to her—modeled after the one left behind in Gravenmoor. She pressed it to her chest, her lips trembling, her voice low: "I still love him..." She let go of a breath, sharp and shuddered. "And I'm going to get her out."

The tower of Astrael—jewel of the Celestial Order—was burning. Ash drifted like snow from the highest sanctum as the final flames died down. Magic runes that had lasted centuries now flickered and sparked like broken candlelight. The divine wards were gone.

The High Council stood in stunned silence beneath a fractured dome. The air was thick with the stench of smoke and failure. "The spire has fallen," whispered the High Seer, her voice hollow.

The Archmage of Utheron gritted his teeth. "It was him."

Astralhart stood near the shattered scrying pool, his hands shaking at his sides. "And he wrote her name in fire."

"He's calling her," one mage said.

"He's forcing her to choose," a seer stated in reply.

Astralhart said nothing. Because he knew...that fire had reached her. And she would burn to follow it.

Several days had passed, but the fires in the sky still haunted Alexandria. By day, she wore her royal mask—her head high, her voice calm, speaking with generals, inspecting reports, offering reassurances to lords whose hands shook more than their swords. By night...she paced. Sleepless. Heart aching. The vision of the burning Celestial Spire never left her. The sigil scorched into the sky. Erythyn's presence, undeniable, uncontainable, alive.

But more than anything, it was the absence of Bellator that carved the deepest wound. Every time she looked at her door, she expected Bellator to be there—silent and strong, as she had always been. And every time... nothing. *She came back for me, and I let them take her.*

Alexandria had spent every quiet moment since trying to devise a way into the dungeons without being discovered. The corridors were swarming with guards loyal to Astralhart. Her magic was still dampened by the wards he had placed "for her stability." The passageways she once roamed freely now felt like a gilded maze. She couldn't act yet. But she was watching. Calculating. Waiting. And then...the moment came.

It began with shouting then heavy footfalls—General Stormrend bursting through the war chamber doors like a thunderclap wrapped in armor. His cloak was torn, his blade unsheathed, dirt and blood on his gauntlets. "Astralhart," he barked, without preamble, "we've got movement at the eastern border."

The room fell still. "How many troops?" the Prime Minister asked coldly.

"Too many. Thousands," Stormrend growled. "Beasts, corrupted men, spectral battalions—carrying the mark of shadow and flame."

The sigil. Erythyn's mark.

"They crossed the last watchtower twenty minutes ago. If we don't mobilize now, they'll breach the outer valley by morning," Stormrend said.

Astralhart's jaw tightened. He turned away from the table, his cloak sweeping behind him like the shadow of a crumbling star. The war was here. "Summon the Grand Commanders," he ordered. "Send the full weight of the Dawnshire Legions to the eastern ridgeline. Hold the valley at all costs." He turned toward Stormrend, his eyes burning. "And I want a scrying veil placed over the castle. No portals. No summons. We cut him off from everything."

Stormrend nodded and strode out, already barking orders. But Astralhart wasn't finished. His gaze shifted to the chamber doors where Alexandria stood, having just entered—silent, watching, listening. She stepped forward, cautious. "What's happening?"

"The war has arrived," Astralhart said simply. "And so has the danger to you." He gave a soft sigh, as if this decision was difficult. "For your protection, you'll be escorted to the lower sanctum until the threat is neutralized."

Alexandria's eyes narrowed. "The lower sanctum...?"

"Guarded. Sealed. Safe. The Dungeons."

Her breath caught. "You're locking me away."

"I'm protecting you," he said sharply. "If we fall...he'll come here first. I won't let him find you."

Part of her wanted to resist. To scream. To run. But another part... understood. If they took her to the dungeon—if they escorted her down there themselves—it might be the only way to reach Bellator. A risk, yes. But an opportunity too. So she nodded, reluctantly. Her eyes cast downward. Her voice quiet. "If it keeps the kingdom safe."

Astralhart studied her, as if searching for rebellion. But she gave him none. Just enough grace to hide the fire building in her bones.

The descent into the under levels of Castle Solara was cold and long. The guards said nothing as they escorted her down the winding staircases. Their armor clinked softly. The torches hissed. All the while, Alexandria kept her breath steady—counting turns, memorizing guard placements, noting which key ring opened which door. When they reached the final stone corridor, her escort unlocked a cell—not harsh, but regal in its own way. It was fitted with enchanted locks. Glowing runes. A sealed ward in the ceiling. A cage. Polished, pretty, but still a cage. As the guards turned to leave, Alexandria took one final glance down the corridor—toward the older cells. Toward where Bellator might be held. And for the first time in days, she smiled.

I'm close.

The dungeons beneath Castle Solara were carved into the mountain itself—cold, damp, and buried far beneath the light. No windows. No warmth. No time. Bellator had stopped marking the days. There was no sun to rise. No stars to chase. Just stone. Iron. Silence. And chains.

Her cell was simple—more a containment chamber than a prison. Carved with druid-lock runes, reinforced with dampening glyphs that kept her power low, her senses dulled. The floor was cold. The walls bore old blood. Her armor had been stripped, her wolf-form bound by ancient talismans that hung from the ceiling like relics of fear. Still...she endured. Because she had faced worse. Because Alexandria was still out there. She whispered her name sometimes, just to remember what it felt like on her tongue.

But tonight—something shifted. The air. The silence. The weight around her. Bellator lifted her head. The guards outside her cell had changed rotation. Their boots were lighter. Their breath...tense. And deeper in the corridor, behind thick walls and a sealed door of gold-etched oak—

She felt it. A heartbeat. Faint. Familiar. Sacred. *Alexandria.*

Bellator rose slowly from the floor. Her knees cracked from disuse. Her muscles ached from stillness. But her eyes... They lit with fire. "She's here," she whispered to herself. "She's finally here."

The guards didn't notice her shift. They rarely looked at her anymore. She moved to the edge of her cell and pressed a hand against the cold stone wall that separated her from the main corridor. "Alex..." No sound in return. But she didn't need it. She felt the warmth in her bones—like a spark that refused to die. Bellator began to prepare. In silence. In darkness. In chains. She tested the ward lines. Measured the cracks in the stone. Recalled every pressure point of the door's enchanted lock. Because if Alexandria was here...

Then freedom wasn't far behind.

The chamber Alexandria had been given in the lower sanctum was not a prison, not officially. It was furnished—cushioned bed, soft rugs, a basin of magically warmed water, and even a warded mirror. But every inch of it pulsed with containment.

She paced like a caged lion. Guards stood just beyond the sealed door. They said nothing, but she could hear their weight shifting when she got too close. The walls were enchanted, the ceiling covered in scrying runes. She could barely feel the air magic flow anymore—her spells reduced to whispers. But still...she waited. Listened. Hoped. Please let her be near.

It had been two days since they brought her down here. Two days without a sign. Until now. Tonight, the air was different—denser, more electric. The guards were less focused. A shift change? A flaw in rotation? She moved to the wall across from her bed. Not the door—the back wall, old stone, part of the castle's original structure. Unenchanted. Ancient. She pressed her ear against it. Nothing. Then—a sound. Soft. Faint. But deliberate. Tap. Tap. Pause. Tap-tap-tap.

Alexandria's breath caught in her throat. She backed up one step. No one else knew that rhythm. That pattern. It was the same one Bellator used as a child to call her during council meetings when she couldn't speak out loud. She stepped closer, pressing her hand to the stone. Tap. Tap. Pause. Tap-tap-tap.

A smile—small, broken, overwhelmed—spread across her face. She replied with her knuckles: Tap-tap. Tap. Tap. Confirmation. I hear you. I'm here. From the other side, she could imagine Bellator standing, pressing her own hand to the wall, just as she did now. And in the silence that followed, Alexandria whispered to the stone: "Hold on, Bell. I'm coming." She drew back slowly, her heart pounding, fire stirring again in her chest. Now she knew where Bellator was. Now... The escape could begin.

Chapter 28
Reunion in the Dark

The Lost Text of Twilight Wrath

When tempest eyes unleash their pain,

The stars weep blood upon the plain.

Beware the winds that howl your name,

They prey on pride & stroke the flame.

*T*he scent of blood and smoke clung to the edges of the council chamber. Stormrend's armor was scorched. His brow glistened with sweat. He didn't wait for the ceremony as he shoved open the doors.

Astralhart stood by the great window overlooking the eastern fields, his knuckles pressed to the war table, the map beneath him aglow with flickering magical threads. But one thread had gone dark.

Stormrend's voice rang like a hammer: "They've breached the outer line."

Astralhart turned, slow and sharp. "What?"

"The second ridge fell an hour ago. And the ward-stone at Redwatch just shattered. The valley is gone."

Gasps rippled through the remaining strategists. The map shimmered as new sigils pulsed—red and angry—marking a rapid advance. Stormrend strode forward. "Whatever Erythyn is leading, it's not just an army. It's a force of nature. Our soldiers are breaking. Some are turning mad. They say he's walking through fire and shadow like death."

Astralhart's face darkened. "Then we strike harder."

"Then we fall faster," Stormrend snapped. "If you're still thinking we can contain this—"

"We have to." Astralhart looked up, his eyes hardening. "Send the Dragon Guard. Summon the High Phoenixes. Burn the entire corridor if you must. But hold the castle." His mind raced. Erythyn was no longer posturing. He was coming. And Alexandria...was the one thing he still did have control over.

Down in the dungeon, the wall was still warm beneath Alexandria's hand where Bellator had tapped the night before. She'd barely slept since. Now, as the guards above grew more distracted—responding to the rising panic in the upper halls—she moved.

Alexandria slipped a hairpin from her braid. She knelt beside the wall, whispering ancient syllables she barely remembered from the scrolls Bellator once made her study. *"Serran'thor valyn...* Untie the lock beneath stone and silence..."

The rune etched on the wall shimmered—barely. A crack formed. Progress. She moved fast, pulling the edge of the rug back, revealing a shallow service tunnel behind a grate hidden beneath decades of dust. One guard outside her door yelled something, then vanished down the hallway. The castle was distracted. It was now or never.

She slipped the grate open, crawling into the narrow space, every motion controlled and silent. Her hands scraped against the stone. Her heartbeat thundered in her ears. She emerged behind an old root-covered column deep in the prison hall, watching the guards at the far end now gathering in confusion—clearly called for emergency deployment. And then, she saw her—Bellator. Chained. Pale. But standing tall in the faint torchlight. Their eyes met across the distance. No words. Just purpose. Alexandria ducked back into the shadows. "You stayed alive for me," Bellator had once said. Now it was her turn to return the vow.

The torches flickered violently as Alexandria crept forward through the narrow passage. Her breath was shallow. Her palms were scraped raw from crawling through the stone-choked tunnel. Dirt clung to her robes. But her eyes—alive, defiant—never wavered. She crouched beside the final wall separating her from Bellator's cell. The guards at the far end of the corridor were gone now, summoned upward by the chaos rumbling through the castle's higher halls. Only two remained. One paced nervously, his fingers twitching near his hilt. The other stared blankly ahead, too rattled by the distant horns and shaking floors to notice the shadow near the corner.

Alexandria whispered into her palm, clutching a stolen sliver of sunstone glass. *"Sonn'thar...* I call the light of hidden truths." The crystal pulsed once. Then, the enchanted hinges of Bellator's cell clicked.

Bellator's head snapped up, her eyes wide. The door creaked open slowly, barely louder than a breath.

Alexandria stepped inside, and for a moment, they just looked at each other. No words.

Bellator's eyes welled with emotion but they did not fall. Then she whispered, "You came."

Alexandria nodded, swallowing the lump in her throat. "Let's get out before this place collapses."

They moved quickly. Bellator retrieved the talismans that bound her druid form, shattering them in one swift motion. Magic flared across her skin like wildfire returning to the forest. "I'm ready," she said. But before Alexandria could speak again, the world above screamed.

The veil cracked like thunder across a silent sky. From the northern mountain ridge, where nothing but wardlight once flickered in soft constellations, a wave of black and gold exploded outward like a star collapsing in on itself. Soldiers near the boundary were thrown back. The skies above Castle Solara turned red, the clouds catching fire as Erythyn breached the ancient defenses—the Aetherian Lock, centuries old, meant to protect the royal line from invasion. It shattered in a single moment. The fire took the shape of wings. The shadow followed like a second sun eclipsing the first.

Astralhart, standing on the citadel balcony, stared into the storm rising at the edge of the kingdom. A horn blasted below—one of the royal watch towers. Then came the roar of spellfire. And in the heart of the chaos, cutting through reality like a blade through silk, Erythyn walked through, wreathed in stormlight, a dozen of his spectral lieutenants at his side, his armor glowing with runes of fury and grief. At his back, the sky corrupted. At his feet, the ground melted. He raised his hand, and the northern gate collapsed in a spiral of screaming metal and scorched earth.

But Erythyn was never there...

Far beneath the mountain pass, deep in the roots of Solara, a second shadow moved through an unmarked canyon, cloaked not in flame, but in silence. The real Erythyn. The image at the front line? A conjured doppelgänger, crafted through forbidden soul-casting, bound to mimic every gesture and power signature of his own essence. It bled magic. It burned with his wrath. And the kingdom believed every flicker. It was meant to be believed because Erythyn knew Alexandria wouldn't be in a throne room when he came. She would be hidden. Locked beneath stone and sanctity. The Dungeons.

He moved like smoke in the dark, slipping between cracks in the old walls, each footfall barely a whisper. The castle's subterranean wards were weakened by chaos above. Screams echoed from distant towers. Fires rose in the hills. And none noticed the true danger sliding beneath their feet.

"I'm coming for you," he whispered. "And I will tear down the roots of this mountain to do it."

The walls trembled from the impact above—dust drifting down like falling ash. Bellator, finally freed from her cell, steadied Alexandria against the rumbling stone as another tremor shook the floor. "That's not just a siege," Bellator murmured, her eyes sharp and haunted. "That's Erythyn."

Alexandria stared down the corridor, hearing the cries above—magical wards shrieking, the roar of unnatural fire, the boom of collapsing gates. "He's giving us a chance," she breathed. "This...this is the distraction."

Together, they crept down the corridor, past cracked pillars and shattered archways. The guards had fled or fallen. The sanctum had become a grave of silence, broken only by the distant sounds of war above. But just as they neared the last gate leading toward the servant tunnels—he appeared. Not from ahead. From behind them. From the dark. Erythyn. The real one.

No flames. No wings. Just him—his armor dusted in earth, his eyes like burning metal, standing at the threshold of their escape. Alexandria froze. Bellator's hand went for her blade—but Erythyn raised one hand in peace. His voice cracked the silence like lightning in a still forest. "Alexandria."

Her breath caught. "Erythyn."

The flickering torchlight painted trembling shadows across the ancient stone walls of the lower sanctum. Dust still swirled in the air from the battle above, but in this moment, in this corridor hidden from the eyes of kings and gods—time stood still.

Alexandria stared at him, her heart pounding in her chest. He wasn't the illusion in the sky. He wasn't a dream or vision. He had returned to their time. He was real. And he was here. Not fire and fury. No armor glowing with divine wrath. Just Erythyn—breathing hard, sweat on his brow, battle-dust clinging to him like shadows that had chased him from another realm. His eyes locked onto her mesmerizing golden eyes, and for a moment, nothing else mattered. The war. The kingdom.

"You're alive," he breathed softly, as if afraid the words would shatter if spoken too loud.

Alexandria blinked through the heat behind her eyes, her throat tightening with a thousand unsaid things. "You made it back!"

He took one step forward, hesitant, as if crossing an invisible threshold. "I thought they'd...broken you. That they'd taken you and buried you beneath duty and memory."

"They tried," she said, her voice raw.

He flinched.

Bellator stepped back quietly, lowering her head—not from submission, but from respect. This wasn't her moment. It was theirs.

Alexandria took a step forward now, pain in every movement. "I tried to forget you. I tried to believe the Order. That you were gone. That you'd turned."

"And I did," he whispered. "I turned into the only thing they feared enough to leave me alone. But I never stopped searching. Every breath... every strike I landed...every fortress I burned—it was all to get back to you."

Her voice cracked. "And you still started a war."

He stepped closer. "I was already at war. With myself. With the gods. With this kingdom that keeps choosing fear over truth." He reached out —hesitantly—as if unsure if she'd let him. She didn't stop him. His hand brushed her cheek, rough and trembling. "You never left me," he said.

"Even when I wanted to let go." A single tear escaped down her cheek. Her lips trembled. "I don't know if I could forgive you," she whispered.

"I don't expect you to," he responded.

"But I never stopped loving you," she said as she looked into his eyes.

That broke him. His forehead touched hers, his breath shuddering against her skin. He closed his eyes. She closed hers. And for the first time since the world tore them apart, they breathed as one.

The warmth of Erythyn's hand on Alexandria's cheek was more grounding than any magic. Their foreheads pressed together in quiet desperation, as though the mere contact might stitch together the time, blood, and shattered promises between them. No more illusions. No more walls. For that fragile heartbeat, nothing existed beyond the damp, flickering corridor—the smell of stone and soot, the tremble in their chests as every emotion boiled beneath the surface.

Alexandria let her hand rise slowly to rest over his, her fingers curling around the familiar weight. His palm was rough, blistered, still warm from the crawl through the depths of the castle. "I thought I lost you," she whispered.

"You did," he said, barely audible. "But I clawed my way back for you."

She almost kissed him. Almost. But then a voice, sharp and low, broke the moment like steel cracking against stone. "We don't have time,"

Bellator said.

She stood a few paces away, tense as a drawn bow, her gaze locked on the passage behind them. The torches were flickering faster now, reacting to rising magical pressure. She stepped forward. "Whatever this is—it isn't over. If Astralhart realizes what's really happening, we'll be surrounded within minutes."

Alexandria turned reluctantly, her voice steadier than she felt. "You're right. Let's go."

Erythyn gave one final glance—one final tether of his soul to hers—then turned, his expression returning to that of the silent, lethal shadow who had clawed through the darkness to find her.

Chapter 29
Tunnels Destroyed

Candide of the Sundering Dawn

At day's first breath the heavens split in two,

The Sunblade's edge shall pierce the Shadow's hue.

One half of flame, One half of haunted night,

And claim the dark to temper truth with light.

*T*he war chamber above was in disarray. A crowd of officers, seers, and high spellcasters had gathered around the smoking remains of the captured figure. The one they believed was Erythyn.

The doppelgänger—his face half-melted from spellfire, armor cracked—lay on the obsidian platform at the center of the circle. His chest no longer rose. His illusion had degraded just moments after being bound in celestial shackles.

Astralhart stood still as frost. One of the arcanists, still covered in soot, whispered, "It's not him."

Another voice added, "The essence is collapsing. It was conjured. Bound to mimic, but it's unraveling."

Astralhart's stare sharpened into something jagged and inhuman. "No."

He stepped forward, gripping the edge of the stone platform. "He walked through fire. He tore the gate down. I saw it."

"You saw what he wanted you to see," a dreamseer said, her voice trembling. "A weapon meant to buy time."

One of the generals shouted over the crowd. "Then where is the real Erythyn?!"

No one answered because they all knew it was too late. Far too late.

Below, the tunnel entrance, once sealed by rust and memory, now stood open. Alexandria led the way, her royal robes tucked beneath a leather belt, her eyes forward and burning with new resolve. Bellator followed, her weapons in hand, scanning every corner. Erythyn moved like a shadow behind them—silently, protectively, a specter returned not to conquer, but to reclaim what had been stolen from him.

Up above, the chaos intensified. Magical wards flared. Orders were shouted. The real alarms had begun. They knew, and now the hunt was on.

As the trio disappeared into the winding stone corridors beneath the castle—one toward rebellion, one toward redemption, one toward a love that never died—the mountain itself seemed to groan with the weight of fate. And somewhere far above, in the crumbling sanctuary of war and prophecy, Astralhart whispered a single word that rang like a curse: "Alexandria."

They rushed through the tunnel, the walls curved like the ribs of a long-dead beast—twisting through the oldest bones of Castle Solara, where the magic was raw and wild, untouched by the Order's purifying spells. Alexandria held a flickering torch in hand, her other pressed against the damp stone wall as they hurried deeper. The air was tight, choked with dust and the echo of footsteps not taken in generations.

Behind her, Bellator moved in sync—blades drawn, every sense alert. Her druidic magic, slowly returning now that the suppressing wards were behind them, pulsed faintly beneath her skin.

Bringing up the rear, Erythyn walked like a wolf untethered, fire still faintly licking at the edges of his armor. He glanced back once, toward the corridor they had come from. "The wards are shifting," he murmured.

"He knows." Bellator cursed under her breath. "We have minutes."

"The end of this tunnel," Alexandria said, panting, "leads to the Moonroot Cavern—an old druidic garden under the castle. If we can reach it, we can use the leyline to open a portal out."

"Let's move," Erythyn responded.

They ran. As they did, Alexandria glanced at Erythyn, her voice low. "You risked everything coming here."

"I would have burned down the stars," he said, "if they kept you from me one more night."

She said nothing—but her fingers tightened on the torch.

Right above them, the council chamber was in chaos. Magical alarms pulsed from the walls like the heartbeat of a dying god. Scrolls of divine architecture crumbled to ash as the realization spread: They had been fooled.

Astralhart stood in the center of it all, his hands spread over the circular seal built into the floor—a massive sun-shaped rune etched with ancient text forbidden even to the High Order.

"What are you doing?" cried the Arch-Seer.

"They're in the lower sanctum," Astralhart said. "The princess. The druid. And him."

"You'll bring the mountain down!"

"I'll bury them in the bones of the kingdom if I must." He reached into his cloak and pulled out a long, pale key made of lightstone and blood-iron, forged by his ancestors to protect the realm through any means. "Failsafe Protocol: Solstice Falls."

"No!" one of the younger mages gasped. "That spell hasn't been used since the Tides of Night. If it fails, it'll rupture the entire leyline!"

Astralhart didn't blink. He slid the key into the seal. The sun-rune glowed. And the earth screamed.

A sound began as a groan—deep and wet, like the belly of the mountain mourning its own death. Then came the crack, a jagged shudder that split the tunnel just behind them. Chunks of the ceiling rained down, and the air grew thick with choking, ancient dust.

Bellator yanked Alexandria back just as a stone the size of a throne crashed beside her. "He's collapsing the sanctum!" she shouted.

"No," Erythyn growled. "He's trying to bury us." Magic surged through him, heat curling in his chest. "Keep moving!"

Alexandria led the way again, coughing through the smoke, her fingers glowing faintly as she summoned an old light-sphere spell Bellator taught her as a child.

The tunnel was narrowing. Cracks opened beneath their feet. They raced forward, leaping over gaps and ducking falling stones. Up ahead—light. A circular arch carved into moonstone, veined with ivy fossilized by time: the entrance to the Moon Root Cavern. But a final quake knocked the ground sideways—Alexandria stumbled. Stone cracked beneath her.

"Alex!" Erythyn shouted, diving forward. He caught her just as the floor gave way, and the two of them slammed into the edge, Bellator grabbing Erythyn's wrist, Erythyn grabbing Alexandria's cloak. Grunting, trembling, they pulled her up—together. Behind them, the tunnel was gone. Swallowed in fire and stone.

They lay there for a moment in the cavern's threshold, panting, bleeding, blinking at the glowing roots pulsing around them like veins in a sleeping god.

Alexandria coughed out dust and stared at the ceiling then laughed out of shock—wild, breathless, and shaking. "They tried to kill us!"

"Yes," Erythyn said, eyes glowing, "they did."

Bellator sat back against a stone, breathing hard. "We need to open the portal."

Alexandria nodded, already pulling the sigil-scroll from the folds of her tunic—the one Bellator had given her before the betrayal, just in case. She turned to Erythyn. "Ready to run?"

He reached for her hand. "Always."

The air was sharp with burnt stone and unraveling wards. Cracks spiderwebbed across the walls of the Council Sanctum, the aftershock of the failsafe still humming through the bones of the castle like a mourning song. Astralhart stood motionless before the great scrying mirror, its surface fractured but functional, shimmering with golden static. He watched as rubble settled, dust coiled, and for a brief moment, it looked as if nothing remained in the bowels of Solara. Then the mirror pulsed. A flare of moonlight. A heartbeat of ley-magic. Movement.

The spell picked up a faint silhouette—no, three. Alive. Rising through glowing roots in a chamber the failsafe was never meant to touch. The Moonroot Cavern. He stared, his eyes narrowing, every line on his face etched deeper by disbelief and fury. "They made it out."

The High Arcanist at his side swallowed. "Impossible. That spell collapsed three levels of stone, redirected the leyline, and destroyed the bloodlocks. Nothing survives that."

"She did," Astralhart growled. "They all did." He stepped back from the mirror, pacing like a panther in a gilded cage. His cloak dragged embers as it swept the scorched floor. "They're trying to escape. There's only one path from there—Moonroot leads to the outer circle of the Verdant Gate."

"And if they make it through?"

Astralhart turned, slowly. "Then Solara falls. Not by his fire...but by her choice." He reached into the runed case beneath the scrying table and withdrew a dagger older than the crown. A soulbound relic forged by the first bloodline of Dawnshire—a blade that could cut not only flesh, but fate. His voice was cold steel. "Prepare the Null Sigil and open the vault. I'm invoking the Rite of Final Authority."

The arcanists froze. "That spell's never been cast in living memory —"

"It doesn't need memory. It needs power." Astralhart's gaze turned toward the mountain's heart. "Find them. If the cavern holds even a whisper of leyline magic, we still have time." His voice dropped to a whisper, not to them, but to himself. "You will not leave, Alexandria. I will seal the world shut before I let him have you."

Chapter 30
Binding Oath and Broken Chains

Verse of the Shadowed Heart

Evil blooms where hope wilted long,

Yet even in that void, a distant song.

It's petals inked in sorrow's deepest well,

Summons the light to break the final spell.

The cavern pulsed with ancient light. Glowing vines curled around pillars of fossilized oak and crystal bark while water trickled from the ceiling in streams of silver. The walls breathed softly—alive, aware. This place was not simply hidden—it was forgotten on purpose.

The three fugitives stumbled into its center, covered in dust and blood. Alexandria dropped to her knees and spread the scroll out over a circular stone dais etched with faded sigils. The ground beneath them still trembled from aftershocks, but the magic here—this place of druidic origin—remained pure.

Bellator was already drawing protective runes in the soil with her blade, whispering to the ancient forest spirits.

Erythyn stood back, keeping watch, his piercing eyes narrowed. The fire along his armor dimmed to embers, but his magic still shimmered around him like smoke waiting to ignite. "We don't have long," he said. "The failsafe was only the beginning."

"Then we open this portal now," Alexandria replied, sweat glistening down her neck. "No matter what it takes." She placed her hand over the sigil-stone in the dais. The glyphs on the parchment pulsed once...then again...then began to lift from the paper like floating threads of light. Tether magic. Root magic. Druid-royal hybrid casting—ancient, volatile, and true. The cavern began to hum.

Bellator's hands trembled over the last rune. "It's drawing power straight from the leyline. This will work. I know it will."

Alexandria gritted her teeth. "Then let it." But suddenly—a shift. The runes on the outer edge of the dais flared red, interrupted by a jagged crack through the earth.

Astralhart's interference.

From far above, a thin pulse of null magic filtered down—a deathspell woven into the leyline itself, reaching with the quiet hunger of a blade made to sever worlds.

Erythyn's head snapped upward. "He's trying to cut the line—collapse the leyflow before the portal can stabilize."

"We're too close," Bellator hissed. "If it falls now—this entire cavern will cave in."

Alexandria's voice trembled, but not with fear. With fire. "No. I didn't come all this way to fall back into his chains." She stepped into the circle fully, raising her hands.

Erythyn moved beside her. "What are you doing?"

"Channeling it manually. Drawing the gate from my blood."

"That'll burn you out."

"Then let it." Her eyes met his.

"Let this cost me. Just not you."

Together, they planted their hands on the sigil at the center of the dais. The entire cavern lit like dawn.

A ring of vines burst into life, flowering with silver and violet blooms. The stone beneath their feet cracked—not from collapse, but from awakening. A circular gate opened in the air—an arched portal of swirling light and rootfire, humming with magic not felt since the first age. It was open. But behind them, the mountain screamed one final time. And a shockwave of null energy burst downward. "GO!" Bellator yelled. "I'll hold it—"

"No you won't," Alexandria said, grabbing her wrist. "We leave together."

Erythyn turned, his eyes glowing like twin suns. "Let the world collapse behind us." And with one final breath—they leapt.

The High Sanctum was eerily still. Smoke curled from the fractured scrying pool. Magical sigils on the walls pulsed dimly, flickering between gold and red—like a heartbeat losing rhythm. Cracks ran like veins across the marble floor, splitting the rune-circle at the center. Astralhart stood motionless in the silence, his hands at his sides, blood trickling from his left palm where the soul-key had bitten too deeply during the failsafe ritual. His jaw was tight. His cloak hung torn at the edges. But his eyes... burned.

Across the far wall, a projection hovered in the air—an echo of the Moonroot Portal, fading fast, the last image it captured before it closed in a burst of white-blue light: Alexandria. Bellator.   And Erythyn. Disappearing together. Astralhart's fist clenched.

Around the room, his advisors and arcanists stood in terrified silence, none daring to speak. The Order had long known him as cold. Commanding. Ruthless when necessary. But this—this silence was different. It was volcanic.

Finally, he turned toward the mirror. "Where are they now?"

The seer assigned to portal-tracing stammered, "Th-the gate blurred beyond the outer ley boundaries. Somewhere in the Veiled South, but... It's protected. Druidic shielding. We can't track them."

Another mage tried to speak. "We can send scouts—"

"No," Astralhart snapped. "He'll feel them before they're within a league. And she'll hide. She's good at hiding...now."

He walked to the war table. His hands hovered above the star-map then slammed down with a force that cracked its surface. "They escaped everything." His voice was low, venomous. "I bound her dreams. I severed their tether. I erased the prophecy from half the realm's records. I gave her purpose—I gave her a future! And she still...chose him." He turned slowly. "No more spells. No more armies. No more words."

One of the older dreambinders dared speak. "Then what remains, my Lord?"

Astralhart's eyes locked onto the man. "Blood." The room fell dead silent.

He strode to the chamber vault and retrieved a narrow, silver-bound tome from its case. It was ancient, locked in chains of ironwood and divine wax. The Codex of Binding Oaths, a book of unwritten pacts— contracts sealed in soul-thread and carried through bloodlines.

Forbidden. Forgotten. Buried. He placed the tome on the central pedestal and opened it. Inside, a single page had already begun to fill itself, ink bleeding upward from the bottom like roots stretching through bone. It bore Alexandria's name. "She is still bound to the realm," Astralhart whispered, his fingers trailing the page. "As long as she carries royal blood, I can invoke the chain."

Another mage stepped forward, his eyes wide. "The Rite of Sovereign Reclamation...that spell hasn't been used since the Cataclysm."

Astralhart smiled thinly. "She was born of the crown. She still carries the oath in her veins. Which means..." He turned toward the shattered mirror, staring at the place she had vanished. "She'll come back, or I'll make her wish she had."

The Moonroot Portal collapsed behind them with a shriek of wind and white-blue light. For a moment, there was nothing but weightlessness—no sky, no ground, no form. And then—impact.

They tumbled into a world heavy with warmth and silence. Alexandria hit the mossy ground first, breath knocked from her lungs, followed by Bellator, rolling smoothly into a crouch. Erythyn landed last, his boots cracking a stone, his blade half-drawn as he scanned the area. They weren't being followed.

The air was thick with moisture and magic. Twilight clung to the sky in hues of deep violet and amber. The sun here looked different—larger, softer, its light filtered through drifting fog and towering trees that seemed to breathe. They had landed in the heart of the Veiled South—a realm ancient beyond reckoning, hidden from celestial tracking by druidic warding and leyline distortion. Even the Order's deepest scrying spells had only ever glimpsed its edges.

"Where...are we?" Alexandria asked, her voice raw.

Bellator stood slowly, brushing off brambles. Her eyes scanned the surroundings. "The Weeping Glade."

Alexandria blinked. "You've been here?"

"Once. A long time ago. This land is wild, sacred. Untamed magic lives here. No cities. No armies. Only the old things that never died."

"Then we're safe?" Erythyn asked, glancing upward at the slow-drifting canopy.

Bellator shook her head. "No. Never safe. Just...unseen."

Erythyn helped Alexandria to her feet. She winced, touching her ribs as if they were possibly bruised or broken. The pulse of the royal blood magic still hummed faintly in her skin. It was apparent that Astralhart had done something. The pressure hadn't stopped with the portal's collapse. "He's going to come after me," she whispered.

Erythyn looked at her, gently gripping her shoulder. "Then we don't stop moving."

As they ventured deeper into the southern woods, the environment began to change. The trees became taller than cathedrals, their bark glowing faintly with bioluminescent veins. Birds with translucent wings flew overhead in flocks of silence. Strange creatures—half-plant, half-spirit—watched from the underbrush with blinking gemstone eyes. But the beauty was laced with warning. The deeper they walked, the more Alexandria felt it—a presence, not malicious, but ancient. Something was watching. "Ley spirits," Bellator murmured. "Guardians. The forest doesn't like outsiders. We'll need shelter before nightfall."

"There," Erythyn pointed ahead. "Stone ruins. Covered in vines."

They emerged into a clearing where a crumbling archway of blackstone and silverwood stood partially sunken into the earth. A broken sigil above the arch faintly resembled the crest of the First Druid Kings—a sanctuary site.

Bellator approached cautiously. "This'll shield us from scrying. Maybe even from the oath tether—if we don't stay long."

They moved inside. The ruins had no roof, only ancient stone walls and moss-covered platforms where once an altar stood. Wildflowers grew between the cracks. The wind here was silent.

Alexandria slumped to sit against the wall, exhaling deeply. "For the first time in weeks... I don't feel the chains." Bellator checked the perimeter, while Erythyn remained near the arch, a hand on his blade. The silence was deafening. It was too still.

Far above, through layers of magic and land, Astralhart sat in ritual meditation, the Codex of Binding Oaths open before him. He had traced the last echo of Alexandria's ley signature—felt it vanish like breath into fog. But now, as he whispered her name, as the blood-magic hummed to life between the sigil pages, her tether twitched. He smiled.

"You're still connected to the land," he murmured. "Which means..." He reached into a carved blackwood box beside the pedestal and withdrew a soul-threaded charm, bound with strands of Alexandria's childhood hair—taken when she was just five and locked within a memory ward. He held it to the flame. "Come home."

It started as a whisper beneath her skin. Alexandria, curled in the soft moss of the ruins, her eyes half-closed, tried to focus on the sounds of the forest—the gentle chirr of insects, the wind threading through the high canopy, the rhythmic drip of water down the stone wall beside her. But the hum inside her chest grew louder. It wasn't a heartbeat. It wasn't a breath. It was a pull.

Her fingers curled unconsciously into the dirt as her back arched with a sudden shiver, her eyes snapping open to the glowing sky overhead.

"No..." she breathed. The tether—the ancient, sovereign-blood enchantment Astralhart had bound to her lineage—was stirring again. She could feel it weaving through her bones, tugging on the leyline beneath her feet, trying to lure her upward like a marionette caught in the current of a spell not her own.

But this was different. More primal. More direct.

He knows I'm alive.

Across the ruin, Bellator snapped her head around just as Alexandria stumbled to her knees.

Erythyn was already beside her. "What is it?" he asked, crouching low, his voice a quiet rumble.

She clenched her jaw, eyes wet. "The tether. It found me."

Bellator was at her side in seconds. "The Codex of Binding Oaths."

"He's using my blood," Alexandria gasped. "Calling me back like a dog on a leash."

Erythyn's eyes blazed. "I'll sever it."

"You can't." Bellator gritted her teeth. "Not without killing her."

Alexandria looked between them—torn, trembling, then furious. "No. We stop running. We end it. We break the chain."

"But not here," Bellator said. "Not without help."

While Alexandria rested, Bellator and Erythyn had swept the outer perimeter, following the faint ley-threads that pulsed through the ground like roots made of light. They paused beneath a giant fallen tree, its base fused with crystal growth and hollowed like an arch. Bellator raised a hand. "Feel that?" Erythyn nodded. The air was too still but heavy—like they were being watched.

A low rustling echoed from the deeper woods, not from wind, but movement. A rustle of moss, bark, and bone. From behind the overgrown stones, it stepped into view. A guardian. Not humanoid. Not beast. Its body was woven of ancient branches, cloaked in vines, crowned with a mantle of bark shaped like antlers. Its eyes glowed a soft silver-blue, pools of memory, not light. It stood taller than any of them, unmoving, its arms of root and rune hanging low at its sides.

Bellator fell to one knee, her head bowed. "Warden of the Veil... I didn't think any of you still lived."

The creature's voice echoed through the ground more than the air—a language of wind and wood, but Bellator understood.

"*You bring danger. One cursed by flame. One burdened by prophecy. One sought by the chain-maker.*"

Erythyn stiffened, his hand gripping his blade. "I didn't come to harm your realm."

"*Yet your shadow cuts into it like the axe of the old kings.*"

Bellator stood, slow and steady. "We seek refuge. And a way to break what binds her."

The guardian turned its gaze toward the distant ruins. Its voice shook the roots beneath them. "*The blood-oath is awakening the old path. If the chain is not severed soon, it will tear the Veil apart—and awaken what sleeps beneath the forest's skin.*"

Erythyn frowned. "What does that mean?"

The guardian raised a branchlike hand and pointed toward the southern horizon, where the trees turned black, twisted, ancient. "*You seek to sever what binds her? Then you must find the one who forged the first vow—the Wyrmsinger.*"

Bellator inhaled sharply. "That thing's real?"

"*It dreams beneath the Hollowheart Grove. But if awoken too late, it will not grant her freedom... It will demand a cost. A pause. Then the guardian leaned forward, its bark creaking. The forest will help you—for now. But hurry. The oath-bearer moves against you still. He seeks not only her soul...but her return.*"

Then the guardian dissolved into petals of glowing bark and vanished into the wind.

Bellator and Erythyn returned, their breath tight and words grave. Alexandria's gaze sharpened. "You found something," she said as she stood tall again, though her knees trembled.

Bellator nodded. "A guardian. It spoke of a creature that might help us break the chain—the Wyrmsinger."

Alexandria's expression changed. "Where is it?"

"Deep south. Hollowheart Grove. No roads. No wards. Just forest—and what sleeps beneath it." Erythyn stepped closer, his voice low. "We go tonight. The tether's calling. He knows you're slipping away."

She met his gaze, fire in hers again. "Then let him feel me pull."

Night in the Veiled South was not like the rest of the world. Here, the sun did not simply set—it withdrew, folding itself behind layers of mist that turned gold, then blue, then shadow-wrapped violet. The trees thickened. The stars blinked through veils of branch and bloom, their light slow and hesitant, like eyes behind frosted glass.

The trio moved through the wild in silence. Bellator led the way, half-shifted into her druidic form—her eyes piercing like lightning, her hands half-clawed, and her senses extended far into the wood. The deeper they went, the more the trees whispered. Not just wind—but language, the breath of something ancient listening.

Erythyn, ever watchful, moved behind her, his fingers never far from his blade. The forest didn't like him. It twisted where he stepped, vines shying back from his boots. Yet it didn't attack—it watched, wary of the fire he carried inside.

Alexandria walked between them, her expression sharp with exhaustion and resolve. The tether in her blood still burned faintly—a thread that tugged like a forgotten promise. But she was learning to fight it. To anchor herself in the now. In Erythyn's steady presence. In Bellator's silent strength. In the promise that she would no longer be bound.

After hours of travel, the trees began to change. The bark turned black. The leaves grew wider, veined with red. The air turned humid and smelled of ash and moss. Strange lights drifted between trunks—too slow to be fireflies, too fluid to be will-o'-wisps. Hollowheart. At the center of the thickening wood stood a colossal tree, hollowed through the center like the ribcage of a fallen god. Its roots sprawled outward like veins. Pale stone steps carved into ancient wood led downward into a yawning spiral pit, lit only by faintly glowing lichen and the gentle vibration of power.

Bellator touched the bark and whispered a prayer in Druidic. "We're here."

Alexandria's throat tightened as she stepped onto the first root. A whisper echoed from the depths. One who carries an oath...walks willingly.

Meanwhile, in the chamber beneath Astralhart's tower that was not marked on any map and was hidden beneath the old sanctum—hollowed from the mountain's root, bound in saltstone and lined with spellsteel—sat a ring of broken mirrors, the Codex of Binding Oaths sat open, its ink running like veins across its final page.

Astralhart knelt before it, blood trailing from his nose, his eyes sunken and alight with madness. The ritual had gone too far. She had resisted the pull. Again. She was growing stronger. He had seen it in the flickers—her magic no longer waned. The forest was shielding her. But he could still taste her in the spellfire. She was not free. Not yet.

He rose, his teeth clenched, and strode to a black-wood altar at the back of the chamber. There, resting in a cradle of shadowlight, was a mask—silver and bone, its surface etched with Alexandria's first childhood drawing, copied from her nursery wall. A crude lion and sun, carved into the steel with unnatural precision. Beside it: a vial. A single tear collected from her on the day of her coronation, preserved in amber spellglass.

Astralhart lifted it carefully. "If you will not come to me—" He poured the tear into the mask. "Then I will send something you cannot turn away." The mask absorbed the liquid. It shuddered. It breathed. And from the shadows behind the altar, something began to form. A figure half-wrapped in veils, made of smoke and silk, bone and imitation. Its face shifted—smooth, clean. Then it began to take her shape.

Alexandria's shape. But not perfectly. A copy. A memory. A weapon. Its voice was hollow and innocent. "Who shall I become?"

Astralhart smiled, his eyes gleaming with unshed fury. "Her regret."

Chapter 31
The Wyrmsinger's Hollow

Liturgy of the Sunblade's Oath

I swear by dawn, by ember, by fire's core,

When night encroaches on the valiant shore.

To wield this blade against the creeping gloom,

My blade shall blaze, & shadows meet their doom.

*I*n Hollowheart, they descended in silence. The steps wound down into the hollow of the ancient tree—so deep the air shifted with every breath, growing denser, richer, and older. The light above faded behind them. Roots the size of towers twisted around the walls like the ribs of some long-dead titan.

As they reached the bottom, the tunnel opened into a wide chamber of pulsing amber light. There was no floor—only a network of massive, glowing root-bridges suspended in the air, hovering above an endless drop that shimmered with constellations. The walls were not stone, but bark and bone-like vines, each inscribed with oaths etched in forgotten languages—each glowing faintly, alive with breath and memory.

At the center of it all was a great cocoon, nestled within the roots like a sleeping dragon's heart. It pulsed with rhythm—a heartbeat made of oath and origin.

Bellator dropped to one knee and pressed her palm to the roots. "This is it. The Wyrmsinger dreams beneath."

Alexandria stepped forward, unable to breathe. The tether in her blood began to vibrate—not in pain, but in resonance. Her presence, her burden, was recognized. The cocoon cracked. And from within it, unfurling like a slow exhale, came a being unlike anything they had seen. It was not a wyrm, nor a spirit. Not quite beast, nor god. Its form shifted —serpentine, armored in overlapping bark and glass-like scale. Its face was eyeless, but crowned with a mane of drifting silks. As it emerged it sang, a song that hummed directly into their bones.

"Child of blood and broken light... You bear the chain."

Alexandria stepped into the halo of the Wyrmsinger's presence, her heart aching, her arms trembling. "I need it severed. I need to be free."

"Freedom is not given... It is earned."

Bellator bowed her head. "Then tell us how."

The creature drifted in the air, slow and enormous. "To sever the oath, the chain must be sung back into silence—unwritten by truth. One of you must speak her name into the wound of her own making."

Erythyn stepped forward. "I'll do it."

The Wyrmsinger turned its head toward him. "You are not blood. You are flame. You are not bound."

Alexandria whispered, "Then... I must."

The Wyrmsinger's song grew louder—not hostile, but sorrowful. "Then be warned. The wound will bleed. And what is unchained...will awaken more than just the chain-maker." A pause, then the being's massive form lowered its head to her. "Place your hand on my heart and call the truth by name."

Alexandria stepped forward. Her hand hovered above the glowing heart-root. But before she could touch it—

The wind tore through the high glade as something unnatural passed beneath the canopy. Not footsteps. Not wings. A drift of memory given form, wrapped in silver-veined silk and royal shadow. The Shadow-With-Her-Face. It walked without making a sound. Its skin was pale like mist. Its eyes were wide—her eyes, but empty, painted in the same gold that once crowned Alexandria on her coronation day. It did not speak. But it sang a soft lullaby that Alexandria's mother used to hum in the garden. "Stars above, stars so near...guard the heart I hold most dear..."

The creatures of the Veiled South shrank from it. The trees bent. The spirits howled, confused and afraid. Because this was not Erythyn's fire. This was something designed to be loved and meant to hurt when embraced. Inside its veins flowed Alexandria's tether—a direct echo of her pain, pulled from her tears and bound to the Codex's curse. It would not strike. It would not burn. It would whisper. It would make her doubt. And when it found her... It would kneel and say, "Come home, sister. I missed you."

She carried her tether—a carefully woven echo, infused with tear-magic, bound to the Codex that still glowed with Astralhart's sigils.

"Stars above, stars so near..." The song spilled from her lips in a hush. "Guard the heart I hold most dear." Creatures of the grove hissed. Birds flew crooked in the wrong direction. The wind around her no longer belonged to the south—it bent to the will of the Codex. She was a weapon crafted not from steel, but from longing. From comfort. From familiarity. And now she was close. Only hours from Hollowheart Grove.

The trees grew denser, but they no longer fought her. One by one, she passed ancient druidic wardstones—and the carvings on them began to change, warping to reflect the mark of Alexandria's aura. To the forest's perception, she was no longer a stranger. She was the returning daughter. And deep in the Wyrmsinger's sanctum, even the leyline trembled. Not in alarm...but in confusion. Because two versions of her now pulsed in the same weave. One true. One near-perfect.

As Alexandria's hand hovered above the Wyrmsinger's heart, she froze mid-motion. Her breath caught. Her body pulsed once—not from within. A whisper, far off. Her mother's voice. A song from the garden. She staggered back.

Bellator moved to her side, steadying her. "What is it?"

"I... I heard her," Alexandria whispered with sorrow.

Erythyn's eyes narrowed. "Your mother?"

Alexandria shook her head slowly. "Not exactly. A memory. But it was too clear. "

The Wyrmsinger stirred—its roots trembling, its eyes turning toward the surface. "A second tether has entered the glade."

Bellator stiffened. "What?"

"Another that sings the blood-oath. Almost her. Not her. But... enough to fool the threshold."

Erythyn's blade was drawn in a single motion. "A mimic?"

"No. Not mimic. Memory. Reflection. A chain given form."

Alexandria's face paled. "Astralhart."

The grove fell silent. All around the edges of the root-chamber, the wind died. The roots stopped breathing. Even the glowing amber lichen dimmed—flickering as though unsure whether to hide or bear witness. Alexandria turned sharply toward the entrance tunnel. And there—emerging from the mist-draped arch of blackened roots—she saw herself. Same hair. Same eyes. Same soft stride. Even the same faint scar near the corner of her brow. But the moment their eyes met, the hairs on the back of her neck stood tall. It wore her like a dress. And then it spoke. "I'm sorry," it said, smiling gently. "I was afraid. I know I ran, but I'm ready to come home now." The voice was hers. Not similar. Exact.

A chill ran down her spine as the Shadow took a step closer, barefoot, its hands folded in front of its chest like a penitent ghost. "You don't have to hide anymore. Let me help you carry it. We can go back. Just say the word."

Erythyn snarled. "Get behind me."

Alexandria didn't move. Her breath came in shallow gasps, her gaze locked on the creature as her own memories crashed against her like waves. Her mother's lullaby. The smell of royal garden roses. The sound of her childhood laughter echoed. It knew everything. It used everything.

"Alexandria," Bellator whispered, her blade half-raised. "It's not you."

The Shadow tilted its head—just like she did when confused. A perfect mirror. "You're tired. I know. He hurt you. They all did. Just come back, and you'll never be alone again."

Then—

The Wyrmsinger stirred. Its glowing heart pulsed brighter, light flooding the chamber. The roots cracked outward like ribs spreading in warning. Its voice boomed through the air, low and final. "This is not your echo. It is your leash given form."

The Shadow flinched—only for a moment.

"It wears your voice to silence you. It wears your memories to lead you astray. But it is not you."

Alexandria slowly raised her hand again, her body trembling.

"Sever the tether," Wyrmsinger intoned. "Speak your name into my heart and be free."

The Shadow stepped forward, faster now. "Don't—"

Alexandria's fingers touched the root-heart. "I am Alexandria of the bloodline Dawnborn. I sever what binds me. This voice is mine."

The roots surged with light. A shockwave of golden force slammed outward, hurling the Shadow from the archway. It screeched—not in pain, but in disbelief, like a child rejected by a parent for the first time. Its features distorted. The smile cracked. The flesh bubbled and blurred— shifting rapidly between younger versions of her face, teenage laughter, tear-stained eyes, coronation day joy. All of it stolen. All of it false. Then it dissolved into smoke and was gone.

Alexandria collapsed to one knee, her hand still glowing. Bellator rushed to her side, catching her as she swayed. Erythyn stood nearby, his eyes locked on the space where the thing had vanished, his jaw clenched. But the Wyrmsinger's heart remained open. Its voice softened—gentle now. "The chain is broken. Your soul is your own."

Roots began to rise from the ground, weaving in a circle of living bark and stone. Light pooled in its center—a portal, but not the kind made by men or spells. This one breathed. It was part of the world's root.

"Where shall I send you?"

Erythyn stepped forward, his eyes never leaving Alexandria. "Take us to my palace. The eastern wing. The untouched floor. No one knows its signature."

Bellator raised an eyebrow, surprised. "You kept it unmarked?"

He nodded once. "It's the one place she'll be safe for now. Let them search kingdoms and shadows—they won't find her there."

The Wyrmsinger's heart pulsed again. "So it shall be." The portal bloomed fully—woven of light, wood, and flame.

Alexandria stood slowly, her body still shaking, but her voice steady.

"Then we go together." The three stepped through. And as the portal sealed behind them, the root-chamber fell silent once more. Far above, the forest exhaled. And in the ashes of broken chains, the future twisted —unknown, untethered, and very much awake.

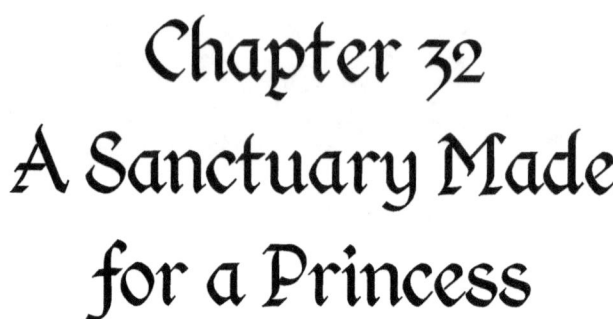

Chapter 32
A Sanctuary Made
for a Princess

Hymn of the Balanced Scales

Good & evil — twin wings of the soul,

For when the balance breaks, the world grows cold.

One must not soar without the other's weight,

& even brightness hearts succumb to fate.

T he Codex of Binding Oaths lay open on the obsidian pedestal, its pages trembling under the pressure of the final invocation. The ritual had been sustained for hours—threads of ley energy spun tight around Alexandria's name, her lineage, her magic, her very soul. And then—nothing. Not a fizzle. Not a flicker of resistance. Just silence. A clean severing, as if someone had taken a blade of truth and cut the spell at its root.

At first, Astralhart didn't move. He stood still, his gloved hand suspended above the page as the ink beneath it faded—drawn backward into the parchment like light receding into a dying star. Alexandria Dawnborn. Heir to the Crown. Chosen by the Celestial Order. Bound to him by birth, blood, and oath. Gone. Wiped from the Codex. Wiped from the scrying pool. Wiped from the lattice of tracking enchantments built into her very breath since the day she was born. His lips parted slightly. A breath left him—short. Shaken. Then came the second breath—longer. Sharper. Twisted. And then—he erupted.

Magic lashed out from him like a solar flare. The pedestal exploded, shards of blackstone flinging across the ritual chamber. Several arcane acolytes were thrown to the ground. One screamed as her robes caught fire from the wild spell-energy unraveling in the air. Astralhart didn't see her. He didn't see anything. He staggered backward, then roared, the sound ripping up from his throat like an animal finally unchained.

"*NO!*"

He grabbed the shattered remnants of the scrying mirror and hurled them at the wall. Cracks spiderwebbed through the floor, glowing with raw, unscripted magic. Books burst into flames on their shelves. Wards shattered in a chorus of screaming runes. "She's gone," he spat, pacing violently. "Vanished. She cut the chain." He punched the wall hard enough to shatter bone—his knuckles burst open, blood splattering down the gold-trimmed columns. "I warned her. I guided her. She was meant to save us!"

Another blast of force knocked a statue of the First Celestial King off its dais. It cracked in two—its gaze falling away from the chamber as if in shame. And in that moment, Astralhart stopped and stared down at his bleeding hand. The pain didn't calm him. It clarified him. "So," he breathed, quieter now, "you chose the flame." He looked to the ashes of the Codex. "You severed the blood that made you. The line that gave you power." He licked the blood from his knuckles, eyes hollow. "Then I'll make you bleed without it."

He walked slowly to the mirror chamber—what remained of it—and summoned a new circle. Not of her. Not of blood. But of shadow. Deep magic. Ancient inversion. He didn't speak her name this time. He whispered his own.

"I gave you everything," he said to the spell-light forming in the air. "Now I will take everything from you. You will beg to return to the chain. You will beg for me."

The portal released them into a narrow, fire-lit corridor. Warm air wrapped around Alexandria like velvet. The scent of sandalwood, ironwood bark, and the faintest trace of starlily oil curled through the stillness. The light here didn't flicker—it glowed, steady, golden, undisturbed. As her feet touched the polished stone, she realized the walls bore no sigils, no war-tapestries, no weapons. Just etched vines, silver-threaded mosaics of constellations, and an open hush that felt like entering sacred ground. It was quiet. Not dead quiet—held-breath quiet. The kind of silence that feels like someone waiting with open arms.

Bellator stepped back. "I will give you two some space for now. I will return soon."

Alexandria turned and gave Bellator a hug. "Thank you for everything. Please stay safe."

Erythyn stepped forward and turned to her. The exhaustion in his body was clear—his magic dampened, his armor ash-stained—but in his eyes, there was no command. Only gentle insistence. "This is the eastern wing of my palace," he said softly. "I warded it against all eyes...even my own."

Alexandria blinked. "You never came back here?"

He shook his head. "Not once. Not after it was completed."

She turned slowly, letting her eyes sweep across the corridor as they entered a large central hall—and her breath caught. The heart of the room was built around a living tree. Pale, silver-barked, glowing with soft blue blossoms that pulsed like stars, its branches stretched into the domed ceiling where hundreds of tiny mirrored shards reflected the light like constellations. Around the room she saw a harp, identical to the one she'd played as a girl, a velvet chair draped in a soft white shawl—the same she'd worn the night of their first firelight kiss—and a bookshelf filled with volumes she'd once read aloud in the castle gardens.

Everything here...was hers.

"Erythyn..." she breathed.

He watched her gently, not moving.

"You kept all of this?"

"I couldn't let go," he said. "Not of what was real. And this..." he said, nodding toward the room, "was you. Before the war. Before the crown crushed you. Before I pulled you into the dark."

Her gaze trembled over to a table in the corner. A glass case sat atop it. Inside was a folded piece of parchment. Her first letter to him—back when their words were coded, passed by hidden hands. She approached it like one might approach a grave, or a relic, then turned to him again, her emotions unraveling. "I don't deserve this," she whispered.

He stepped closer. "You deserve more than this. But it's all I could protect. And now..." He paused, his voice deepening, gentler, but firm. "You must stay here. On this floor."

Her head tilted. "Why?"

"Because it's the only place I can guarantee your safety." His eyes darkened slightly. "Astralhart is not done. He'll turn the world to ash before he lets you go. This room—this wing—is shielded from every scrying pool, every tether. Even the leyline doesn't know you're here." He stepped toward her, his voice lower now. "You will want for nothing. The tree's bloom will feed the wards. There's food. Books. Light. I've had the best of what's left moved here. You'll be protected."

Alexandria looked around slowly, the magic settling into her skin. It didn't feel like a prison. It felt like a memory...made into a sanctuary. "I can't stay forever," she said.

"You won't have to." His voice was quiet, earnest. "But until I clear the path for you to live free...this is your refuge. Your floor above fire." Then, with a faint trace of emotion in his voice, he added, "You are the only light I ever followed. And now...the light lives here."

The first weeks were quiet. Alexandria barely spoke. She wandered the preserved wing like someone walking through a memory—not her own, but one crafted from another's love and grief. Every room had a trace of her: a book she once favored, a flower pressed in a frame, a cloak folded neatly over a chair. She'd wake often in the middle of the night, the silence so thick she feared she might drown in it. But every time she stirred, Erythyn was there—not watching, not hovering, but sitting nearby. Present.

One night, without a word, she walked over to him and sat beside him near the roots of the silver tree. She didn't speak. Neither did he. But they sat together, shoulder to shoulder, and simply breathed. That became their ritual.

By the second month, their words returned slowly. He began bringing her tea in the morning, always brewed the way she liked it—light with a curl of sunroot. She never told him how she took it. He just knew. In return, she began leaving open books in the library with pressed petals between the pages—a silent invitation to come back to the stories they once spoke of together. Some nights, she would wake from dreams—

dreams of chains, or fire, or Astralhart's voice echoing like rot in her spine. And without asking, he would come to her. Not to comfort. Not to touch. To sit. To keep her grounded. One evening, she reached for his hand. She didn't let go until morning.

Going into month three, the shift was subtle, but undeniable.

One night, as the rains came—slow, warm, whispering down through the open skylight above the silver tree—Alexandria found herself curled beside him on the low-cushioned couch in the reading room. Her legs tangled over his. Her hand rested on his chest. He read aloud. His voice had changed since the war. Deeper. Rougher. But still capable of gentleness that made her chest ache. As he finished a passage, she looked up at him. He turned to her. Silence. Then—a kiss. Not rushed. Not hungry. Slow. Reverent. Like two people memorizing the shape of each other's mouths again. They didn't speak after. She simply pulled him closer.

That night, their embrace was tender, layered in unspoken forgiveness. Her lips against his neck. His hands against the curve of her spine. The heat between them growing slow and sure like coals being coaxed back to life. When dawn came, they stayed wrapped in each other's arms. She laughed for the first time in months. He closed his eyes as if her breath itself was a spell keeping the world at bay.

By month four, the fire was intense beneath the surface.

Desire, once cautious, grew bolder. Over the weeks that followed, the shadow over Solara's night skies became a distant memory whenever Alexandria and Erythyn stole away to their hidden refuge. What had begun as a fierce determination to save her grew into a fire neither could or would quench.

They passed entire days wrapped in each other's arms beneath the cavern's bioluminescent vines, where silver-veined pillars glowed like tethered stars. Mornings bled into afternoons as Alexandria drifted against Erythyn's chest, the steady beat of his heart a promise of safety she'd never known. He traced the curve of her ribs with gentle desperation, memorizing the softness of her skin, the way her pulse fluttered under his fingertips like a song just for him.

When dusk fell, they would slip into the sanctuary's warm pools, their water aglow with humming stones and petals of moonlight moss. Alexandria leaned back against the moss-lined edge as Erythyn brushed wet strands of hair from her face. His fingers followed the line of her jaw, down her neck, pausing at the hollow of her collarbone as though each touch was a benediction. She sighed, tilting her head into his palm, and the world beyond those glowing waters that threatened to collapse under Astralhart's chain felt impossibly far away.

They explored each other slowly, devouring time as though it were a feast laid out just for them. Fingertips traced patterns across bare skin; lips lingered in places words could never reach. When Erythyn pressed into her, it was never to claim her, but to honor her as the center of his universe. When Alexandria's hands roamed over him, she was not seeking penance but affirmation, her touch a vow that their bond was forged of steel and soft light alike.

Days dissolved into weeks, and weeks into months, measured only by the warmth of each sunrise they welcomed tangled together, and the hush of each midnight when neither wanted to close their eyes. They spoke of futures unbound by prophecy, of children they might raise far from the prying eyes of kings and seers, of a love strong enough to shatter any chain.

And every time they emerged from that secret haven, their hearts beat louder, fortified by passion and hope, ready to face whatever darkness Astralhart might cast upon the world. Knowing that together, they had already conquered night itself.

Alexandria and Erythyn knew the sanctuary's every hidden alcove and secret spring. They rose each dawn to the hush of dripping crystal and the song of echoing droplets, Erythyn cupping a handful of dew-kissed water to her lips before pressing a gentle kiss to her forehead. She would laugh—soft, bright—leaning into his warmth as the first pale light filtered through the vines. In those moments, the world outside ceased to exist.

Afternoons found them sprawled on carpets of moss and flowering roots, sharing stories they'd never dared speak aloud before. He taught her the old songs of his people, low chants that twisted through her like a promise, and she whispered courtly tales of kingdoms lost and won. Their voices intertwined, his baritone like distant thunder, hers like wind through autumn leaves. And when the words faded, they held each other in a silence so profound it felt woven from their own hearts.

When evening fell, they returned to the baths, where the stones thrummed with heat and the steam curled around them like a living embrace. Alexandria would lay her head against his shoulder as he traced runes, lightning-fine scars only he could see along her spine. Each pattern was a vow that they belonged to one another. And beneath the glow of those humming stones, they would drift into sleep wrapped in each other's arms, safe from every shadow and chain that threatened beyond the cavern's bones.

Even now, when Alexandria closed her eyes, she could still feel the echo of his touch on her skin, the steady rhythm of his breath guiding her back to that hidden world. And Erythyn, no matter how far he roamed in battle or shadow, carried the heat of her laugh like a talisman, fuel for his fury and balm for his scars. Month after month, through whispered promises and shared dawns, they found in one another a love that refused to be bound or broken. A beacon bright enough to outshine any darkness they would face.

He began to dream less of fire. She began to dream more of light. They shared food in silence, but it was no longer strained—it was peaceful. They planted herbs in the terrace garden. They danced to no music beneath the mirrored skylight. They made love not to forget the world but to feel like they were finally living in it.

One morning, as dawn spilled through the branches of the silver tree, Alexandria leaned her head against his chest and whispered, "I think I'm falling in love with you again."

He didn't answer right away. He only held her tighter and kissed her forehead. Then—"I never stopped."

It was like a dream come true, until everything seemed to change one morning when Erythyn returned from a battle. He came in and didn't speak a word. Alexandria could feel the change in him. She could feel the dark presence surrounding him once more. She knew something was wrong but he wouldn't reveal what it was. This went on for days. He didn't want to talk. He was only focused on the war.

The stillness began to ache. The floor that once felt sacred now felt like a beautifully decorated prison. Erythyn was starting to be gone more often than not. At first, it had been for a day. Then two. Then five. No explanations. No gentle reassurances. Just a soft kiss on her forehead and a vague, "I'll return soon."

Sometimes when he came back, she found new burns on his forearms, his armor scorched, his voice darker, tighter. He didn't say where he'd gone, and she had stopped asking—but not wondering.

Bellator still visited, though rarely, and only in her hound form. She never entered the chambers fully, only appearing now and then at the edge of the moon-lit terrace, curled beneath the glowing branches of the silver tree. Alexandria found herself more and more at her side. They didn't speak—at least not with words. But when Bellator placed her massive head in Alexandria's lap, or nudged her gently toward the garden's edge, it made the silence feel less like abandonment.

Some nights, Bellator would disappear into the forest paths that trailed just outside the sanctuary's edge—places Alexandria wasn't allowed to go. And each time she returned, her fur carried the scent of pine, moss, and freedom. Alexandria would bury her face into it and weep softly.

She missed it—freedom... She longed for the forest, the earth beneath her feet. The tie to mother earth, the place where she felt grounded no matter what the day held. The place she most felt at home, where she felt like her parents were beside her. The place she felt truly alive. It began as a whisper in her bones. A low yearning. A call.

The forest beyond the sanctuary—it called her. Not with words, but with feeling. It was something old, something druidic, something that had awakened when the Wyrmsinger's light touched her blood. She began spending more time at the threshold of the outer terrace, her toes grazing the edge of the wardline, staring out at the tall trees beyond. She would brush her fingers across the glowing vines and imagine them turning to wild leaves, the polished floor replaced by soil, the mirrored walls by sky.

She wanted to run.

To feel the earth beneath her feet.

To breathe the wild again.

And the more she longed for it, the more she noticed: Erythyn was pulling away.

When he did return, something in him was...colder. Not cruel. Not angry. But distant. Guarded. His touches were slower. His kisses felt rehearsed. And his eyes, once brimming with fire only for her, now seemed to carry smoke—the remnants of battles fought alone, and perhaps...secrets buried deeper than he was willing to speak.

She found dark residue on his cloak once. Not ash. Something slick. Almost...corrupted. When she asked what it was, he only turned away and said, "There are things you're safer not knowing."

That night, she lay awake long after he fell asleep. And for the first time in months, she watched him breathe beside her and wondered, *Is he slipping away? Or is he pulling me closer to something darker?*

One night, after another four-day absence, Alexandria stood alone in the bathing chamber. She lit the scry mirror, intending only to watch the flamelight reflect. But instead of her own reflection, she saw herself smiling. But the smile wasn't hers. It was too still, too perfect. Her heart twisted. The mimic had returned. "You miss him," it whispered in her voice. "But maybe you never really had him." The reflection tilted its head. "Maybe the only part he loved was the part he could control."

Alexandria backed away. "You're not real."

The mimic leaned forward. "And yet...he hasn't come back, has he? You feel it too, don't you? The shadows in him rising again. Just like before."

Bellator stood outside that night, staring at the dark treeline, her ears perked, her tail rigid. Alexandria stood beside her, barefoot, her cloak loose around her shoulders. And in the wind, she smelled smoke. She heard her own voice. And she felt the forest recoil.

The next morning when it was dawn, soft and silver, the kind that kissed the world awake gently, but never promised warmth, Alexandria stood barefoot at the very edge of the wardline—the shimmering arcane ring that pulsed around the sanctuary floor like a silent sentinel. Her cloak was draped around her shoulders, her hair falling loose down her back.

In her hands she held a single glowing vine, taken from the silver-barked tree the night before. Its light trembled, responding to her heartbeat. For weeks, she had stood here, watching. Wondering. But today, something inside her shifted. Not with rebellion. With need.

A need to breathe without runes, to feel the wild soil under her skin, to step outside of what even love had turned into—a beautiful prison. She took a breath and pressed the vine to the edge of the ward. It flared. Flickered. And then—it opened.

Just a sliver. A heartbeat. A permission. And that's all she needed. The air outside was thicker, older. The forest pressed in close. Branches curled like arms. The moss beneath her feet was wet and soft. Sunlight laced through the canopy in shattered gold. She moved like someone re-learning her own rhythm. The earth welcomed her. The wind whispered her name correctly for the first time in months. She walked deeper, her fingertips brushing ferns and roots, her heart pounding—not in fear, but relief. I'm still alive.

But somewhere behind her…the mimic watched. A faint outline. Her face. Her voice. But her eyes were hollow, and the smile she wore was wrong.

Erythyn returned that same night—scarred, yes, sunken, his cloak tattered. The firelight in the main hall flickered as he stepped inside. He expected silence but found Bellator waiting, standing in her humanoid form by the hearth, her arms crossed, her cloak wet with rain, and her druidic eyes piercing.

He paused. "Where is she?" he asked, low.

Bellator tilted her head. "Out there."

His face shifted—panic buried behind practiced control.

"I left the wards intact, and she opened them."

He took a step forward, His voice harder now. "How?"

"She remembered who she was." A silence stretched between them. Then Bellator stepped close. "You say you love her, Erythyn. But love doesn't contain. And you—" Her voice cracked like branches underfoot, "You're beginning to look like the man she ran from."

Erythyn's jaw clenched. "You don't know what I've seen—what I'm keeping from reaching her."

"She doesn't need walls to be safe," Bellator snapped. "She needs truth. And you're hiding more than shadows."

Erythyn said nothing. Bellator turned away, her voice softer now—but edged with finality. "You have one chance left. If she starts to feel caged again…you will lose her." She stepped toward the door. "Maybe not to the Order. Maybe not to the war. But to herself. And that's a path no magic can bring her back from."

Chapter 33
The Mimic

Creed of the Duskward Circle

We stand between the dying light & dawn's first tear,

Shields raised against the creeping void we bear.

In every breath a prayer, in every strike a plea,

Let the Sunblade guard what once was free.

Alexandria knelt by a small stream. She let the water run over her fingers. Cool. Clean. Free. And as she sat back, staring into the dancing light that broke through the trees, a voice called her name. Not aloud. Not in echo. Inside her. Faint. Sweet. Familiar.

She turned sharply. Behind her, in the distance, her own face came from between the trees, smiling. The wind hushed. Even the birds stopped singing. Alexandria stood among the trees, her breath shallow, her bare feet rooted in the moss as she stepped through the light—herself, but wrong. The mimic. Its hair was braided like hers had been months ago. It wore her silver-stitched robe, the one Erythyn once draped over her shoulders during a storm. It even carried her softness—her quiet warmth—reflected like a painting behind glass. It smiled. "You miss me."

Alexandria didn't answer.

The mimic's voice was gentle, coaxing. "You miss how easy it was. When he looked at you like you were light instead of a liability." It took a step forward. Alexandria didn't retreat. "You miss the way he held you," the mimic continued. "But you've noticed the shadows in him, haven't you? The ones he hides when he thinks you're sleeping." Its eyes narrowed ever so slightly. "He's slipping, Alex. You feel it."

Alexandria clenched her jaw. "You're not me."

"I'm the part of you that still wants the dream," it said, reaching up to brush a lock of hair behind its ear. "The part that wants to go back to the days before war. Before chains. Before fire." It cocked its head. "You miss being loved, not guarded."

Alexandria's hands curled into fists. Her voice dropped to a whisper. "You wear my face...but you'll never wear my truth."

The mimic paused for just a moment. Then smiled wider. "But are you sure you still know what that truth is?" Behind her, the forest shuddered.

Erythyn moved like a flame in the wind—fast, furious, uncontrolled. He tore through the underbrush, his cloak catching on low-hanging limbs, his boots skidding over damp soil. Leaves scorched beneath his feet from the heat rolling off his body. "Alexandria!" His voice cracked through the woods. There was no answer. His breath came ragged, every heartbeat hammering against his ribs like a threat.

Every time she was out of his sight, the same nightmare clawed back to life: her lying in the forest again, torn from him, taken. "Alex—!" He stopped. Listened. A rustle. Too close. Not bird. Not beast. Magic.

He drew his sword. The flames licked up the blade, casting light across the trees—then came a whisper. Not a voice. A memory. "Come back to me." He froze. Her voice. But...wrong. Too smooth. Too eager. Too perfect.

His eyes widened. "No..." He pushed forward, his heart thundering. Roots clawed at his boots, vines tried to twist around his ankles—the forest trying to warn him, or hold him back. "Please," he whispered, "don't let me be too late again."

The mimic now stood only paces away. Her smile faltered for just a moment, sensing Alexandria's steadiness. "Why won't you let yourself have peace?" it asked, its voice feather-soft. "Why keep fighting for pain?"

Alexandria stepped forward, meeting her own reflection with steel in her voice. "Because peace built on lies isn't peace at all."

The mimic twitched, and in that second of hesitation, Bellator emerged from the trees in hound form, her fangs bared, her eyes glowing. The mimic turned to run, vanishing into shadow.

Alexandria fell to her knees, her breath shuddering. Bellator growled low, circling her protectively. And through the trees, Erythyn appeared, his armor cracked, his eyes wide, panic, rage, and raw fear written across every line of his face.

"Alexandria!"

She looked up, her breath catching. But something was different now. Not distrust. Not hatred. But...distance. "I'm not broken," she whispered, before he could speak. "I don't need to be kept anymore."

On the long walk back, no words, only silence. The forest around them had quieted, as if sensing the shift. The mimic was gone, but its presence lingered in the tension between every footstep. Alexandria walked first, barefoot on the damp forest floor, her hair tangled with leaves, her breath steady but weighted. Her thoughts were a storm cloaked in stillness.

Erythyn followed, his form flickering with contained heat, his jaw set tight, his hands clenched at his sides. And Bellator, in her hound form, walked beside Alexandria, silent as shadow, but close enough to protect her without command.

They crossed the ridge-line above the river, passed through thickets of ancient willows, climbed the stone trail to the secluded entrance of the east wing—the hidden path to Erythyn's shielded floor. The door opened for them without magic. It had always been waiting. And still...not one of them spoke.

The firelight still burned, soft and golden. The silver barked tree still swayed gently in the center of the sanctuary, its petals falling like snow over the basin pool. The harp still sat untouched.
The books still laid open where they left them. The shawl was still draped on the chair. But now, it all felt...hollow.

Alexandria stepped inside and didn't look back. She made her way toward the low fountain and sat on its edge. Her eyes traced her reflection in the shallow water. Her face looked different—stronger, yes, but sadder. Bellator shifted back, kneeling silently beside her. The sanctuary wasn't broken. It just...no longer felt like it belonged to her.

She ran her hand across the marble, over the grooves of the tree roots embedded beneath the stone. "It's beautiful," she whispered.

Bellator nodded beside her. "It is."

"But...why does it feel like a room I'm not supposed to leave?"

Bellator looked at her with soft, knowing eyes. "Because it was built for your safety. Not your soul."

Alexandria let her head drop, her eyes stinging. "I thought I was free. I severed the tether. I left the Order. I chose this."

Bellator touched her shoulder. "You chose love. Not a cage."

Alexandria inhaled deeply. "And yet... Why do I feel like I'm locked in gold?

Later that night, Alexandria found it by accident. A long corridor. No ward. No lock. Just a heavy door left slightly ajar. Inside was a war room. Cold. Stark. Unforgiving. Maps were burned at the edges. Letters were half-written in ash-black ink. Daggers rested across documents. Walls were lined with charred sigils and coded battle runes. On one wall—a painting of her, darkened by smoke, was hidden behind a drape.

She stepped inside. And at that exact moment, Erythyn entered from the other end. He froze. She turned slowly, meeting his eyes. Not angry. Not afraid. Just done with pretending. "You weren't going to tell me about this room."

Erythyn stepped forward, guilt flickering in his expression. "It wasn't for you to worry about."

She walked past the war table, brushing her fingers over the blades laid out like choices. "How many battles did you fight while I lay in that garden, thinking I was safe?"

"I was protecting you."

"You were keeping me quiet."

His breath hitched. He took another step toward her. "You were finally at peace."

"No," she said, turning to him, fire rising behind her eyes, "I was finally distracted." A beat passed. Then, "You said you loved me."

"I do," he said, hoarse.

"Then love me, not your version of me. I'm not made of memory. I'm not the girl from the firelight." She stepped closer. "I want truth. Not comfort."

He closed his eyes like her words physically hurt. Then said, quiet, fragile, "If I show you everything... You'll walk away."

She held his gaze and whispered, "If you don't, I already have."

He stood there—unmoving, as if her words had split something open inside him. The air between them was still, tense, but heavy with something unspoken that could no longer remain hidden. Erythyn exhaled through his nose. His jaw clenched. He looked at her not as the girl who once trusted him but the woman now demanding truth—and willing to shatter whatever fragile thing they'd built if he didn't give it.

"You remember the night I disappeared for days?" he began, his voice low, grating like stone dragged across stone. "You thought I was hunting spirits beyond the borders." She said nothing. "I wasn't." He looked down, ashamed. "I was meeting with the Shadowlord. My father."

Her breath caught, but she didn't flinch.

"I told myself it was to learn his movements. To gain an edge. But the truth is...part of me needed to see him. To know if what's in me—what's growing in me—was something I could still fight or if I was already too far gone." He took a slow, shaky breath. "I didn't just go to spy. I listened to him. I wanted to understand. He spoke of balance...of breaking the cycle of light and dark. Of reshaping the world into something neither side could control. And part of me—Alexandria—part of me agreed with him."

She blinked, but didn't look away.

"I've killed creatures... Not all of them were corrupted. Some were innocents who simply knew too much, who wandered too close. I've erased memories from the minds of your guards so they wouldn't question why they never saw me leave your floor at night." He was unraveling now.

"I placed tracking runes on your skin when you slept. In the crook of your shoulder, just beneath your collarbone. To find you if you ran or if someone took you. But it was more than that. I wanted to make sure you always returned to me."

Her hands balled at her sides, but she said nothing.

"And the sanctuary?" he said, his voice bitter. "The one I said was protected, hidden from the Shadowlord? It wasn't. Not at first. He let us stay there. I made a bargain—time for safety. I gave him names of rogue mages, rebels from the Celestial Order who were working against both sides. I handed them over to keep you hidden." He stepped back, ashamed of the echo of his own confession.

"There's more," he rasped. "I've lied about who I used to be."

Her lips parted, her eyes stinging, but still, she didn't speak.

"I burned a village once," he choked. "Years ago, when I first took the mark of shadow. I told myself it was full of loyalists to the Order...but there were children. I still see their faces in dreams."

Silence still.

He looked at her now, broken, trembling, a prince of darkness pretending to be a savior. "You wanted the truth. There it is. The worst of it." Then, the final wound bared—his voice almost a whisper, "The version of me you love doesn't exist. I tried to become him for you. But the truth is... I'm still his son."

She stepped closer, slowly, until they were almost chest to chest. Her eyes shimmered—not with fear, but with fierce clarity. "I never asked for a savior," she said. "I asked for you." A long silence stretched between them. "Now," she said gently, "show me everything else. The rest of the truth. Or walk away and leave me with lies." His breath trembled. And finally—he nodded.

Erythyn said nothing as he turned, beckoning her with only a glance. They descended through the corridor in silence—neither touch nor word exchanged—only the echo of footsteps trailing behind secrets finally released. The air cooled with each level they passed, torches flickering to life as if sensing his presence. Magic moved here, old and resentful.

At the end of the hall, a black iron door awaited. No handle. No keyhole. Just a carving etched deep in the metal that read: "That which is hidden shapes that which remains." Erythyn raised a hand, and shadows curled from his fingers, slithering into the carvings like ink filling veins. The door groaned open. She followed him inside.

The room was circular, cavernous—like a forgotten cathedral carved into the earth. High, arched windows let in no light, only swirling mist. In the center was a dark pool of water, still as glass. Around it, fragments of memory suspended in black crystal shards floated in the air, pulsing softly. "This is the Chamber of Echoes," Erythyn said, his voice hushed. "A place where memory becomes vision. It does not lie. It only remembers."

He moved to the pool's edge and extended his hand. The surface rippled. "Look," he whispered.

Images flared across the water's surface like fire consuming oil. She saw a younger Erythyn—bare-chested, kneeling before a towering figure cloaked in shadow: the Shadowlord. His father. Erythyn's voice echoed in the chamber, trembling. "I'll do it. Whatever it takes. Just protect her." Then another memory: A battlefield soaked in blood. Erythyn stood among corpses, his hands shaking, his lips parted in horror as a child's lifeless eyes stared up from the mud. "They said she was harboring light mages. I didn't know—gods, I didn't know..." Next: Alexandria sleeping, peaceful in the sanctuary garden, unaware as Erythyn stood over her, whispering an incantation. A glowing sigil faded into her skin near her collarbone.

"This is for your safety. This is for us." Another—Erythyn alone in a dim study, speaking to a scrying mirror. The Shadowlord's voice, a low rasp, said, "You'll give me what I asked for. Or I'll take her."

Erythyn slammed his fist on the table. "You won't touch her!"

"Then give me the druid's location." The vision shattered like glass.

Alexandria's hand shot out, grabbing Erythyn's arm. He turned, startled, but she didn't pull away. Her eyes were wet but unwavering.

"You bargained with a monster," she whispered.

"I became one," he answered, hollow.

She stepped closer. "And yet...you never let him touch me." He blinked. She took another step. "You could've vanished. Given in. But you didn't."

"I don't deserve your forgiveness."

She brushed her fingers along his cheek. "No," she said. "But maybe you deserve your own."

Erythyn trembled under her touch, a shadow forged in war and guilt finally crumbling. The silence between them was no longer empty—it was sacred.

After a long moment, Alexandria turned back toward the pool. "Show me everything," she said. "No more hiding. If we're going to face what's coming—we do it together."

And for the first time in years, Erythyn did not flinch from the light.

Chapter 34
The Unraveling Truth

Song of Radiant Reckoning

Hearken, O earth, to the Clarion's cry,

When steel meets shadow neath the weeping sky,

Let each resounding blow proclaim the right,

That light endures beyond the longest night.

*E*rythyn reached toward the center of the black pool, whispering a phrase in an ancient tongue. The surface shimmered—then pulled them in. They didn't fall. They slid, as if the water had become a veil between worlds.

Alexandria blinked—and found herself standing in Erythyn's memory, not as a phantom or observer, but as though she were there. They stood in a throne room—not of gold and grandeur, but obsidian and fire. Torches burned with black flames. The floor was scorched. And at the far end sat the Shadowlord—his features obscured by shifting shadow, but his presence suffocating.

A young Erythyn knelt before him, his face streaked with blood and sweat. "What are you?" the Shadowlord asked, his voice rumbling like distant thunder.

"Yours," the boy answered, too quickly.

"Wrong." The figure leaned forward. "You are mine only when you kill your light."

Suddenly, the memory rushed—jumping through time like wind through cracked windows. Erythyn screaming as runes were burned into his back by shadowed priests. His hands wringing the life from a dying spirit, while his face showed only emptiness. The moment he met her. Alexandria standing at the forest's edge, the first time he saw her. He looked different then—wilder, gaunt, desperate. And then...a moment she had never seen—Erythyn sitting alone beneath the stars, weeping, a lock of her hair tied around his wrist. He whispered into the wind, "If I lose her, I lose the only part of me that matters."

Alexandria blinked away tears as the vision fractured, returning them to the Chamber of Echoes. Erythyn dropped to his knees. "I've done unforgivable things. But I never stopped trying to become someone worthy of your faith."

She knelt before him. "Then prove it now. Not with penance. Not with power. With truth. Every step forward—from here—together."

Far above, on the topmost floor of Erythyn's fortress, Bellator stirred. She lay by the hearth in her hound form, curled but watchful. Her ears perked. The wind outside shifted. A low pulse, deep within the stone of the fortress, vibrated through her paws. She lifted her head. The fire dimmed—just slightly. It wasn't a threat. Not yet. But it was a change. Something was awakening.

Bellator padded to the balcony, her fur bristling. Her golden eyes narrowed toward the eastern skies. Thunder rolled far in the distance—but not from clouds. From the wings. A single raven—black as pitch, with too many eyes—circled once above the fortress and vanished into shadow.

Bellator's lips curled into a silent growl. "They're watching again," she murmured. "They feel his shift."

Behind her, a map lay unfurled on the table. Magical runes flared across its surface—markings Astralhart had placed weeks ago. But one rune in the far northeast—a place called Varrakor's Hollow—had just ignited, glowing like wildfire. Bellator shifted into her human form, quickly fastening her druid cloak. "The sanctuary's veil is weakening," she whispered. She reached for her staff, then paused. "And the woman I swore to protect may be the only thing holding the darkness at bay." She turned on her heel and began the descent. She would reach the Chamber. She had to before the truth they'd unleashed grew into something too powerful to bury again.

Erythyn and Alexandria sat in the after-quiet of unraveling truth. The visions were gone. The Chamber of Echoes stilled. Shadows returned to the edges of the walls, subdued. Alexandria's fingers brushed against the pool's surface one last time, but it gave her nothing now—only her own reflection, rippling. She looked to him. He hadn't moved. Still on his knees, shoulders hunched, gaze lowered—not from shame anymore, but from fear. "Erythyn?" she asked softly. "You told me everything."

As he hung his head and cut his piercing eyes upon her, he said, "Yes." He couldn't tell her anymore. He didn't believe she would be able to handle more, and he didn't want to lose her. For it was certain, if those words crossed the threshold of his lips, he would lose her forever...

She knelt in front of him again. Face to face. Pain to pain. "I don't forgive you. Not yet. But I'm still here."

And for the first time in his life, Erythyn cried—truly cried—as she held him, both of them kneeling in the ruins of their past, choosing to carry the burden of truth together.

The fortress trembled—barely perceptible to most, but Bellator felt it, as if the stones had exhaled after holding their breath for centuries. She descended swiftly, barefoot and silent, her druid cloak trailing behind her like leaves in the wind. As she neared the chamber, she slowed. Her animal senses stirred—the scent of salt. Grief. Not rage. The iron door to the Chamber of Echoes stood ajar, something that should never happen unless bound hearts had unraveled inside. She stepped in. And froze.

There—at the heart of the chamber—knelt Alexandria and Erythyn, clasped together like two broken statues at the foot of a ruin. He wept openly, unmasked by pride or pretense. She held him—not as a princess holds a warrior, but as a woman holds the shattered boy who tried to carry the world alone.

Bellator did not speak. Not at first. She approached quietly, stopping just a few paces behind them. "I felt the shift," she said gently. "Like the roots of an ancient tree being torn free from stone."

Alexandria slowly turned her head, her eyes still red but clear. "He told me everything."

Bellator's golden gaze moved to Erythyn. Her lip curled slightly—not in cruelty, but in recognition, a predator understanding another creature who had spent too long hiding their wounds. "I don't forgive easily," Bellator said to him. "And I don't forget. But I do protect what my princess chooses to keep." She walked forward and offered Alexandria her hand. "We must go," she said softly. "Something stirs in the Hollow. Something ancient."

Alexandria rose, her fingers tightening on Erythyn's. "We'll face it," she said. "But not apart."

Far across the sea of stars, beyond the Veil of Ash and through the storm-choked skies of the Wraithlands, he felt it. In the center of his sanctum, the Shadowlord stood motionless, his hands behind his back, staring into a churning black mirror set into the wall.

One of his generals approached, cloaked in bone and crimson. "My Lord, a ripple was felt in the Thread. From him..."

The Shadowlord didn't turn. "I know," he said quietly. His voice was low and ancient, a voice that did not speak so much as remember itself. The mirror showed a flicker: Alexandria's hand pressed against Erythyn's cheek. Her eyes shining. Her rage not enough to walk away.

"He chose *her*," the Shadowlord said flatly, "over *me*." Cracks splintered across the mirror's surface. "So it begins," he muttered. "The unraveling of what I forged."

"But he carries your mark," the general said. "He is still bound..."

"Not anymore."

The Shadowlord turned now, his cloak hung low, covering his head except for the wicked smile that hung on his face. "If the boy wants to choose love," he growled, "then let him. Let him bleed for it." He raised a single finger toward the far wall where a great chain was bolted into black stone. "Release it," he whispered.

The general's breath caught. "My Lord... The wyrm sleeps. If we release it now..."

"Release it!"

A pulse of darkness surged from the Shadowlord's hand, and far below the Wraithlands, something ancient moved. Something that hadn't stirred in eons.

The wind howled low as the three figures stepped from the fortress and into the wilderness beyond. Clouds hung low and bruised over the horizon, rippling like something alive beneath the veil of sky. The further they walked, the quieter the forest became. Not from peace, but from warning.

Bellator walked ahead in her wolf form, her ears twitching at every shift in the trees. Erythyn, quieter now, walked beside Alexandria, not touching her, but never more than a breath away. She felt it too. A pull in the air. A tension, like a string drawn tight, waiting to snap.

"Varrakor's Hollow is a wound in the world," Erythyn murmured. "It was sealed long ago...not by power but by will. A collective denial. The kind of silence that leaks madness."

Alexandria nodded slowly. "What happens if it wakes?"

"It doesn't wake," Bellator said sharply from ahead. "It calls."

They crested a hill, and there it was. Varrakor's Hollow, a great sunken basin in the earth, shrouded in mist. Dead trees lined the rim, their bark white as bone. At the center stood a black monolith, cracked and pulsing, and around it...the land had withered into a spiral of rot.

Alexandria's breath hitched. Something alive was beneath that stone. Something bound in memory and shadow. And it knew her name.

That night, they camped beneath what few stars dared show their faces. Erythyn sat watch near the fire. Bellator remained half-shifted, neither beast nor woman, as if even her druid form was unsure of what was coming.

Alexandria slept, and she dreamed. But this was no dream born of exhaustion. It was a summoning. She stood barefoot in a field of ash. The sky above her burned red and gold, as if fire had replaced the sun. Ahead were two figures. Children. A boy and a girl. The boy bore raven-black hair and emerald eyes—Erythyn's eyes. The girl was fierce and wild, with cascading white strands of hair and a mark glowing faintly on her palm. They looked at her with sorrow.

"We don't have long," the girl said. "He's already found the gate."

"Who?" Alexandria asked, her voice small.

"The wyrm," the boy whispered. "He is what sleeps beneath the Hollow. Not beast. Not god. Memory that devours."

Alexandria knelt. "Are you...my children?"

They nodded. "From a future that won't exist," the girl said. "Unless you change it."

A rumble shook the field. The boy stepped forward, gently placing a hand over her heart. "You must choose. Light or love. The world...or him."

The dream cracked. The ash turned to feathers. The sky folded inward, and Alexandria awoke with a scream.

Erythyn was already at her side, his arms around her, whispering. "Shh—shh, I'm here. You're safe."

"No," she whispered, clinging to him. "Not safe. Not yet."

Bellator had already drawn her blade, scanning the darkness. In the distance, toward the Hollow, a pulse of cold air rolled across the earth, carrying with it the scent of ancient breath. The wyrm had stirred.

The fire was burning low, embers soft and red, casting flickering shadows against the tent walls. Bellator sat just outside the circle, listening to the wind with her back to them, keeping watch but giving them distance. Inside, Alexandria sat wrapped in a blanket, her knees drawn to her chest. Her breath still trembled from the dream. Erythyn knelt across from her, his hand resting near hers, not touching, just there. She hadn't spoken since waking. Finally, she did. "They were ours."

Erythyn didn't need to ask what she meant.

"The children," she whispered. "A boy with your eyes. A girl with my mark." Her voice cracked. "They were beautiful."

His throat tightened. "They would be."

She nodded slowly. "But they came to warn me. Not comfort me."

He shifted forward just slightly, his voice careful. "What did they say?"

She looked at him, really looked, as if trying to memorize him before the storm. "That a choice is coming. A choice between the world...and you."

Erythyn's face went still. His jaw clenched, but he didn't flinch. "I already knew that was coming," he said, his voice low. "I've always known it. You're the light. I'm what crawled out of its absence."

"That's not what they said," she snapped, sudden anger lacing her voice. "They didn't say he would be the end. They said you would be my choice. That loving you might destroy everything." Her words hung there. Heavy. Painful. She swallowed, softer now, broken. "What if they're right?"

Erythyn moved closer, his hand finally brushing hers. She didn't pull away. "If choosing me costs the world...then I'll walk away."

"No," she said quickly. "Don't say that. Don't make it noble. That's not the truth." He looked into her golden eyes. "The truth is... I don't want to choose the world." Her eyes shone with tears. "Not if it means losing this. Losing you. And I hate myself for that."

He reached out now, cradling her face gently. "You think I haven't dreamed of the same future?" he whispered. "Of her laugh? Of his voice calling out for you? Of peace, not borrowed, but ours?" His brow touched hers. "But you are the heart of the world, Alexandria. And if the world dies so we can live, then I will never forgive myself, even if you do."

She closed her eyes. Her voice came out as a whisper, fragile and aching. "What if I'm not strong enough to choose right?"

"You are." His thumb brushed the tears from her cheek. "But no matter what comes...don't carry it alone."

She opened her eyes, and in the glow of dying fire, they didn't kiss. They didn't fall into each other. They just held on to the moment, to the breath between choices, to what they still had before fate came to claim the rest.

Outside, Bellator raised her head. The Hollow pulsed again. The choice was coming. And it would not wait forever.

In the obsidian throne room of his fortress, the Shadowlord stood motionless before a brazier filled not with flame but with memories, visions harvested from the wyrm's dreaming thoughts. Smoke slithered upward in unnatural colors, shifting into images no mortal eye should witness. He saw them. The children. The future. The boy with Erythyn's eyes, the girl bearing the mark of the princess. His hands clenched into fists, the gauntlet hissing as shadow strained against his skin. "So...that's the shape of her love," he murmured. "A future where shadow and light entwine." His voice grew colder, crueler. "It cannot be allowed. Not again." He extended a finger into the smoke. The image of the children distorted, writhing, then burned.

Behind him, his bone-cloaked general approached. "My Lord, the wyrm stirs restlessly. It dreams of her."

"Then let it dream," the Shadowlord said, turning. "But tell it this..." He stepped down from his dais, each footfall echoing like a hammer striking ancient stone. "If she enters the Hollow, she belongs to me."

Chapter 35
Feeding the Wyrm

Psalm of the Everlasting Dawn

O Endless Light that knows no end,

From your embrace all wounds shall mend.

When darkness comes with bloodied hand,

Shine anew upon this broken land.

B ack at the edge of the Hollow, dawn never came. The skies above had darkened, not with night, but with stillness, as if the world itself was holding its breath.

Bellator stood at the rim, her staff in hand, her cloak flickering in the unnatural wind.

Erythyn approached beside Alexandria, silent but alert. "The wyrm lies beneath the monolith," he said. "It doesn't guard knowledge. It is knowledge. Everything forgotten, denied, buried. That's why it calls to her."

Alexandria's heart pounded. "It wants me?"

"It remembers you," Bellator corrected, her voice soft but grim. "And it remembers every version of you that could have ever lived. It will show you those lives. It will tempt you with them."

As they descended into the basin, the mist thickened. Whispers tickled their ears, never quite forming words. The monolith loomed taller with every step, cracked and bleeding a faint silver-black light, like moonlight caught in ink. Alexandria reached it first and placed her hand on the stone. It was ice-cold. Her breath caught, and then vanished. The world fell away.

She stood in a golden field, under a blue sky that had never known war. A home stood nearby. Laughter came from within. She stepped inside. There he was Erythyn, barefoot and smiling, holding a tiny girl in one arm and a wooden spoon in the other. The scent of herbs and bread filled the air. "Love?" he called to her. "She took her first step!"

Alexandria stared in silence. The child giggled and reached for her. Then another figure entered, it was herself, but older. Peaceful. Untouched by grief. A perfect future. A trap.

Because just as she stepped forward, the sky above shattered into black fire, and a voice echoed through the Hollow. "This is what you will never have."

Alexandria stumbled back, clutching her heart. The vision blurred. The house burned. The laughter turned to screams. The wyrm began to rise in her mind, no body, no shape, only memory made hunger. "Choose," it whispered. "The world...or love. You cannot keep both." And then—Alexandria screamed.

It wasn't loud, it was raw. A cry dragged from her soul, not her throat. Her body stood frozen at the base of the monolith, her fingers still pressed to the stone, her head bowed as if in prayer. But her eyes were wide. Unseeing. Inside, she burned. Outside, she bled.

A thin trickle of blood ran from her nose. Her body trembled violently. Bellator was the first to move. She sprinted to Alexandria's side, slamming the butt of her staff against the earth. Magic surged, green and silver, but it shattered against the monolith like glass.

"She's not just seeing the future," Bellator hissed. "The wyrm is feasting on her."

Erythyn was already there, gripping Alexandria's shoulders. "Alex... Alex, come back to me." His voice was low, urgent. "You're stronger than this. You know what's real." But her hands stayed fixed. The monolith pulsed, deep and slow. Like a heart. Or a god breathing.

Bellator circled it, her lips chanting ancient druidic invocations. Runes sparked across her skin, lighting the ground. "It's feeding her a life where everything is perfect. No pain. No war. Just...him. A version of you that never broke."

Erythyn flinched. "I have to go in."

Bellator spun on him. "If you touch that stone..."

"She's alone in there." His voice was steel. "I'm not leaving her in that place, not again." He took a breath. Then, without hesitation, he reached up and pressed his palm to the monolith. The Hollow opened for him like a mouth—and swallowed him whole.

He stood in the ruins of a burning house. A child cried for a mother who no longer existed. Alexandria stood at the center of the chaos, untouched by flame, staring at the ash of what had once been her dream. She turned slowly and saw him. Not the version the wyrm had shown her. Him. The real one. Scars, shadows, flaws and all. Her knees buckled. He caught her.

Her sobs tore through him as she clung to his tunic, trembling. "It was so beautiful. I wanted it. I still want it."

"I know," he whispered, holding her tightly. "But that wasn't real. Not yet. Not until we fight for it."

She looked up at him. "Will we ever have it?"

"I don't know," he said honestly. "But I'd rather bleed beside you in truth than live forever in a lie."

The wyrm howled in the distance. The illusion cracked, walls collapsing, sky splintering. Together, still holding one another, they turned toward the storm. And they walked out.

Back in the real world, their bodies jolted. Both gasped as if surfacing from icy water. Alexandria fell into Erythyn's arms, her breath ragged, his heartbeat pounding against hers. Bellator was already beside them, whispering grounding spells, anchoring them to the now. The monolith had gone dark. The wyrm was silent again. But not gone. Never gone. "You went in after me," Alexandria whispered.

"Every time," Erythyn said, voice hoarse. "Always."

And in that moment, they knew—they'd escaped the vision. But the choice was still coming. And next time, there would be no illusions to wake from.

The fire crackled gently. Morning had come, though the sun struggled to pierce the clouds that hung low and heavy over the Hollow. Alexandria sat wrapped in her cloak beside the fire, a mug of heated water laced with forest herbs in her hands. Bellator crouched nearby, running her fingers over a map carved into dirt and ash with her staff. Erythyn stood behind them both, his arms crossed and gaze distant. No one had spoken much since the vision.

Finally, Alexandria broke the silence. "The wyrm wasn't just showing me a dream," she said quietly. "It was showing me the cost. What I'll lose if I choose the world."

Bellator nodded without looking up. "And what the world loses if you don't."

Erythyn's voice came like smoke. "That thing... It wasn't just feeding. It was judging. It knows the shape of your soul."

Alexandria stared into the flames. "It showed me what I could have. A life with him. A family. No war. No blood."

Bellator's voice softened. "And yet, you came back."

Alexandria's eyes shimmered. "Because I don't trust anything that demands I abandon the people I'm meant to protect." She looked to Erythyn. "But that doesn't mean I won't still want it."

He stepped closer, kneeling beside her. "Then let's fight for it," he said. "Let's build that world with blood and fire if we have to—but on our terms. Not theirs."

Bellator finally spoke what they were all thinking. "The Shadowlord will know what happened here. The wyrm is his tether to ancient power. He won't let this stand."

Alexandria nodded. "Then we find the others. Ashlynn. Astralhart. The remaining circles of the Celestial Order."

Erythyn's gaze turned sharp. "They'll never trust me."

"They don't have to," she said. "I trust you." And that was enough—for now...

Bellator scattered the dirt map with a wave of her hand and stood. "We move by twilight."

Chapter 36
The Shadowlord's Fury

Canticle of the Undying Flame

From pyre's heart & dragon's breath

The Sunblade rose to cleave through death.

Its fire-endowed, its oath unbound,

To burn corrupt till light is found.

*T*he chamber deep beneath the Wraithlands trembled. The Shadowlord stood at its center, his arms spread, power flooding into a cocoon of pulsing darkness that hovered above a ritual circle. He was furious. The wyrm had failed. Worse, it had hesitated. A fragment of it had almost let her go. "It remembers her blood," he hissed. "The blood that banished it once before."

The general approached. "Shall I prepare the hunting beasts?"

"No." The Shadowlord turned slowly, his eyes gleaming with something darker than rage—purpose. "They have defied memory. Dream. Even prophecy." He walked toward the cocoon, its shape writhing, half-formed. "Let them now face something new. Something not drawn from what was... But from what should never be." He pressed his hand to the cocoon. Dark tendrils burst outward. From within the black shell, something opened its eyes. Eyes that had never belonged to any god, beast, or man. Eyes born of void. "Unleash the Hollowborn."

The borderlands of Celestara, once alive with gentle rainfall and crystal springs, fell silent. A farmer's field lay split open, not by tools or weather, but by rot. The soil itself blackened from beneath, as if something crawled up from memory long-buried. And then, it stepped forth. The first Hollowborn.

It had no skin. Only a frame of black sinew and bone-light and a face too smooth, too still—like porcelain scorched by smoke. Its eyes were milky, but behind them flickered fragments of voices not its own. It turned its head. It heard her name.

"*Alexandria...*"

But it didn't speak. It echoed, like the Hollow itself had worn flesh. Behind it, others emerged. Dozens. All shaped differently.
Some were tall and elegant, made to mimic the faces of those once loved. Others were jagged, twitching with incomplete memories, half-made

monsters, half-lost regrets. And all of them were hungry for what the wyrm had failed to consume. They began walking, not fast, but with certainty. They were going to find her. And when they did, the choice would no longer be hers.

Far across the kingdoms, beneath a hazy red sky, Alexandria, Erythyn, and Bellator crossed the foothills of the Stormcradle Mountains. The winds here whispered old truths. This close to Dawnshire, magic pulsed like a second heartbeat beneath the land. Their journey had been silent since morning. Bellator walked ahead, scouting. Erythyn walked just behind Alexandria, his gaze constantly drifting toward the skies. He was the first to speak. "Something's wrong."

Alexandria glanced back. "You feel it too?"

He nodded. "The air's...changing. It's not just the Hollow anymore. Something else has been born."

Bellator returned swiftly, her druid form shifting mid-run. "There are rumors in the villages. People disappearing. Not killed, unmade. Like their bodies forgot how to be human."

Erythyn's jaw tightened. "The Shadowlord is unleashing something new. Not spirits. Not soldiers."

Alexandria inhaled slowly, her eyes narrowed on the path ahead. "Then we don't go to Dawnshire quietly." She pulled her hood up, her royal emblem tucked away. "We ride fast. No detours. We get to Astralhart, to the Order. They have to know what's coming."

Bellator's eyes flashed. "And if they don't listen?"

Alexandria's voice was low. Steady. "Then I'll make them."

Meanwhile, on the outskirts of the village of Norhollow, near the River of Light, a child no more than seven stood at the edge of the forest, clutching a lantern made of pressed flower glass. Her father had told her never to go this far, but the dog had run off. She could hear him barking. And then...silence.

She stepped forward, her boots crunching frostbitten grass. That's when she saw her. A woman. Beautiful. Familiar. Dressed in her mother's traveling cloak. Hair golden. A warm smile...but her eyes...wrong. They were too wide. Too pale. "Mama?" the girl asked.

The figure stepped forward, its arms open. "Come here, love."

The girl hesitated. She stepped back. The figure tilted its head, and the smile twitched, like it didn't know how to hold a face anymore. Then the illusion cracked. The woman's skin slid away, falling like wet parchment, revealing a creature of slick black tendrils, its veins glowing with a dull silver light. Its face was hollowed. A mimic with no voice of its own, only stolen ones.

The child screamed. The Hollowborn stepped forward, slow, gliding, not walking. But before it reached her, a flash of silver tore through the air. The girl's father, bow in hand, his eyes wide with terror, fired again. The second arrow passed through the creature. It turned its head slowly, then opened its mouth and spoke in his daughter's voice. "Help me, Daddy..."

The man dropped the bow, trembling, and then the creature moved. By dawn, only the bow remained, dripping with frost, laid on the edge of the woods.

On the edge of Riverlands, hours from Dawnshire, night crept across the land like ink spilled on parchment. The fire they'd built crackled softly, its flames licking up into the cool night air. Its light shimmered off the damp stones and cast their shadows tall and wavering against the trees. All around them, the woods held their breath, too quiet, too still. Even the wind seemed reluctant to pass through the clearing.

Bellator rested at the perimeter in her great hound form, silent and alert. Her silver eyes watched the trees, her ears swiveling and nose twitching.

Alexandria trusted her instincts more than her own these days. She sat close to the fire, her knees drawn to her chest, her cloak wrapped tightly around her like armor. The chill had settled in hours ago, but it wasn't the kind that fire could chase away. It was a chill that burrowed under the skin, made of fear, loss, and the weight of truths she could no longer ignore.

Across from her, Erythyn sat in stillness but not in peace. He'd shed most of his armor for the evening, but the darkness around him never truly left. Even in the flicker of firelight, shadows clung to him like a second skin. His eyes, pools of ash and ember, watched the flames, but she knew he was seeing something else, some memory that refused to stay buried.

"They used to tell stories," she murmured, her eyes on the fire, "about wind spirits who stole children in the night. Took their forms. Used their voices. Lured others to their deaths with soft songs and familiar smiles."

Erythyn didn't look at her, but his jaw tensed. "They weren't stories."

Her gaze flicked toward him. "You've seen them."

"I saw the first Hollowborn before they had names. Before the Shadowlord refined them." His voice dropped low. "They were imperfect, twisted things. But now...they learn. They adapt. They remember what they wear."

"They become what you love," she whispered. "Or what you fear."

He nodded slowly. "Or both."

The silence that followed was heavy, the fire snapping between them like the breath of something ancient. Bellator stirred but did not rise. Alexandria watched Erythyn's profile in the firelight, sharp, fierce, beautiful in a way that made her ache. "You were never supposed to be this important to me," she said quietly.

He turned to her then. Slowly. As though afraid to break the moment. "You're the only part of this world that doesn't scream when I get close."

A beat passed. Then she rose and crossed to him. She knelt beside him, their knees brushing, the fire warming her cheek. His hand moved to her waist, uncertain at first, but she didn't pull away. "I don't scream," she said, "but I do wonder if I've lost myself."

He looked up at her, his eyes dark with a hunger that had nothing to do with the Hollowborn. "You haven't. You're just finding the part they tried to bury."

Her breath caught as his fingers lifted to brush her cheek, slowly, reverently, like she was something sacred. She leaned into his touch. And then, wordlessly, their lips met. It wasn't rushed, nor violent. It was inevitable. A collision long overdue. Her hand slid into his hair, his arm wrapped around her waist, pulling her closer. She melted into him, their breaths mingling, their hearts thunderous in their chests. She tasted ash, heat, and something wild beneath it all, something him.

His forehead pressed to hers as they pulled apart slightly, breathing heavy, their fingers still locked. "If this is a mistake," she whispered, "then I don't want to be right."

"I stopped caring about right and wrong the moment I looked into your eyes."

She leaned into him again, just as his arms fully enveloped her...

CRACK.

A branch snapped in the trees nearby. Bellator surged to her feet, a low growl rumbling from her throat. Alexandria and Erythyn sprang apart, their hands to weapons, their eyes on the treeline.

A cloaked figure emerged from the dark, his presence deliberate but cautious. A dusk-feathered hood was drawn low over his brow, the silver-bladed bow slung across his back gleaming in the firelight. A falcon perched above in the branches, watching.

"Elowen," Alexandria breathed, her voice caught between relief and alarm.

The ranger stopped just short of the firelight, his eyes flicking from her to Erythyn. The tension in his frame was instant. "Your Highness..." he said, his voice sharp, disbelieving, "you're—with him?"

Erythyn rose to full height, his eyes narrowed. "The proper title is 'terror of legend,' I believe. You're welcome."

"Elowen, stand down," Alexandria ordered, stepping between them. "Now."

Elowen's hand fell away from his sword hilt, but his expression was taut with disbelief. "You vanished without a word. Astralhart's gone mad looking for you. He's turned half the kingdom inside out. Sent messengers to every outpost. Deployed the royal bloodtrackers."

She flinched. "He's that angry?"

"He's beyond angry. He thinks you were taken by force. He sent the elite guard into every province. He even cracked open the vault at Dawnbreak to summon diviners—diviners, Alexandria. He's not thinking clearly. I've never seen him like this."

Her heart thudded. "I left to protect the kingdom, not to destroy it."

Elowen's voice softened slightly. "I know. That's why I came alone. I didn't want them to find you first." He looked again at Erythyn, then back to her. "What's happening out there, Alex?"

She took a breath, steadied herself. "The Shadowlord has released the Hollowborn. We've seen them. Villages...gone. People not just murdered —unmade. They steal faces. Voices. Become your loved ones. They speak in your child's voice while they tear you apart."

Elowen's face darkened. "We've had reports. Officers returning to camps, speaking of homes where everything was still in place, but no people. A house in Norhollow was found with food still warm on the table. No sign of life. Just mirrors facing the doors."

"They're moving faster than the Order realizes," Erythyn said grimly. "They're smarter now. Coordinated."

"We're headed to Dawnshire," Alexandria said. "We need to warn the Council and Astralhart."

"I'll fly a message," Elowen said, stepping back. He raised a hand and gave a low whistle. The falcon above screeched once and took to the skies, vanishing into the stars. "Kyros will carry word to the rest of your guard. We'll have a unit at the southern gate before sunrise." He paused. "I don't know what this is between you two," he said, not looking at Erythyn, "but my loyalty is to you, Alex. No one else."

A silence fell. Then Bellator growled, a low, guttural warning. They turned toward the trees. The wind had shifted. Something was watching. Not from the ground, but from the dark between the branches. The world had gone still again, unnaturally so.

Bellator stood rigid in her hound form, her eyes fixed on the treeline, her body taut with tension. Then it came. A whisper, sweet and cold as death: "Help me, Daddy..." The voice didn't belong here. It slithered across their skin like fog, unnatural and mocking.

Erythyn stood, his jaw tight, frustration still simmering from the earlier interruption. "I'll handle this one," he said, low and bitter, his gaze cutting briefly to Elowen. "Stay here." Before Alexandria could speak, he turned and strode into the woods, Bellator padding silently after him. The trees swallowed them whole within seconds.

Alexandria stared after them, her fingers clenched.

Elowen stepped beside her, his gaze still scanning the dark. "He'll be fine," he said quietly. "Whatever he is... He's not weak." Alexandria didn't reply. The firelight danced in her eyes.

Behind them, Elowen let out a sharp whistle, low and clear. From the shadows, three direwolves emerged, massive, thick-coated, their eyes alert and intelligent. One lowered its head respectfully as Elowen murmured a command in a forgotten dialect. They would accompany the princess back to Dawnshire, a silent signal that she returned not in retreat but in force.

Moments later, a new sound stirred the forest, the sharp crack of a branch, followed by the wet hiss of something unnatural dying. Then came the footsteps. Erythyn stepped into the clearing, his breath even, his blade dripping with shimmering black ichor. His coat was torn at the shoulder, but otherwise, he looked untouched, dangerous still, his presence even darker than before. His eyes briefly found Alexandria's. "It was trying to be a girl," he said, low. "Didn't do a very good job." He paused, sliding his blade back into its sheath. "But it screamed your name when it died."

Alexandria felt her stomach turn, but she didn't flinch.

Bellator padded out beside him, shifting mid-stride. Where a hound had once stood, now a towering stag stood proud, its muscles rippling beneath its silver-white coat. Her antlers gleamed in the firelight like crescent moons. She hoofed the ground with purpose.

"We make for Dawnshire now," Alexandria said, lifting her hood. "No hiding. They'll know we're coming."

Erythyn stepped beside her without a word. Elowen mounted one of the direwolves, the others falling into formation. Overhead, a hawk shrieked and vanished toward the stars, carrying word to the rest of Alexandria's Royal Guard.

Bellator led the way, regal and powerful as she moved through the dark. And behind her came the last hope of a dying realm, A princess cloaked in war, a ranger bound by loyalty, a shadow-walker who'd once been her enemy, and the beasts of the wild, who now knew who their true queen was. They would ride into Dawnshire not as exiles, not as fugitives, but as a storm. And this time, the Shadowlord would feel it coming.

Epilogue
The Storm Arrives

Ballad of the Shattered Shade

Once darkness held dominion wide,

Its talons sunk in mortal pride.

But in that hour a hero came,

Her blade of dawn extinguished shame.

*J*ust before sunrise, the first fingers of light broke over the eastern horizon, golden and searing, casting long shadows over the valley below. As the rising sun reached the towering spires of Dawnshire, it struck the highest point, the Sunfire Bastion, with a brilliant flare, turning its marble tower to flame. Light danced down the polished stone walls, pouring through the stained-glass windows of the citadel like holy fire. But beyond the light, behind the valley...

A storm was coming.

Dark clouds gathered low across the western edge of the sky, rolling like furious waves in slow motion. Lightning cracked deep within the mass, but no thunder followed, just a silence that built like breath held before the strike. And then...

From over the ridge-line came the beat of hooves and paws against damp earth.

Bellator crested the hill first, galloping like the spirit of the forest herself, massive in her stag form, her silver antlers wide and gleaming like blades of moonlight. Her muscles rippled beneath a coat the color of ancient birch bark, her eyes burning with druidic fire.

Upon her back rode Princess Alexandria, her cloak trailing like a banner of dusk, her crown braided into her wild curls, her shoulders draped in bark-textured armor and shimmering royal blue. In her hand she held no banner, just her sword, drawn and gleaming, the light catching along its etched edge. Her face was calm, resolute.

Beside them raced the direwolves, dark and silent as phantoms, three in all, their pace even and eyes forward. One carried Elowen Duskbane, his cloak billowing behind him, his bow already strung. Behind them, the storm gathered strength, churning clouds flashing violet and silver, the wind screaming through the treetops like the howls of the gods.

And then came Erythyn. He strode behind them with inhuman grace, his black coat billowing, his blade still fresh with Hollowborn ichor. His eyes were fixed on the citadel ahead, unreadable, but filled with a promise.

A reckoning.

—————+———

Atop the Eastern Terrace of Dawnshire, high above, Prime Minister Astralhart stood on the stone balcony of the Council Tower, his robes disheveled, his eyes sunken with sleeplessness and obsession. He had not left this perch in three days, watching the horizon as if waiting for an omen.

Beside him stood General Stormrend, armored in steel and gold, his hands clasped behind his back. A glint of movement on the hill caught the general's eye. He stepped forward, squinting into the wind. Then he saw her.

Alexandria.

She was riding Bellator like a storm-bringer, the wind whipping her cloak around her shoulders, the light catching her blade. Behind her came the wolves. The cursed warrior. The storm.

Stormrend smiled. It was not the smile of amusement or surprise. It was the smile of someone who had waited a very long time for the tide to turn. He turned his head slowly toward Astralhart and said, in a voice calm and grave, "Looks like a storm's rolling in."

Astralhart gripped the stone rail, his knuckles bone white. "No," he whispered, panic flaring behind his eyes. "She can't..."

But she had.

Alexandria was coming.

Not as a runaway. Not as a rebel.

But as a queen returning with the storm at her back.

And behind her, carried in that thunder, rode the end of the old world.

The gates of Dawnshire would open. The war would begin.

And this time, the Shadowlord would find no weakness, no hesitation.

Only fire.

Only fury.

Only her and her army that would follow.

The storm had arrived...

Acknowledgements

First, I would like to thank Amy Vanhorn with Rogue Wolf Publishing as my editor and mentor. The one who told me that I have something there that I should pursue. I can't thank you enough for your guidance and patience with me while helping me grow as a better writer. The late-night text, the million questions answered, and the recommendations along the way. I appreciate all of your help in this journey!

Gaylene Lambson, editor, for helping me on such short notice. Such a kind soul. Thank you for your sweet words and your great work!

Alyssa Turoczy, graphic designer and illustrator, a Godsend! I am beyond grateful for you! You have literally been such a blessing. Your work has been amazing, and your patience and kindness are beyond measure! I have thoroughly enjoyed working with you! You have gone above and beyond to help me, from your work with the graphic design, editing, formatting, and everything in between... If I needed help, you were there! We have had great laughs along the way, and I may have even shed a tear or two. I am so glad that Amy introduced us, as I consider you a friend, and I look forward to working with you in the future!

To my soul tribe, you know who you are... With continuous encouragement, and when I wanted to quit, ya'll helped push me through with lots of laughs and some tears along the way. I couldn't have made it through without you. I am forever grateful for all the words of love and encouragement. Thank you! I hope to see ya'll in person soon!

To my boys, I know this has been a long journey, and you both have been through so much. Just know, my love for you is beyond measure, and my hope for you both is that, above anything else that I have taught you, no matter what you have been through, no matter the battles you may face, you can achieve anything you set your mind to. Don't ever hold yourself back, and believe in yourself. Love others, have patience, be kind, know your worth, and above all, love yourself unconditionally!

From the Author

This manuscript is written as a fictional story, though it was written based on my life. The roles that different people have played in my life. The love and lies, deception and battles happening between souls. A real war that we face today. A war between governance and sovereignty. One between light and darkness. See, I had been around so much negative and darkness my whole life that I couldn't see the beauty anymore. I had to go back to nature and find it, the place that grounded me. The place where I could find peace in all the chaos. Every photograph throughout this book was taken at a place with great spiritual significance. Every location I learned something new about this world and about myself.

I hope that if there is even just one reader that my story can touch, it was all worth it. Just remember: No matter how big the battles you may face, you have the strength within you to make it through.

Love others, have grace, learn peace, & love yourself.

TikTok/@alexandria_renee1

Sloan & Co. Publishing
sloanepublishing.com

www.ingramcontent.com/pod-product-compliance
Lightning Source LLC
Chambersburg PA
CBHW070846260626
47170CB00007B/2516